PLAYING FOR KEEPS

Josh ran a finger down her arm. "You are no stranger to me, love. I know every inch of you by heart.

His touch made her tremble, and she quickly moved away. "What is your horse's name?" she asked.

"Gambler's Lady." He smiled at her obvious attempt to change the subject. "Why?"

"She'd make a beautiful match for Rapscallion. I'll make a deal with you," she said, moving toward Rapscallion's stall. "If Rapscallion beats Gambler's Lady tomorrow, you breed her to my horse and I get the foal. If your horse wins, we'll give you stud rights for three seasons, and I keep the foal the third season."

"That means you win either way," he said. "I'd rather make a different wager." He pulled her into his arms. "If I win, you come to my bed. If you win, I come to yours."

"No, you can't have me," she screamed, trying to break away from his embrace.

"Come here, Wildcat. Let me love you," he said gently.

She darted toward the stable door, but he was there before she could open it. He turned her around and pinned her against it, his arms like steel bands on each side of her. "Don't fight me, Wildcat. It won't do any good."

PASSION'S PRISONER

CASEY STUART

ZEBRA BOOKS
KENSINGTON PUBLISHING CORP.

ZEBRA BOOKS

are published by

Kensington Publishing Corp.
475 Park Avenue South
New York, NY 10016

First printing: February, 1989

Printed in the United States of America

This book is dedicated with love to my husband and family, especially Kyle and Cory, and to the wonderful, helpful staff of Romantic Times, *and the great friends we made at the May Conference.*

There is always
a comforting thought
in time of trouble when
it is not our trouble

— Donald Robert Marquis

Prologue

On A Mississippi Riverboat
1859

Josh Rawlings leaned back in his chair and drew deep on the long thin cheroot he held in his mouth. He studied Will Gregory across the poker table, noticing the beads of sweat that had broken out on his brow as he stared at the amount of money in the pot. He had played poker with the man several times before, but had never seen him so nervous.

Josh ran a hand through his curly blond hair, wishing the man would make up his mind. He took out his pocket watch and glanced at it. They had been playing for nearly six hours since boarding the *Fulton Queen,* and he was looking forward to calling it a night and stretching out in his cabin. Five of them had started out playing when they left St. Louis, but now it was down to only the two of them with the rest spectators. The ship's whistle sounded loud in the night, bringing his attention back to the game.

Will Gregory's eyes finally met his, and he smiled confidently as he reached into his pocket and pulled out a folded piece of paper.

"This is the deed to a gambling casino in Natchez, Mississippi. Will you accept it to cover the bet?"

"What am I going to do with a casino in Mississippi?" Josh laughed. "I'm on my way to New Orleans to sell off some real estate I won a couple of weeks ago."

"I don't think you have to worry about going to Natchez, Rawlings. I have the winning hand," Gregory said in a confident tone.

"All right, put the deed on the table," Josh agreed, "but I hate to take advantage of you."

Gregory threw the paper on the pot, then leaned back and examined his cards for a final time. "I've called your bet, Rawlings. What have you got?"

Josh laid his cards on the table. "Can you beat three jacks, Gregory?"

"Damn," Gregory swore, slamming his cards facedown. "You certainly have been lucky this trip."

"I'm always lucky, my friend."

"I know, I've heard about you up and down the river. Do you ever lose, Rawlings?"

"Occasionally." Josh pushed away from the table. "I'll be here tomorrow night, Gregory. I'll give you a chance to win it back."

8

"No, I don't think so, Rawlings. You have Lady Luck with you on this trip. I should have seen it earlier."

Josh leaned against the railing of the *Fulton Queen,* enjoying the cool night's air and the sound of the paddle wheel cutting through the water. The river was calm at the moment, but he was well aware of its capricious nature. He had seen the damage done to the land and structures near Cairo after a week of heavy rain.

"It looked like you were the big winner again tonight," a voice said behind him.

"I was, little brother." Josh turned and faced the man who was as tall as he.

"It certainly seems Lady Luck is still riding with you." Matt laughed. "I wish a little of it would rub off on me."

"There isn't any such thing as Lady Luck," Josh snorted. "A man makes his own luck."

"I suppose you're right, but you have to admit everything has been going your way since the strike at the gold field in California. It seems you can do no wrong."

Josh was silent as he lit up another cheroot. "I know we had talked about staying in New Orleans for a while, but what would you think about stopping off in Mississippi first?"

"Mississippi?" Matt laughed. "What did you win now, big brother?"

"A gambling casino in Natchez."

Matt let out a whistle. "A lumber company in

9

Idaho, a steamboat company in St. Louis, several warehouses, a shipping business and a house in New Orleans, and now a gambling casino in Natchez. This has been a very profitable trip for you. But tell me, big brother, how do you plan to run all these businesses when you never stay in one place longer than a month?"

"I'll do it with good people, Matt. People who are honest and dependable, and who want to share in the profits."

"What about this house in New Orleans? I thought you wanted to take the time to sell it."

"I can still talk to a banker about selling it before we sail. Or who know, maybe I'll keep it. I think I'd like New Orleans."

"Then why go to Natchez? Why don't you just sell the casino?" Matt asked.

"I don't know; I suppose the idea of running a gambling casino appeals to me. Maybe it's the black side of me. Anyway, it won't be for long."

Matt fell silent, staring out into the darkness. "What's bothering you, little brother?" Josh asked.

"I was just wondering when we were going home."

"Home?" Josh snorted. "Where the hell is home?"

"You know what I mean, Josh. When are we going back to California? It's one thing to leave these other businesses in the hands of employees, but it's a little different letting someone else run a gold mine."

"I trust Whitney with my life, Matt. The man hasn't missed making a deposit in the Bank of California a single month."

"I know, I know," Matt said, running a hand through his unruly brown hair. "I suppose I'm just tired of moving around so much. I don't have the talent for gambling that you do. I'm going through my money at a rapid pace. I should start looking for work."

"Hell, Matt, you have enough gold to last you a lifetime without ever having to worry again. Enjoy life, little brother. By God, we certainly earned it after nearly starving as kids."

"You know, Josh, no matter how rich you get, you can't change the fact that we grew up poor. I remember when we didn't know where our next meal was coming from, or if we would be shut out of the house because Stella was entertaining some man while Dad was working the fields."

Josh threw his cheroot into the water, remembering bitterly what life had been like after their mother had died in childbirth. A year later their father had brought home his new bride, a girl he thought was sweet and innocent, but who turned out to be a lying whore. "I remember, too, little brother, and that's why I intend to enjoy life now. When I find something worth settling down for, then I'll think about it. You can do whatever you like."

Even in the darkness Josh saw the hurt look on his brother's face. "What I'm trying to say, Matt, is that I enjoy your company, but I'll understand if you want to go back to California and Georgette."

"Naw." Matt sighed, leaning his elbows on the railing. "Georgette is just a friend. Besides, the Rawlings brothers have to stick together like we always have."

"You're right." Josh laughed, slapping his brother on the back. "Look out world. When the Rawlings

11

boys stick together, there isn't anything we can't do."

"Gentlemen, I hate to interrupt, but I'd like to talk to you both in private, if I may," Will Gregory said.

"He must want his saloon back." Matt laughed.

"No. On the contrary, I was hoping your brother would win it. It makes my job much easier."

Josh raised one eyebrow, his curiosity peaked. "What are you talking about, Gregory?"

"I represent some very important people in Washington who have an interest in what's going on in the deep South."

"What does that have to do with us?" Josh asked.

"Our first intention had been for me to run the casino, but there are people in Natchez who know my connections in Washington," Gregory admitted. "It would not be easy for me to learn what a stranger could."

"Come on, Gregory." Josh laughed. "This is still a free country. You can go anywhere you want. Whether people choose to talk to you or not is your problem."

"Part of what you say is true, my friend, but things are changing rapidly. There is talk of secession all over the South. Natchez seems to be a gathering place for many of the groups advocating breaking away from the Union and going to war. We need someone who is neutral who would keep his eyes and ears open and report who the troublemakers are."

Josh angrily threw his cheroot over the side. "You're right about one thing, Gregory, I am neutral, and I plan to stay that way. You can have your damned saloon back and find somebody else to do your dirty work."

"You don't understand the importance of this assignment, Rawlings. We may be able to keep the country from going to war if we can expose the individuals who want war for their own greedy purposes. There are senators from the cotton states who sit in the Capitol of the Union dreaming about a new empire of Southern states—at any cost. They are the ones convincing the planters that secession would benefit everyone, and all the while they are buying weapons and stockpiling supplies so they can become even richer. My job is to convince the Southern people otherwise, but I have to know who I can trust before I can do any good."

"Hell, man, there isn't any way one man can prevent what's happening in the South," Josh said in disgust.

"I told you, Rawlings, I represent a lot of people. We need your help. All I'm asking is that you keep your eyes and ears open and let me know what's going on."

"It couldn't hurt, Josh," Matt said. "War between the states can't benefit anyone."

"Damn it all, I didn't plan to become involved in this conflict. . . ."

The troubles of our proud and angry dust
Are from eternity, and shall not fail
Bear them we can, and if we can we must . . .

— Alfred Edward Housman

Chapter One

Lansing Creek Plantation
Natchez, Mississippi

"Child, you git down off dat horse and git into some decent clothes!" The black woman shook her finger at the girl sitting atop a large black mare. "Your grandfather should be horsewhipped for letting you gad-about de countryside dressed like a boy."

"I have business to take care of, Martha," Cassandra Lansing, better known as Shadow, explained.

"Business," the black woman snorted. "Wat kinda business a young snip like you got?"

"Important business, Martha. I'll be back tonight. Now please stop worrying about me. I promise to-

15

morrow I'll wear a dress all day. I can't very well ride astride if I have skirts flapping around my legs."

"You're not s'pose to be riding astride," Martha scolded. "If you was my child, you wouldn't be on dat big animal. It's jus' not ladylike."

"Here comes Toby, Martha. I have to go now."

"Miss Shadow, you better be back here 'fore your grandfather gits home." The girl gave a wave as she disappeared down the tree-lined drive. "Lordie, Lordie." Martha shook her head. "Where dat child git her stubborn streak. It's gonna git her into trouble yet . . . and going off with the overseer . . . what is dis world coming to. Lordie, Lordie, de master better spend more time wit dat girl and less time gambling. . . ."

"Where are we going, Shadow?" Toby McAllister asked.

"Under the Hill." She laughed as she kicked her horse into a gallop.

"Hold on a minute, Shadow," he shouted. "Why are we going there?"

"To play cards."

"No way," he shouted, pulling his horse to a halt. "Dammit, Shadow, it's one thing to have our poker games at the stable, but if we go into town and try to play, someone is bound to recognize you. No, sir, this is pure and simple foolish," he said, his jaw squared firmly. "If your grandfather caught us, he'd have my job and my hide."

Shadow reluctantly drew her horse up, certain a few sweet words would convince her long-time friend to go with her. "There isn't any reason for anyone to get suspicious." She smiled at him in the way that usually got her her way. "We always have fun together."

"Of course we do." He squirmed uneasily, feeling the blood rush to his face. How could he tell her that anything he did with her was fun.

"For heaven's sake, Toby. Why should anyone get suspicious if they think we're just a couple of fellows in town to play a few hands of cards? I certainly don't look like a girl dressed up in this git-up, now, do I?"

He stared at her in the oversized jacket and baggy pants, and he gulped. Her tall, willowy figure was disguised, but he could still remember how she had looked when he came upon her swimming nude in the river one hot steamy day.

"Is there something wrong, Toby?"

"No, nothing," he lied. He took his hat off and ran a hand through his red hair. He was a few years older than she, but she had always been the leader in everything they had done. Up until this past year, it had always been innocent fun and pranks, but now this gambling thing had him unnerved. And the damndest thing was, she usually won, thanks to her grandfather's tutoring. If Noble Lansing ever imagined that his granddaughter would use the skill he had innocently taught her, to gamble in the casinos "under the hill" in Natchez, he would have a fit—to say nothing of Toby's hide for going there with her.

"Let's do something different, Shadow. I don't feel like playing cards. I hear Allen Middleton had a new foal sired by Black Demon. Let's go see it."

"Tomorrow, Toby," she said stubbornly. "I have to play cards tonight."

Toby looked at her suspiciously. "What's this all about, Shadow?"

"What do you mean?" She laughed.

"Why do you have to play cards tonight?"

"I didn't mean I had to, but I want to. Come on, Toby." She smiled, her cornflower blue eyes pleading. "Tomorrow we'll go see the foal."

Toby studied her for a long moment. "Does this have anything to do with your grandfather losing Rapscallion?"

Shadow leaned forward, stroking her horse's neck. "Grandfather played cards with the new gambler in town, Toby, and I'm sure he was cheated. I mean to win my horse back. You of all people know what he's worth."

"Of course I do," he said irritably. "Rapscallion is the most valuable stud in Mississippi, not to mention the fastest horse around here. But apparently your grandfather didn't think so or he wouldn't have bet him."

"I told you, Grandfather had too much to drink, and this gambler, Josh Rawlings, took advantage of him," Shadow stated emphatically.

"Well, there isn't any way you're going to be able to beat him if your grandfather couldn't. From what I hear, not too many people have walked away a winner after playing any kind of a game of chance with him. He's a born gambler."

"He's only a man," she said, urging her horse on.

"My God, Shadow, haven't you listened to a word I've said. The man's a professional gambler," he shouted after her.

"I don't care. I have to do this, Toby. If you don't want to come with me, I'll go alone."

Rose Jardine admired Josh Rawlings' strong profile as she watched him pull his jacket on. He was the most beautiful man she'd ever been with, and she always dreaded when the time came for him to leave. Despite being exhausted from hours of lovemaking, she still yearned for his touch.

"Are you sure you can't stay and have supper with me?"

"I'd like to, Rose, but I really need to get back to the saloon."

"Have there been any more robbery attempts?" she asked, drawing her knees up to her chest as she continued to admire him.

"Not since last week."

"Maybe there won't be any more."

"I'd like to think there won't. It sure as hell isn't good for business."

"I don't know why you want to bother with that little ole place. Why, I'd love to take care of you, and then you wouldn't have to worry about a thing," she drawled.

"A kept man?" He laughed. "Thanks, but no thanks." He kissed her briefly on the lips.

Rose wrapped her arms around his neck. "I'm serious, Josh. My late husband left me very well off. You'd never have to worry about a thing."

"You don't know me very well if you think I'd enjoy living like that," he said, not bothering to tell

19

her how wealthy he was.

"I remember how excited you were about winning that gray horse from Noble Lansing. Marry me, darling, and I'll buy you a dozen fine horses, and anything else your little heart desires."

Josh touched her ivory cheek. She was a beautiful woman, but he had made it clear from the start that he wasn't interested in anything permanent. "You are a very generous woman, Rose, but I'll buy my own horses. I don't know how long I'll be staying in Natchez, so let's just enjoy each other's company for now."

"Oh, please, darling, don't even talk like that," she pleaded, her green eyes filling with tears. "I would just perish if you left here. I have enjoyed your company so much."

Josh lifted a strand of her dark brown hair. "I've enjoyed your company, too, Rose. And I must admit, I've enjoyed seeing eyebrows raise when you introduce me to your socialite friends."

"Just think how they'd raise if we married."

"Forget it!" Josh said, abruptly pulling away from her.

"You needn't run from me, darling," she teased. "I knew from the beginning marriage wasn't in your plans."

"Then why do you keep bringing it up?"

"Because I can think of nothing I'd like more than to claim you for my own and enjoy you all to myself for the rest of my life."

"Being married doesn't assure that." He laughed bitterly, remembering his stepmother's dalliances.

"I know, darling, it was just a thought. I guess

what bothers me is why you find it necessary to sleep with that . . . that saloon girl who works at your place."

"What I do is none of your business," he growled.

"I know, darling, but why would you want to take her to your bed when I'm here for you any time day or night," she persisted.

"I'll see you later, Rose."

"Josh, wait, please. I'm sorry . . . I didn't mean to push—"

Rose found herself talking to an empty room. "Oh, damnation," she swore, leaning back against her pillows. "When am I going to learn not to force the issue. I can't lose him. I just can't."

The sun had gone down over the muddy Mississippi as Josh made his way from the elegant splendor of Natchez to the infamous section known as Under the Hill. Because of his conversation with Rose, thoughts he had tried to avoid came flooding back. Vividly he recalled the sounds that would come from his stepmother's bedroom when she was entertaining while his poor father worked trying to strike it rich. God, how he hated her for the pain she had caused his father. In the end, the poor man had taken his own life. No woman would ever do that to him, he swore silently. Women had only one use to him and that was to satisfy his needs. It didn't matter to him if it was the rich widow or one of his girls at the bar. None of them would ever get close enough to hurt him.

As he crossed the street, he could hear laughter

and piano music coming from his saloon. He smiled, thinking how the gentlemen from uptown spent their evenings beneath the bluff of Natchez, making him even richer, while their wives played miss high and mighty in their fancy mansions.

As he headed for the bar, he noticed his brother seated at a table with a young lady. "Who's that with Matt?" he asked the bartender.

"I don't know her name, but she came in here a little while ago wanting to see the owner. Matt's been with her ever since. He told me to ask you to join him when you came in."

Josh turned back to the table and watched his brother pat the girl's hand in a sympathetic gesture, then offer her his handkerchief, which she used to dab at her eyes. There was a very strange look in Matt's eyes.

"I better save him before he proposes marriage," he mumbled as he headed toward the table.

Matt saw Josh coming toward him and smiled sheepishly as he stood up. "Josh, I'd like you to meet Miss Mandy Cameron."

"Miss Cameron." Josh bent over her uplifted hand. "What brings you to Yancey's?"

"Please, sit down, Josh," Matt suggested. "Miss Cameron is looking for a job."

Josh turned a chair around and straddled it. "A job?" He laughed. "Surely you don't mean here at Yancey's."

"That is exactly what I mean, Mr. Rawlings."

"Take a look around you, Miss Cameron. Do you see the type of women who work here? Now, I could be wrong, but you don't strike me as that type of woman. Surely you have friends, or perhaps you could find a job as a governess or—"

"A maid?" she prompted. "I'm not from around here, Mr. Rawlings, so I don't have any friends who can help me. My father and I came from England several years ago. We've traveled all over the country performing. We were on our way to New Orleans when my father died suddenly. I'm a singer, Mr. Rawlings, and now I must find work for myself."

Josh studied the girl and wondered if she had any idea what she was getting into. Natchez Under the Hill was certainly no place for a lady. "I just don't know, Miss Cameron . . ."

"Mr. Rawlings, all I'm asking is for an audition. If you don't like what you hear, then I'll go down the street to another saloon."

"You've put a lot of money into this place, Josh. If we add a singer it would really give it class."

Seeing the look on Matt's face, he knew he'd have to give the girl a chance or he'd never hear the end of it. "All right, Matt. Why don't you take Miss Cameron uptown to one of the boardinghouses and arrange for a carriage to pick her up in the morning for an audition."

"That isn't necessary, Mr. Rawlings. I can take care of myself. I have a little money left. Just tell me what time to be here."

"I insist, Miss Cameron. If we find we can't use you as a singer, you'll need that money."

"Thank you, Mr. Rawlings. You and your brother have been most kind."

Josh then joined Patience at the bar. He laughed at the pouting look on her pretty face. "Do you have a problem, love?"

"Surely you're not hiring Miss Prim and Proper."

"I may." He laughed. "Matt seems to be smitten with her."

"That doesn't mean she'd fit in here," Patience persisted, worried that Josh might become interested in the girl. "It's bad enough having to share you with that Miss High and Mighty widow woman."

Josh laughed. "Women, you're all alike."

Natchez Under the Hill was where the riverboats docked. It was mostly inhabited by gamblers, rogues and ladies of the evening. Certainly not a place for a proper young lady to be, but that didn't bother Shadow Lansing when she had her mind made up to something.

She and Toby stood in the doorway of Yancey's Saloon and Gambling Hall taking in the new furnishings. The place that had been known for years as Yancey's dump Under the Hill, now sparkled with green velvet furniture and bright crystal chandeliers. A painting of a beautiful nude woman covered the wall behind the massive bar.

Toby let out a low whistle. "I had no idea it had changed so much."

"Neither did I, but if this gambler cheats everyone like he cheated my grandfather, it isn't any wonder he can afford to fix this place up."

"Maybe we should go to O'Hara's," Toby whispered. "This place looks too fancy for my blood."

"You forget why I'm here," she snapped. "I'm going to get my horse back."

Before Toby could say more, one of the saloon girls walked up between them, wrapping her arms through theirs. "Good evening, gentlemen. What's your pleasure this evening?"

Shadow was about to tell the girl to get her hands off her, when Toby quickly spoke up. "My friend and I are here to play cards."

"Why don't you buy me a drink, and maybe I'll bring you some luck." She smiled.

"I'll be glad to buy you a drink, ma'am," Toby quickly volunteered.

"What about you, blue eyes?" The girl smiled at Shadow.

Shadow could feel the heat rise to her cheeks. This stupid chit was actually flirting with her. "I'm here to play cards," she said in her deepest voice as she pulled her arm away. "What table does the owner play at?"

"At that one over there—" the girl pointed to a table near the bar—"but you'd be better off playing someplace else. Josh Rawlings doesn't lose when he plays."

"So I've heard," Shadow mumbled as she headed toward the table. There were several empty seats, so she pulled back a chair and sat down. "Mind if I join you?"

"Are you prepared to play high stakes poker, young man?" one of the men asked.

Shadow took a pouch of money out and set it on the table in front of her. "Don't worry about me."

To prove her point, she won the next two hands without any trouble. Feeling secure in her ability to win against more experienced players, she leaned back in her chair and surveyed the room. As she scanned the faces gathered around the bar, she wondered where the owner was. Suddenly her attention was drawn to a handsome blond man leaning against the bar. He was impeccably dressed in a dark brown coat and matching breeches which molded well-muscled thighs. She admired the fitted jacket that emphasized his wide shoulders and narrow waist. Now that's how a man should dress, she thought silently. One of the saloon girls clung to him, and his gold eyes sparkled as he laughed at something she said. She wasn't the only one to notice him, she realized, as several more young ladies surrounded him.

"Are you in?" One of the players nudged her.

"What? Oh yeah." She forced her attention back to the game.

"How many cards do you want?"

"Two," she answered, tossing her throw-aways on the table. She was dealt a queen and a four, giving her three queens. Not too shabby, she thought smugly as she studied the four men, watching for signs that her grandfather had taught her. One man flicked his cards with his fingernail, a sure giveaway that he wasn't happy with his hand. She smiled. One of the others had a frown on his face as he studied his cards. Two down, she thought smugly. Unfortunately the other two men's faces were expressionless, just as her grandfather had taught her to play.

"Your bet, Russell," one of the men said.

The man called Russell pushed his money to the center of the table. The man next to him whistled. "Too high for me," he said, laying his cards facedown on the table.

"I'm out, too," the next man said, leaving Shadow and two other players.

"I'll see your bet and raise a hundred," the man called Fowler said.

Shadow shoved more money into the pot, trying to act confident. "I'll see the bet and raise another hundred," she said.

"I'm out," Russell said in disgust, leaving only her and Fowler.

"You've been called," she said to the remaining player.

Fowler turned his cards up. "Two pairs," he said proudly.

"Sorry"—Shadow smiled smugly—"that isn't good enough. I have three queens."

"You sure are lucky, young man," Fowler growled, as he glared at her.

"Yeah, I suppose I am," she said, raking in her winnings. "I had understood the owner of this place played at this table."

"I do," a deep voice said behind her, "when I choose to play cards."

Shadow turned around and met the smiling amber eyes of the man she'd noticed at the bar. A beautiful woman dressed in red clung to his arm.

"Just why are you interested in my card playing habits?" he asked, a glint of suspicion in his eyes.

"I . . . I had heard about the renovations you had done here at Yancey's," she said in her deepest voice. "I wanted to compliment you on improvements."

One blond eyebrow raised, but he didn't question her. "Deal me in this game, gentlemen," he said, taking the empty seat across from Shadow.

"Josh"—the girl who had been clinging to him pouted—"I thought we were . . ."

"In a few minutes, sweet," he said, patting her on the bottom. "How about getting the gentlemen and myself a drink while you're waiting."

What a nerve, Shadow thought as she picked her cards up. *He stands the girl up, then orders her to wait on him. Serves her right for falling all over him.*

"I understand you were robbed again the other night," Fowler mentioned as he studied his cards.

"Yeah, we were. That makes three times in the past month," Rawlings growled. "When I get my hands on the bastards, they'll wish they'd never heard of me."

"It's strange, O'Hara's hasn't had any problems," another man commented.

"Yeah, I've wondered about that myself," Rawlings retorted as he smoothed his mustache and stared at Shadow. "I'm beginning to think someone would like to run me out of business."

"I'm surprised no one has recognized them," another man said.

"They wear hoods over their faces," Rawlings answered.

The game seemed to move much faster now that Josh Rawlings was sitting in. Shadow was dealt a pair of tens, then drew another ten, a jack and a three. She felt confident as she glanced up and met Josh Rawlings' curious stare. She noticed his cards lying facedown on the table. *If that's meant to scare me, he'll have to try something else,* she thought smugly as she raised his bet.

After two rounds of betting, it was down to just the two of them. When Rawlings called her bet, she proudly spread out her cards, sure she had him beat.

"Three tens," she announced gruffly.

"Not good enough," Rawlings said. "I have a full house, seven over twos."

The girl standing behind Rawlings whispered something in his ear. "Thanks for the entertainment, gentlemen, but the lady is tired of waiting for me. I'm sure you all understand."

"Wait . . ." Shadow said as he stood up to leave.

He turned and looked at her, a puzzled expression on his handsome face. "Yes . . ."

She had his attention, but now she didn't know what to say. "I — I wanted to play another hand. . . ." she stuttered.

"Be my guest." He laughed as he walked away with the girl.

Damn the bastard, she cursed silently. He was just as arrogant and despicable as she had imagined. As she sat there trying to decide what to do now, another hand was dealt. She absentmindedly glanced at the hand, finding three jacks, but she had other things on her mind, and folded. She had to find a way to get Josh Rawlings to sit down and play her again, but it was obvious it wasn't going to be tonight.

She glanced around the room, wondering where Toby had gone. Excusing herself, she went in search of her friend, spotting him just a moment before she heard someone shout a greeting to her grandfather.

Oh God, how was she going to get out of there? Her grandfather and several of his friends blocked the entrance. Glancing around, she noticed a door to the left of the bar. She pulled her hat down further on her head and made her way through the crowd.

Opening the door, she quickly slipped inside, realizing too late that it wasn't an exit, but someone's living quarters. It didn't matter, she told herself. She had to avoid her grandfather. She moved farther into the room still hoping to find another way out, then suddenly froze.

"You lay there, love, and I'll get us some more champagne," a deep male voice said.

The door opened, and the lamplight silhouetted a half-naked male figure coming toward her. He struck a match, and as he brought it close to his face to light the cheroot in his mouth, she could see the handsome features of Josh Rawlings. She took a quick step back toward the door, deciding that she would have to take her chances in the bar, but before she could open it, shots sounded on the other side. In the next second, all hell broke loose.

"What the hell . . ." Rawlings swore as he rushed toward the door.

As Shadow grabbed for the doorknob, the door flew open, knocking her back into Josh Rawlings' arms.

"Josh, another robbery attempt," the man yelled.

"You bastard . . ." Rawlings growled. She glanced up into angry gold eyes. "I knew I'd get one of you sooner or later."

She saw the muscles ripple across his bare chest as he drew back his arm, but she wasn't prepared for what happened next. His fist connected with her

30

jaw, and she collapsed to the floor, blackness washing over her.

"Patience, get out here," Josh yelled. "Keep an eye on this one," he ordered the startled girl. "Don't let him get away!" he demanded as he grabbed his gun and rushed out into the saloon.

"We foiled them this time," Matt Rawlings said, "but they got away."

"Not all of them," Josh mumbled.

"Noble Lansing had just walked in when they showed up. He thinks he may have recognized one of their horses."

"Good. I'll talk to Noble in a minute," Josh said. "Have Chauncey serve a round of drinks on the house, and apologize for the interruption. We don't want to lose our customers."

"All the commotion must have woke Tate Fuller up," Matt commented, seeing the sheriff walk in the door. "We always do his dirty work, and then he shows up to take the credit."

"Not this time," Josh said in a clipped voice.

"What do you mean? How about the fellow you knocked out in your room?" Matt asked. "Aren't you going to turn him over to the sheriff?"

"Hell no!" He laughed bitterly. "A hell of a lot of good he's been to us. No, I'm going to handle this one myself. Don't say anything to anyone about the one we caught."

Josh joined Noble Lansing at the bar and bought his friend a drink. "I understand you may have recognized a horse one of the robbers rode."

"I did, Rawlings, but it must have been stolen from Allen Middleton's stock. I'm sure it was one of his horses."

"Middleton," Josh growled. "I wouldn't put it past that bastard to be involved in something like this. I didn't like the man the first time I met him."

"His place joins mine," Noble said. "His father and I were friends for years. Granted, the young man is far too arrogant, and has had his share of trouble, usually over cards or women, but I don't think he'd be involved in something like this. Besides, coming from one of Natchez's best families, he doesn't need the money."

"Did you get a look at any of the men?" Josh asked.

"No, they all had hoods on. Besides, I was being roughed up by one of them for getting in his way. As I said, I saw the horse as they were leaving. If I were you, I'd check with Middleton. Maybe he sold the horse to someone recently."

"I'll do that. Thanks for your help, Noble. I really appreciate it."

"No problem, my friend. I came by tonight because you promised me a chance to win my horse back. I'm afraid my granddaughter is going to disown me if I don't come home with him."

"I'm afraid I have some business to take care of this evening, Noble, but how about tomorrow night?"

"I suppose I'll just have to face her one more night." Noble laughed. "I'll see you then."

Josh headed back to his room and found Patience standing over the robber, a small derringer in her trembling hand.

"Oh, God, I'm so glad you're finally back." She

32

trembled. "I was afraid he'd wake up before you got here. He moaned just a moment ago."

"You did a good job," he said, "but you better go on back to work, love. I'll handle this one now. I'd appreciate it if you didn't mention that we captured one of them."

"What are you going to do, Josh?"

"I'm going to get some answers."

"Oh, Josh, please be careful. The others might come back for him."

Josh pulled the girl into his arms and kissed her on the forehead. "Thanks for worrying about me, but I'll be fine."

She raised up on her toes and kissed him quickly on the mouth. "Will I see you later?" she asked tentatively.

"Maybe," he answered. "It depends on our friend here."

Men should be what they seem.

— Shakespeare

Chapter Two

"All right, you bastard, on your feet!" Josh swore as he hauled Shadow roughly off the floor. "You've got some questions to answer," he growled. "I want to know who your friends were and where I can find them."

"No, please," Shadow whimpered, feeling as if her jaw had been broken. "This is all a mistake."

"You're damn right it is," he hissed as he grabbed her roughly by the shirtfront. "You're going to wish to God you'd never stepped foot in my place."

Even in her dazed state, she had already wished that with all her heart. She tried to focus her eyes on him. She saw his fist coming again, but there was nothing she could do. "Please—"

The hat she had pulled down snugly on her head flew off as she fell backward over a chair, then slumped to the floor, unconscious. "Get up, you sniveling coward," he ordered, turning her over with the toe of his boot. "I'm not through with you yet."

Suddenly he went very still. "Jesus . . . it couldn't be," he swore as he knelt down. Her reddish-blond hair tumbled over her face and around her shoulders. "Sweet Jesus," he hissed between clenched teeth. "So the bastards rode off leaving a young girl behind to fend for herself."

He studied her pretty face, feeling a twinge of regret as he noticed blood at the corner of her mouth where he'd split her lip. "Damn the bastards for getting a pretty young girl involved in their dirty work," he growled. He picked her up and gently laid her on his bed. On the other hand, he thought, a devious smile on his face, perhaps it was obliging of them. He ran a finger across her swollen jaw. It would be just as easy to get the information out of this one, and maybe even a little more enjoyable.

Shadow opened her eyes when she felt someone touch a wet cloth to her mouth. Her breath caught in her throat as she met the gold eyes of Josh Rawlings. She quickly tried to sit up, then realized she didn't have a stitch of clothes on, and worse, the man sitting on the bed had on very little.

"Oh, God, what have you done?" she asked accusedly.

"Nothing . . . yet," he answered.

"Where are my clothes . . . who undressed

me . . . ?" she asked, her heart pounding.

"I undressed you," he said, pouring her a sip of brandy. "It will deter you from trying to escape."

"Oh, my God," she gasped.

"You're not the first woman I've undressed," he said arrogantly. "Here, drink this. Perhaps it will loosen your tongue and make this easier on both of us."

Shadow accepted the glass, careful to hold the blanket up to her chin. "I don't know what you're talking about," she said, trying to avoid staring at his bare chest and wide shoulders. She gently touched the corner of her mouth and came away with blood on her finger. "Why have you done this to me?" she asked, tears in her eyes.

"Don't play the innocent with me, girl. I know better," he said in disgust as he moved across the room to lock the door. "I'm the man you and your friends have attempted to rob four times in the past month. You're lucky I don't break your pretty neck."

"My God," she exclaimed, "you can't believe I had anything to do with that!"

"Of course not"—he laughed sarcastically—"because you're pretty and a female; I'm sure robbery is beneath you."

"Well, of course it's beneath me," she stated emphatically. "I would never be involved in anything like that. It just happened that I was in the wrong place at the wrong time."

"Of course." He laughed, mockery in his voice. "That accounts for why you were dressed as a man, and also why you were so interested in my card playing habits."

"That didn't have anything to do with the robberies," Shadow persisted. "I was only interested in . . . I mean . . . I wanted to—"

"Yes"—he smiled, his face only inches from hers—"I do want to hear everything, my pet. Why don't we start with your name."

She stared at him, trying to decide what to do. She couldn't give him her name. It would be the talk of the town, and she would be ruined. God, if her grandfather knew how she had gotten herself into such a mess, he would probably strangle her—or worse send her off to live with a cousin as he always threatened when she got too headstrong. Fighting for composure, she took a deep breath. "Sir, you must believe I had nothing to do with those robberies."

"My, my, but you are an excellent actress, my dear. You almost sounded like a lady, but I'm used to dealing with women like you. I've been around them all my life," he said bitterly.

"I am a lady," she insisted impatiently. "And the only reason I entered your room was to avoid running in to someone I did not wish to see."

Josh ran a finger down her smooth neck and across her shoulder. "Would that someone have been the sheriff?"

"No!" she denied, shoving his hand away. "Damn you, return my clothes this minute."

"Ah, now that's more in keeping with a whore. Somehow it suits you better, pretty one." His warm hand touched the skin just above her breast.

"A whore! How dare you," she gasped, as she

kicked out at him. "Damn you, I'm not a whore!"

"Every woman I've ever met is a whore," he growled, "some better than others, but all whores."

"Release me, you bastard!" she screamed. "You can't keep me here like this!"

He grabbed the long slender leg that kicked out at him. "Can't I?" he said, the timbre of his voice suddenly deadly serious as he ran his hand up the inside of her leg. "Lady, I plan to keep you here just as long as it takes to find out who your accomplices are, and why you've been hitting my place and not O'Hara's."

Shadow drew a deep breath. Somehow she had to get herself out of this mess. "I will try to explain calmly one more time," she said in exasperation. "I have no accomplices. I have done nothing wrong, certainly nothing to warrant this type of treatment, and I have no idea why you've been robbed and O'Hara's hasn't. Now, I have answered all your questions, so I suggest that you give me my clothes and let me leave here before you're in a lot of trouble. Kidnapping is a very serious offense."

His deep laughter surprised her. "You have an incredible amount of nerve; I'll give you that, my little thief. But might I remind you that the only one in trouble here is you," he said, his gold eyes glittering dangerously. "Or didn't you know that robbery is a hanging offense?"

Shadow's eyes widened in disbelief. He couldn't be serious. "You've asked your questions, and I have no answers. Now enough is enough, Mr. Rawlings." She tried to sound sure of herself.

His face was only inches from hers. "The inquisition hasn't even begun, my pet. Whatever it takes, I mean to have the truth from you."

The color drained from her face. "You can't mean to hurt me again?" she asked in a faint voice.

"That all depends on you. I don't usually go around beating up women, but I want your accomplices bad enough to do anything that it takes."

"Well, I've told you the truth," she said, turning away from his intense smoldering eyes. "I know nothing about the robberies."

"So you said, but the evidence proves otherwise."

"Evidence? You call my being dressed in male clothing evidence?"

As his fingers clamped on her shoulders, the blanket dropped to her waist. He stared at the beautiful pink-tipped nipples inviting his kisses. It was all he could do to keep his mind on why he had her there. God, she was beautiful with those innocent blue eyes and strawberry-blond hair. But dammit, she couldn't be as innocent as she looked. He'd known women like her all his life—all sweet and innocent to look at, but seething with venom when it served their purpose. Hadn't his stepmother been an expert in that field. This bitch had probably made herself available to all the men she rode with, and that thought angered him beyond reason as he remembered his stepmother coming to his bed when he was only fourteen.

Shadow watched the expressions change on his face and wondered what was going on in his head. One moment his gold eyes smoldered with something she didn't understand, and the next they flashed with undisguised hatred. When she tried to pull away from his grip, he only held her tighter. "Please, you're hurting me."

"Were you supposed to kill me?" he asked between gritted teeth.

"Kill you?" she asked in bewilderment. "Oh, God, how could you think such a thing . . . ?"

"I searched through your clothes, but there was no weapon. How did you plan to do it?" His grip tightened painfully. "Tell me what your part was in this foul plot. I already know you tried to keep me at the card tables, and when that failed, you snuck into my room. If I hadn't discovered you, there is no telling what you would have done. Isn't that right, my sweet?" he asked in a savage whisper. "Who wants me dead?" he asked again, his fingers digging into her shoulders.

Anger and frustration surged inside her. She raised her hand and struck out at him, her nails leaving gashes down the side of his face.

"Bitch," he hissed, grabbing her wrist in a numbing grip. "You will regret that. . . ." Her breasts were flattened against his chest as she panted in frustrated anger. Their gazes locked in silent struggle as each became aware of something strange and powerful building between them.

"I will have the truth sooner or later, my little wildcat. Perhaps I should just slow down and enjoy our little interrogation. We have all the time in the world," he said as his hand caressed her breast. "You know, it was mighty obliging of your friends to leave you behind for my pleasure," he whispered huskily. "Particularly since you interrupted my evening with Patience."

41

He wrapped his fingers in her hair and forced her head back, then with perverse pleasure he slowly lowered his head and ran his tongue along her bruised and swollen lips and down her neck. "You smell and taste mighty sweet for a girl who runs with a band of outlaws."

"I don't . . ." was all she could manage to exhale as his tongue slipped inside her mouth. She felt a queer sense of detachment, as if this were happening to someone else.

"I'm going to enjoy forcing you to tell me the truth," he said before his teeth gently captured a taut nipple.

"No, please no," she cried. This couldn't be happening. This stranger meant to ravage her, and there was nothing she could do to stop him. Fight him, she told herself, but even if she'd had the strength, her body seemed to have a mind of its own. She had lost all feeling in the arm he held so tightly, and for some unknown reason, she couldn't seem to muster the strength or desire to shove him away.

"Sometimes it's easier to make a person talk when you use kindness," he whispered against her mouth. "Is that what you need, little one, a gentle hand? Perhaps you've been mistreated by the men you ride with. . . ."

"I don't ride with men, and I know nothing about your robberies." She forced the words out.

"Your friends don't deserve such loyalty," he said, his breath warm against her throat. "They left you behind with no thought for your safety. They must have known what I would do to you. . . ."

Shadow thought of Toby and wondered if he had

42

gone looking for her. Poor Toby, how would he face her grandfather. Her grandfather. Oh, God, what if they thought the robbers had kidnapped her and had gone after them . . . ?

Seeing the panic in her eyes, Josh smiled. "Good, I can see my words make sense to you."

"Please, you must let me go immediately. My grandfather could be in danger."

"Your grandfather?" he said in disgust. "Do you mean to tell me your grandfather was one of those men who left you behind?"

"Dammit, this is too ridiculous for words." She struggled against his firm grip. "I was not with the robbers, Mr. Rawlings. I was only in your casino to play cards; and I know that isn't proper for a lady, but I don't believe it's a crime. Now I insist you release me this moment!"

"Is that right?" He laughed in soft satisfaction. He couldn't help but admire her. Even though her face was white with fear, her chin was thrust forward stubbornly and proudly. "I like a woman with spirit, little one. Now, why don't you save yourself a lot of trouble and tell me who this grandfather of yours is?"

"Oh," she said in exasperation, turning her head away from his piercing gold eyes. "You are the most stubborn, hardheaded, stupid man I've ever met."

"And you are the most stubborn, hardheaded, beautiful woman I've ever met," he retorted as he moved his hand down over her stomach. "And your skin feels like velvet. You deserve better than the life you've been leading. Tell me the truth, and I'll make life easier for you. I'll make you my mistress and set

43

you up with your own place in town. I'll buy you beautiful gowns to wear . . ."

At the touch of his hand on her naked skin, she began to shake her head back and forth. "No, please, you are making a grave mistake," she warned, fighting back tears. "If you persist, you will ruin both our lives."

"Now, why would my enjoying the favors of a girl who rides with outlaws ruin both our lives?" he asked, staring down into her blue eyes.

She shut her eyes tightly against his questioning gaze. A shudder rippled over her as his hand moved still lower. She was shaken by the surge of desire pulsing through her veins. Oh, God, what was happening to her? Why did his touch make her heart pound in her breast and her blood feel as if it were fire rushing through her veins?

She breathed a sigh of relief as she felt his weight lift from the bed, but when she opened her eyes, she saw him step out of his breeches. The lamp flickered over his skin, making his body look like gleaming bronze. The muscles of his chest rippled as he moved to lie back down beside her.

He leaned up on one elbow, staring down at her. "You know you didn't really want me to leave," he whispered against her cheek. "I can see the smoldering desire in those eyes."

"If you weren't so damn arrogant, you'd know that what you see is fear."

"Come now, you know you have nothing to fear from me as long as you cooperate."

"That's the whole point, Mr. Rawlings," she said in exasperation, "I can't cooperate. I have nothing to tell you."

"You are so beautiful," he whispered, ignoring her struggles. His gaze lingered upon the curling bronze triangle of hair between her long legs, and an image of her wrapping those slender legs around his body made him moan with desire.

"Please don't do this to me," she whispered, even though she had the feeling she would surely die if he stopped. "I . . . I will tell you. . . ."

"I'm afraid any choice in the matter has been taken from both of us, little one," he whispered huskily. "I must have you now. . . ."

She lifted her hands to hold him off as he moved his body on top of hers, but instead she spread her fingers over his broad shoulders and down the corded, steellike muscles of his arms. "You are making a terrible mistake," she murmured.

"I don't think so," he said, parting her thighs. His fingers gently touched her most private part as he knelt above her.

The heat of his hand sent shock waves through her. She felt as if the nerve endings were exposed; everywhere he touched she felt on fire. As he leaned forward to capture her mouth, his swollen manhood pressed against her abdomen. A strange trembling sensation erupted in the pit of her stomach as her response grew. She lifted her hips seeking release. One moment she felt shame that she was reacting to his slow and tantalizing arousal, yet the next she told herself nothing mattered but the feelings he evoked. It was pain and pleasure, refined cruelty, yet she had to know what the conclusion would bring.

"Look at me," he ordered in a husky voice.

Shadow opened her eyes and stared into his smoldering gold eyes as he guided himself into her soft moist flesh. She was surprised at his whispered curse as he met resistance. He tensed above her, but only for a brief moment.

"This is a night full of surprises," he whispered.

A strangled cry caught in her throat as a moment of sharp pain engulfed her. Then it was gone, and Shadow felt as one possessed. She moved with him, matching his rhythm as he moved in and out of her soft moistness. She closed her eyes again and caressed the blond hair that curled at the nape of his neck.

"Open your eyes, little one. I want to see your face when you experience your first time," he demanded.

"I am surely going to die," she cried out, digging her nails into his arms as a wild, stunning wave of exquisite pleasure washed over her, a never-ending wave that took her up, up. . . . She heard herself crying out his name as he plunged into her hungrily.

When at last the incredible emotion had spent itself, Josh cradled her in his arms, amazed at what had happened between them. He smoothed the hair away from her face and realized she had fallen to sleep. "Yes, this night has been full of surprises," he whispered into the darkness. As he studied the girl's beautiful face, he realized he had never enjoyed a woman as much as he had this one. She was an innocent, yet she had matched his passion to the end.

Josh gently touched her bruised jaw. There was one undeniable fact he had to remember: She was an outlaw, and he still hadn't gotten any answers from her. He ran his hand over her breast, touching the nipple with his thumb and feeling it harden. There was still tomorrow; he smiled in anticipation.

Josh joined his brother at the bar where Matt was counting the night's take of money. The place was empty except for Henry, the old-timer sweeping up. Josh poured himself a drink, saying nothing as his brother stared at him, a puzzled look on his face.

"Where the hell did you get those scratches?"

"I ran into a wildcat," Josh said before downing his drink.

"I don't understand . . ." Matt said bewildered. "I thought you had one of the robbers."

"I do," he answered abruptly.

"You mean to tell me the robber you caught did that to you?"

"That's right."

"Well, I hope the hell you got what you wanted out of him," Matt swore.

"I suppose you could say I did," Josh answered as he poured himself another drink.

"Then, you know who the other robbers are?"

"I didn't say that," he answered.

"What the hell have you been doing in there behind locked doors all this time?" Matt asked in exasperation. "Did you end up killing the bastard before you got the information we needed?"

"No" — he laughed — "but I've had to change the way I go about getting information."

Matt stared at his brother, wondering what the

hell was wrong with him. "Do you mind explaining what's going on?"

Josh glanced around at the old man who was slowly sweeping the floor. "Henry, do you think you could get me something to eat. Maybe some of that cold beef Lottie had this evening, and some bread."

"Sure, boss." The old man nodded.

"I don't want anyone to know about the prisoner," Josh said quietly.

"Good, then we do still have a prisoner," Matt said sarcastically.

"Yes, but it turns out it isn't a he. It's a beautiful young woman."

"Come on." His brother laughed.

"Damn it, it's true. I didn't know it was a woman until I hit her and knocked her out. Then all this beautiful blond hair tumbled out from beneath her hat. . . ."

"And you still think she had something to do with the robberies?"

"I'm convinced of it. She refuses to even tell me her name."

"What kind of a woman rides with outlaws," Matt said in disgust.

"A very beautiful one," Josh answered. "And on top of that, she has the manners and speech of a highbred lady."

"I want to see this for myself," Matt said, stuffing the money in a pouch.

"No." Josh quickly stood up. "Not tonight, Matt. She's asleep. I'm afraid I was a little hard on her."

"Here's that food you wanted, Mr. Rawlings," Henry interrupted. "I put some cheese on the plate,

48

too."

"Thanks, Henry. I appreciate it," Josh said as he leaned over the bar and poured a glass of beer. "I'm going to turn in, Matt. We'll talk again in the morning."

"Josh . . ."

"Maybe I'll have some answers then," he said over his shoulder, cutting off any further questions.

As soon as Josh opened the door to his bedroom, Shadow started screaming at him. "Untie me this instant! How dare you tie me to the bed while I was asleep."

"It is only a temporary measure," he said, amused that she should be upset about being tied to the bed instead of losing her virginity to him only an hour before. "I couldn't take a chance on you escaping before I had my answers."

"My God, are we going to start that again?" she asked in utter disbelief.

"Very definitely," he answered as he set the food and beer on the table beside the bed. "You were about to give me the answers I wanted just before your passionate outburst."

She lowered her gaze, unable to look into the gold eyes that taunted her.

"Are you hungry?" he asked.

She was famished, but she wasn't about to tell him that, or anything else, for that matter.

He sat on the side of the bed and examined the plate. "Let's see, I have cold roast beef." He broke off a piece and tossed it into his mouth. "Um . . .

delicious. There's also some sharp cheese and a loaf of Lottie's delicious bread, and to wash it down, a refreshing beer. Does that sound good to you, love?"

Shadow turned her head away and stared at the wall.

"Feeling a little touchy, are you? Well, you shouldn't. You were a delightful surprise in bed, and my offer still stands to make you my mistress."

Shadow's head snapped back around to stare at him. "Your mistress?" she gasped in disbelief. "Is that how you dismiss rape, Mr. Rawlings? Without concern for me, you have ruined my life, and all you can do is offer to make me your mistress?" Her voice rose in anger. "You . . . you bastard . . . you're a blackguard, a scoundrel; oh, I can't think of words strong enough."

"Did you expect a proposal?" he asked, a wicked grin on his handsome face.

"I expect nothing from you," she spat, "and you will get nothing further from me. Now leave me alone. I don't feel well."

"That's a typical reaction to losing your virginity, Wildcat. You're probably a bit sore between the legs now, but by morning you should feel fine."

"You sound as if you've had quite a bit of experience dealing with raped virgins, Mr. Rawlings," she spat sarcastically.

"Regardless of what you think, I don't make it a practice of seducing inexperienced women. Your case was different."

"Would you mind explaining why?" she asked.

"You're very beautiful; but still, you are a common criminal, and you refused to answer my questions. But I'm sure all that is changed now."

"I have no intention of answering your questions," she said defiantly. "There is nothing further you can do to me, so you may as well release me."

"Really, my love? You don't consider being paraded naked before everyone in town on your way to jail just a little bit embarrassing?"

"You wouldn't—"

"You would be wise to believe I will do far worse if I don't have my answers soon," he warned. "But there is time for that. Here, have a bite of food."

Shadow accepted the piece of meat he placed in her mouth as she contemplated his threat. The only way she could see to get out of this predicament was to make him trust her so he wouldn't tie her up everytime he left the room. Then she would make her escape.

"Another bite?" he offered.

"Yes, please. It's very good." She smiled. "Do I still need to have my hands tied?" she asked sweetly.

"You can stop the act, my pet. The hands are going to stay tied while we sleep. I don't intend to sit up watching you all night."

"You don't have to. Just untie me, and I promise I'll stay here until morning."

"You must think I'm a fool." He laughed. "Here, take a drink of this," he said, holding the glass of beer to her lips. When she finished taking a drink, she had a line of foam along her upper lip. "Let me get that for you," he said, leaning forward and running his tongue sensuously along her lip. "You know, Wildcat, I rather like you like this."

"Just don't get any ideas about keeping me like

this," she protested.

Josh studied her tied to his bed, her arms above her head. Animal lust so primitive it frightened him and threatened to take over. "I suggest you eat and then get to sleep. Otherwise I may be forced to enjoy your lovely body again."

"You wouldn't—"

"Don't tempt me, Wildcat. You look mighty tempting tied to my bed."

"You are a depraved animal," she spat.

A grim smile flickered in his amber eyes, and he laughed softly. "You may be right."

Yield not thy neck
To fortune's yoke, but let thy
    dauntless mine
Still ride in triumph over all mischance.

—Shakespeare

Chapter Three

The aroma of strong coffee drifted to her, inviting her awake. Shadow stetched her arms above her head, then with a gasp drew back, suddenly aware of the tenderness between her legs. Oh, God, it hadn't been a dream. Her eyes flew open and met Josh Rawlings' gold stare.

"Good morning. Did you sleep well?" he asked, as if nothing had happened.

"How could I possibly sleep well when I've been dishonored, and now I'm being held a prisoner?" she snapped.

"My, my but aren't we touchy this morning?" He

grinned. "I thought you would be grateful that I had untied your hands during the night — when you were sleeping like a bear in hibernation, I might add."

"I was not! I never slept a wink."

"If you would like to freshen up, there's water and towels in that room," he said, pointing to a door off the bedroom.

"Yes, I would like that. I would also like my clothes," Shadow snapped as she wrapped the sheet around her like a toga.

"Sorry, I had those rags burned. You will find a robe hanging on the door."

"Burned . . . you burned my clothes . . . how dare you!"

"If you're going to be my mistress, you will have to dress decently. Granted, I wouldn't mind keeping you naked all the time, but I'm sure there will be times when you'll want to get out and socialize."

"You can go to hell," she shouted before slamming the door.

Josh smiled, thinking what a delightful little wildcat she was. "As soon as you tell me who your accomplices were, I'll buy you a whole new wardrobe," he shouted back through the door.

Shadow stood in the middle of a small room, looking for some way out, but there was none. Instead she found a large brass tub, items to complete her toilette, a large mirror on a floor stand, an armoire filled with male clothes, and a chest filled with towels and pretty bottles. She picked up a jar and sniffed the contents of perfumed oils and fragrances. The man was prepared for everything, she thought in disgust. She supposed most women he entertained were there of their own choosing. If circumstances had been different, she might even have been attracted to his handsome looks.

Oh, God, what was she thinking; she stared at herself in the mirror. The man was arrogant, cruel and selfish. He was a gambler, beneath her social station —

She let the sheet drop and stared at her own slim body. He was all those things, yet he had made her feel things she never imagined she could feel. How was it possible to hate a person yet feel drawn to him at the same time? If she had met him in a different way and taken him home to her grandfather, would he even have been accepted?

"Grandfather . . . " she gasped in horror. Oh, God, by now her grandfather would be looking for her, along with half of the town. When people found out what had happened to her, she wouldn't be able to hold her head up in Natchez. She had to find a way to escape, then she would worry about excuses.

She finished her toilette and wrapped the silk robe around her. She glanced at herself in the mirror again. *I don't look any different,* she thought, *yet I'm not the innocent girl I was yesterday. I'm a woman now . . . I know a man's touch. . . .*

"Wildcat, are you going to be all morning?" Josh shouted. "Breakfast is getting cold."

Reluctantly she stepped back into his bedroom and found him sitting at a small table casually smoking a cheroot and reading a newspaper.

"Sit down and eat. You'll find Lottie is an excellent cook. I didn't know what you liked, but there are eggs and bacon here, and some of the best biscuits you'll ever taste."

Shadow's stomach growled as the smell of food assailed her senses. She sat down and buttered a biscuit. "Who is Lottie?" she asked between bites.

"She takes care of my brother and me," he answered as he sipped his coffee. "She worked for the previous owner and agreed to stay on to clean and cook for us."

"You have a brother?"

"That's right, love. I'm just your normal run of the mill guy." He laughed.

"I doubt that," Shadow said as she dug into her food with a ravenous appetite.

Josh leaned forward and studied her as she ate. "Why don't we stop this cat and mouse game. Tell me who your friends were, and this afternoon I will have Madame Roget come by and take your measurements for some new clothes."

"No!" Shadow exclaimed, dropping her fork. She couldn't tell him that Madame Roget was her dressmaker. If the woman ever saw her there, the tongues would never stop wagging. "I told you, I have nothing to tell you."

"Dammit, woman, I'm losing patience with you. Last night you were ready to tell me who your friends were," he said angrily, throwing his napkin on the table.

"I lied," she said, her blue eyes sparkling. "So you may as well give me something to wear and let me leave here."

"Not on your life," he growled. "You're going to tell me what I want to know."

Shadow decided a change of tack was needed. "All right. I was with the men who tried to rob you last night," she lied, "but I don't know any of their names. I only met them yesterday."

"Really?" he said, frowning. "That may be, but I do recall you mentioning a grandfather."

Damn him, she thought silently. "I mentioned him because I knew he would be worried about me. I certainly did not mean that he was one of the robbers. I rode into town from Port Gibson, looking for some excitement. The robbers were camped on the outskirts of town and invited me to ride with them," she lied, keeping her eyes averted. "I thought it sounded exciting." She glanced hesitantly at him when he didn't respond. "I had no idea what I'd be getting into."

"You're a liar. A beautiful one, but nevertheless a liar," he said with an icy smile.

"How dare you. I finally tell you the truth—"

"Enough!" he erupted, coming to his feet. "I've dealt with lying, cheating women all my life, and you're not even in the upper ranks of them."

Shadow was stunned at his outburst. She drew back in the chair as he leaned forward, pinning her there with an arm on each side of her shoulders.

"Tell me your name," he growled.

His eyes were cold, and a tight line around his mouth told her he meant business. "It's Cassandra," she admitted.

"Cassandra—the bearer of ill tidings, and never to be believed. It suits you," he sneered.

Cassandra had heard what her name meant from a prissy little girl one morning at Sunday school

when she was only seven. That was why she pre-
ferred the name her grandfather called her.

"What is your last name?" he persisted.

"Russell," she quickly answered, using the married
name of an aunt.

Some of his fury seemed to fade. "Cassandra Russell," he repeated. "We shall soon see if you're telling
me the truth," he said, pulling on his jacket.

"What do you mean to do?" she asked, suddenly
feeling a sense of doom.

"I'm going to ask a few questions about Cassandra Russell around town."

"I told you, I'm not from Natchez," she explained
nervously, knowing that all he had to do was hear
someone's granddaughter was missing, and he'd put
two and two together. "Are you going to leave me
alone?" she asked tentatively.

"Not on your life, my sweet. My brother will be
your keeper while I'm gone."

She managed a smile. "I'll be glad for the change.
He has to be nicer than you."

"He is, sweetheart, but I've already warned him
about you. Besides, he doesn't like being robbed any
better than I do."

She stared at the door as he closed it. This was
her chance, she thought, looking around for something to put on besides the robe. Damn, there wasn't
time to search for her clothes. If she was going to
get out of there, she had to move fast.

She opened the door just a crack and peeked
through it. Good, the place seemed to be empty.
Clutching the robe around her, she stepped barefoot
into the room where she had played cards the night

before.

"I wouldn't advise it," a voice said behind her. "You're sure to catch cold dressed like that."

Shadow spun around and faced a dark-haired version of Josh Rawlings. He leaned against the doorjamb, a steaming cup of coffee in his hand.

"I'm Matt Rawlings." He smiled. "I understand we still don't know your identity."

"I told your brother who I was, but he doesn't believe me," she spat.

"Josh can be a bit stubborn," he said, looking her up and down appreciatively, "but he certainly didn't exaggerate when he said you were beautiful."

"Are you aware your brother is holding me against my will?" she asked, hoping to see some compassion in his brown eyes.

"I've never heard a woman complain about having to stay with Josh before." He laughed. "Usually it's the other way around."

"Please, you look like a nice man. Let me leave here," she pleaded, her soft blue eyes filling with tears. "Your brother has not been kind to me."

Matt opened the door to Josh's room and stepped aside for her to enter. "I'm afraid you will have to bear his company just a little while longer, my dear. Just keep in mind that staying here is better than going to jail. Tate Fuller, our sheriff, is not the most pleasant man in Natchez."

"You are both cruel, cold-hearted bastards!" she spat, storming past him into the room.

"I'm sorry you think so," he said, following her. "My brother is really a very decent person. Most people like him."

Shadow paced, furious that she had been caught. "Your brother is the devil!" she spat.

Matt smiled, taking another sip of his coffee. "I suppose there are some who have thought that; but you know, all you have to do is tell the truth about your involvement in the robberies, and he'll let you go."

"Please," Shadow drawled, holding her hand up. "At least spare me any more of this foolishness while he's not here."

"Of course," he agreed. "May I pour you some coffee?"

"Yes, that would be nice. I didn't have a chance to finish my breakfast with your brother intimidating me."

"Come, sit down," he said, pulling a chair out. "Lottie's biscuits are good even when they're cold. Try some of the jam on one."

Shadow smiled, taking the chair offered. Perhaps this brother wasn't as bad, she thought. Maybe she could win him over to her side and get away. She spooned jam on the biscuit and took a bite. "Um . . . you're right, it's delicious."

Matt took the chair across from her. He picked up one of the biscuits and spread jam on it. "Lottie is one of the best things that happened to us," he said, taking a bite. "I'm sure I've gained ten pounds since we've been here."

"How long have you been in Natchez?" she asked.

"A little over six months."

"You've accomplished a lot with Yancey's in that short a time," she exclaimed.

"Ah, so you were familiar with Yancey's before

Josh took it over."

Shadow's eyes met his. "I didn't say that."

Matt laughed. "Relax. You don't have to be on the defensive with me. I'll leave your interrogation to my brother."

"That is not a very pleasant thought," she said, lowering her eyes coyly. "He has been very cruel to me."

"Isn't that strange; I thought it was the other way around, since he's the one who bears the scars," Matt said, patting her hand sympathetically. "You know, my dear, all you have to do is cooperate with him, and it will all be over."

"Please, you said we wouldn't discuss this," she complained, rubbing her temples in a display of femininity.

"Of course. Forgive me." He smiled.

"Neither of you have a Southern accent," she commented a moment later as she sipped her coffee.

"That's because we're not from the South." He laughed. "We're from California."

"Oh, my, I've never met anyone from California," she exclaimed. "Whatever brought you to Mississippi?"

"We've been traveling around the country for over a year now. When Josh won this place in a card game, he decided he'd like to run it for a while. I doubt we'll be here long. Josh is the restless type."

"I'd like to travel around and see the country," Shadow said, a dreamy look in her eyes. "I went to Europe with an aunt a few years ago. I enjoyed the trip, but I must admit, I was glad to come home."

"I know the feeling. I've been ready to go back to

California for months. Tell me, what did you enjoy most about Europe?"

Shadow thought for a moment. "I think the museums and cathedrals. And there was a grand ball at Sutton Castle that I shall never forget." Suddenly her eyes met his, and she knew she'd made a mistake.

"Josh said you talked and acted like a lady." He smiled. "Why don't you tell me why you're playing this game?"

"I can't." She turned away from him. "It is all too complicated."

"Is it because you're afraid to face the consequences of your crime, or is it because you're enjoying my brother's company?"

Shadow came to her feet. "I have committed no crime!" she screamed, "and I abhor the company of your obnoxious brother."

"I'm glad to see you two are getting along so well," Josh said as he entered the room. "And here I was concerned that Wildcat would try to make you feel sorry for her. I can see my worries were unfounded."

Matt picked up his coffee cup and headed for the door. "She isn't like the others, Josh," he whispered. "Maybe you should listen to her."

Josh laughed bitterly. "When are you going to learn, little brother, that you can't trust a woman. They're all alike. I'm surprised you let this one get to you."

"And she didn't get to you?" Matt asked smugly. He laughed at the look on his brother's face. "Don't forget we have an audition to listen to this morning.

Of course if you're too busy . . ."

"Just let me know when she arrives," Josh growled.

Picking up the bottle of brandy, Josh poured himself a drink. What his brother had said bothered him. This girl was definitely a lady; but why had she been in his gambling hall playing cards, and why had she been looking for him?

Shadow paced the room, wondering if Josh had found out anything. She couldn't stand the suspense of not knowing if her life had already been ruined. "Well, what did you find out about Cassandra Russell?" she asked impatiently when several minutes had passed and he hadn't said anything.

"I'm sorry, Wildcat. What did you say?" he asked, preoccupied.

"Damn you!" she screamed, her hands on her hips. "What did you find out?"

"Find out?" he asked, his mind still on his brother's parting words. "Oh, you mean about the robbery. I didn't have much of a chance to ask questions around town. Somebody's little kid is missing, and everybody seemed involved in that."

"I'm sorry to hear that," she said, turning her back to him. "Whose child is it?"

"I didn't ask," he said, removing his jacket. "I had an image of you seducing my brother, so I hurried back here."

"Bastard," she hissed. "It's too bad you can't be a gentleman like him."

"I've been told that before" — he laughed bitterly — "but then every family has to have a black sheep in it."

"Or a devil," she sneered.

Josh laughed. "I suppose I was born with a bit of the devil in me."

"More than a bit," she retorted.

Silence fell between them again. Shadow paced, studying his handsome features and wondering what was going on in his mind. He seemed preoccupied with something.

"Why have you been lying to me?" he asked.

"I—I had to," she stammered, taken by surprise.

"It has cost you a great deal."

"Yes, I must admit, I wasn't prepared for that," she said, rubbing the silk sleeve of the robe.

"Are you protecting someone?"

Shadow's eyes snapped to his face. "Yes, but certainly not who you think."

"Not one of the robbers?"

"I have told you the truth about that," she said, moving restlessly about the room.

"Now what truth is that?" he said, a gleam of amusement in his eyes. "That you did join them for the excitement, or that you weren't involved in the robbery?"

"You know I wasn't with them," she snapped.

"Yes, I must agree," he said, stroking his mustache. "It defies the imagination to picture you riding with a bunch of outlaws."

"Well, thank you for that vote of confidence, Mr. Rawlings," she drawled sarcastically. "I'm so glad you finally believe me."

"But there is still one thing, Wildcat," he said, moving close to her. "Just who are you?"

She stared at him, trying to come up with something that would satisfy him, yet still protect her. "I told you, I'm Cassandra Russell."

He picked up a lock of her strawberry-blond hair and rubbed it between his fingers. "I don't think so," he said softly.

His touch sent warm shivers down her spine. "I don't care what you think," she whispered breathlessly, her nerves stretched taut. "Since we have come to an impasse, I assume you will now release me."

"An impasse?" He laughed. "Is that what we have come to, love?"

"Well, you said you believed me," she said in frustration.

"About the robberies, yes; but you're still a puzzle to me, little one, and I have no intention of releasing you until I know everything about you."

"You can't mean to keep me here. . . ."

Josh flashed her a lazy grin. "Oh, but I do mean to. At least until I tire of your lovely body, and I can't imagine doing that anytime soon."

His words hit her like a bolt of lightning. "No! Never!" she spat, suddenly sickened at the sordidness of what had taken place between them. "You're a bastard . . . a monstrous beast, and I will not give in to you again."

Josh grabbed her by the wrist and pulled her against him. "And you're a lying bitch," he whispered as he stared down into her damning eyes, "but I still want you."

His lips sought hers, warm and inviting. "No please," she begged against his mouth. "Don't do this. . . ."

"You enjoy my company as much as I enjoy

65

yours," he said, smiling down into her face. "Even though it's very similar to being caged with a wildcat."

"You can't do this," she protested. "I'm not a plaything for you to keep around. I'm a human being, and I have feelings."

"Oh, I'm aware of that, Wildcat. That's why I want you with me."

"Don't you have a conscience?" she screamed as she fought to break his hold on her.

His hands moved inside the robe and caressed her breast. She felt a multitude of emotions as her breathing became rapid. She wanted to kill him for humiliating her, yet at the same time, she felt the familiar start of a shuddering sensation in the pit of her stomach. Oh, God, how could she react this way? She was no better than the dance hall girls that clung to him, she thought shamefully.

"Please leave me alone," she begged. "I will not let you humiliate me again."

He released his hold on her and stepped back. "Look at yourself," he said, unbuttoning his shirt. "Your eyes are ablaze with passion. How can you deny you want me as badly as I want you?"

"Stay away from me, damn you!" she cried, backing away from him. "You have women waiting at your beck and call," she said in a trembling voice. "Why do you insist on harrassing me?"

"I'm not sure, Wildcat," he admitted. "All I know is I want you."

"Well, you can't have me!" she screamed.

Josh understood her fear. She was probably wrestling with her conscience after the passion she had shown the night before, but still he couldn't deny his need for her.

"Come here, Wildcat. Let me love you," he said gently.

Suddenly she darted toward the door, but he was there before she could open it. He turned her around and pinned her against it, his arms like steel bands on each side of her. "Don't fight me, Wildcat. It won't do any good."

"I will not let you do this again," she gasped, struggling against him.

He wrapped his hand in the luxuriant mass of her blond hair and forced her head closer. "Kiss me, love. Put your tongue out and run it over my lips."

"Please don't—"

Fiercely his mouth descended on hers, forcing her lips apart. She could feel the heat of his swollen manhood as he moved his body against hers.

"You are so lovely, so desirable," he whispered, pushing the satin robe off her shoulders. His lips traveled down her neck and across her shoulders, before kissing each pink nipple.

She tried to think of something else, to picture him doing this to one of his saloon girls, but nothing helped. Her body reacted to his touch as if it had a mind of its own.

She opened her eyes, and the first thing she saw was his gun hanging in a holster next to his jacket. Just maybe she could stop him, she thought wildly. She brought her knee up, connecting with a muscular thigh instead of her intended target. Surprised, he stepped back, giving her the chance to dive for the gun before he realized her intent.

She turned and faced him, the silver gun pointed at his stomach. "Don't come any closer," she warned. "I know how to use this, and I will."

"I bet you do," he hissed. "Is this what you had planned all along?"

"No! I just want you to leave me alone. You have shamed me enough," she cried.

"Shamed you?" he said in disbelief. "There is nothing about our lovemaking that should shame you. It was beautiful and natural."

"How will I ever face—" She shook her head. "Damn you, damn you," she said, tears running down her cheeks.

"Come, little one, put the gun down. You're making me very nervous." He held his hand out to her. "I don't think you want to kill me."

"I don't want to hurt anyone," she said, rubbing the back of her hand across her eyes, "but you've forced me to."

"Give me the gun, love," he said, moving a step closer.

"No!" she screamed, pulling the trigger.

A bullet whistled past Josh's head. "Jesus Christ," he swore, grabbing her by the wrist.

The gun clattered to the floor as he shoved her toward the bed. "You're lucky I don't strangle you," he growled, pinning her to the bed with his body. "Yet all I can think about is making love to you."

He had kissed hundreds of women, and probably made love to as many, but this one was different. His feelings for this one confused and staggered him. His golden head lowered and gently touched her lips. "God, Wildcat, what am I going to do with you?"

She wrapped her arms around his neck pulling him closer. There was nothing she could do to stop the wild beating of her heart or the pulsing between her legs. She would give in to him—and she would enjoy it. "I hate you, Josh Rawlings," she whispered against his mouth.

There was a slight grin on his face as he stared down at her. "I don't believe it, Wildcat. I don't believe it for a minute."

Their lovemaking had been tender and beautiful after starting on such a violent note. Now he slept peacefully at her side like a child. He looked so vulnerable in sleep, she thought, gently touching a gold curl that fell over his forehead. Staring at him, she was conscious of the strangest sensation. A feeling of possessiveness overwhelmed her, and she couldn't bear to think of the other women he had enjoyed—or would enjoy.

Oh, God, she was being ridiculous again, she chastised herself silently. She had to get back to Lansing Creek and to reality.

She watched his face as she slowly slipped out from beneath the leg that held her so possessively. He moaned softly, but didn't move.

Shadow glanced around the room. She had to find something to wear, she thought desperately. People would be drifting into the casino about now, and she couldn't draw attention to herself.

The only items of her clothing that she found were her boots. Well, at least that's something, she thought as she pulled them on. She grabbed Josh's white silk shirt and slipped it on, savoring the feel of its softness and the delicious smell of Josh Rawlings. Pull yourself together, she told herself. You're wasting precious time.

Now what, she thought, glancing around the room. His pants would swallow her whole. Hanging on the rack where his gun had been was a beige canvas riding coat which was worn in rainy weather. She lifted it from the rack and held it up to her. It came down to her ankles, but it would have to do, she decided.

When she reached the door, she hesitated. Turning, she took one last look at Josh sleeping so peacefully. She felt a heavy ache in her heart, and a strange sense of loss. "Good-bye, Josh Rawlings," she whispered before slipping through the door.

Forget not yet the tried intent
Of such a truth as I have meant;
My great travail so gladly spent,
Forget not yet!

—Sir Thomas Wyatt

Chapter Four

Shadow stared out the window of her room. Why did she feel so alone when she was back among her own things and in her beautiful room at Lansing Creek. Her grandfather had accepted her story, that she had been thrown from her horse and helped by an old couple on the outskirts of town. Martha was another story though. She could see the black woman shake her head in disbelief as she told her story, but she knew Martha wouldn't betray her.

It was one thing to sneak into town to play cards behind her grandfather's back, but now she was having to lie to him about something so important that it could change her whole life. Oh, God, what if she were with child . . . Damn him! Damn Josh Rawlings! This was all his fault.

Suddenly his smiling face came unbidden to her thoughts. Had it only been yesterday that she lay in his arms? A dull ache suddenly enveloped her as she recalled how his hands had moved over her body, and how his tongue had plundered her mouth.

A knock at the door startled her. "May I come in, dear?" her grandfather asked.

Shadow smiled at the white-haired man she loved more than anyone else in the world. "Yes, of course, Grandfather."

"Martha tells me you haven't eaten a thing all day," he said, concerned.

"I'm sorry, Grandfather. I'm just not very hungry."

"I understand," he said, hugging her. "I'm sure tomorrow you'll feel more like eating. I have some business to take care of in town this evening," he said, kissing her on the forehead. "Will you be all right?"

"I'll be fine." She smiled through her tears. "I plan to retire early."

Noble pushed back a strand of her blond hair, still wondering if what she had told him about her night away from home was the truth. "I hope to have a surprise for you in the morning. Will you plan to go riding with me?"

"Yes, of course," she answered, but her heart wasn't in it. "But I don't need any surprises, Grandfather. Really, I'll be fine."

"Now don't you go arguing with me, girl," he

said, hugging her. "I know what's best for you."

Shadow forced a smile. "I know you do, Grandfather."

Noble headed for the door, but hesitated. "Are you sure you're all right?"

"Of course." She forced a laugh. "Go on and take care of your business. I'll see you in the morning."

When she was alone again, she collapsed on her bed. "No, I'm not all right," she cried into her pillow, "but how can I tell you? How can I tell anyone?"

Suddenly she heard something hitting against the French doors. She jumped off the bed and rushed to the balcony. As she had expected, Toby was standing below.

"Good Lord, Shadow, what in the world happened to you? I've been out of my mind with worry over you."

"I know. I'm sorry, Toby. When I saw my grandfather enter Yancey's, all I could think about was getting out of there."

"I figured that, but what happened to you. I thought you would come back for your horse."

Shadow suddenly realized she couldn't even confide in her friend. "I had . . . I had an accident."

"For God's sake, Shadow, what kind of accident? Are you all right?"

Shadow was seized with a sudden urge to tell him everything, but she took a deep breath, knowing he wouldn't understand. "I'd rather not talk about it right now, Toby. I'm really very tired."

"Did someone hurt you, Shadow? he asked angrily. "If they did, I'll kill them."

Shadow couldn't picture Toby going up against Josh Rawlings, nor would she want him to.

"Don't be silly, Toby. Let's just forget it."

"I hope you won't be wanting to play cards at Yancey's anymore," he commented.

"You don't have to worry about that." She forced a smile. "I'm going back inside now. It's getting a little cool out here."

"Will I see you tomorrow?" he asked.

"I'm going riding with Grandfather in the morning. Perhaps later in the day."

"All right, Shadow," he said, wishing he could kiss her good night. She looked so frail and troubled. "Sleep well." He waved.

I'm afraid that may be impossible, she thought as she closed the French doors.

Matt Rawlings greeted Noble Lansing as he entered the saloon. "Good to see you again, Noble. Hope it will be a little more peaceful in here tonight."

"I hope so, too." Noble laughed. "Is Josh around? He promised me a chance to win my stallion back."

Matt glanced at Josh's closed door. "I'm not sure this is a good night for that, Noble. Josh has been out of sorts today."

"Is that right?" Noble laughed. "Sounds to me like the odds may be with me, then. Is he in the back?"

74

"Wait, Noble . . ." Matt tried to stop him, but Noble was already on his way. "I tried to warn you," Matt muttered to himself and shook his head. "I wouldn't advise anyone to bother Josh when he's in one of his black moods."

Noble knocked on the door, then stuck his head inside. It was dark in the room, and he thought Matt must have been wrong about Josh being there. "Josh, are you here?"

"Yeah, who is it?" Josh asked in a slurred voice.

"It's Noble Lansing," he said. "You haven't forgotten our card game tonight?"

"I can't tonight, Noble," Josh said, lighting the lamp next to him.

"Josh, as one gentleman to another, I need to win that horse back. I can't face the look of disappointment on my granddaughter's face another day."

"Take the horse, Noble. I have no use for it."

"I can't do that, Josh," Noble said, moving into the room. "You won the horse fair and square. All I'm asking for is a chance to win it back the same way."

Josh took a deep breath. He opened the drawer of the table next to him and withdrew a deck of cards. "Is five card stud acceptable?"

"Of course," Noble quickly agreed as he took the seat opposite Josh. "I have nine hundred dollars to put up against the horse," he said, removing the money from his pocket. "Does that sound fair?"

"That's fine," Josh said, unconcerned as he dealt them each five cards. "What do you have?" he asked, barely looking at his cards.

"Damn, only an ace," Noble answered, certain it wasn't good enough to win.

"You win," Josh said, laying his cards facedown. "Now, if you'll just leave me alone."

Noble stared at the man he had come to respect in the short time he'd known him. "Is there anything I can do for you, Josh? You look like hell."

Josh laughed bitterly. "I feel like hell, but thanks for asking. This is a personal problem. Rapscallion is at Hampton's Livery. Just tell Hampton you won him back."

Noble headed for the door, then turned back. "Josh, I don't feel right about this. . . ."

"You won fair and square," he said, pouring himself a drink.

"Thanks, Josh. You're making a young girl very happy, and I won't forget you for that," Noble said, closing the door behind him.

"That's good," Josh mumbled as he turned his hand over and stared at the pair of aces he had folded with. "I'm glad somebody is happy."

Noble joined Matt at the bar and ordered a drink. "What the hell is wrong with your brother?" he asked.

"Woman trouble," Matt answered. "Josh isn't used to a woman leaving him."

"Too bad. He seems really upset," Noble said, taking a drink. "Well, I've a horse to get back to my granddaughter. Why don't you see if Patience can make him forget his trouble," he suggested, still worried about his friend.

"We've already tried that. He told her he wanted to be alone."

"Too bad," Noble said, shaking his head. "I hate to see a man hurt that way."

"Yeah, me too," Matt agreed. "Particularly when you think that person is invincible."

Noble downed his drink and headed for the door.

"Why don't you stick around for a few minutes?" Matt said. "We have a new singer coming on I think you'll enjoy. Her name is Mandy Cameron."

"Really. Well, maybe I will. My granddaughter is probably already in bed anyway."

Josh sat on the bed and leaned back against the headboard. The girl's beautiful face loomed before him, her blue eyes shining with passion. He could remember every detail of her lovely body, and he ached with the longing to have her there in his arms.

He suddenly jumped off the bed. What the hell was the matter with him, he wondered in frustration. He was going on about this girl like a lovesick schoolboy. Why should she be any different than the other women in his life? He closed his eyes and took a deep breath. But dammit, she was different. In the eighteen hours she had been with him, she had managed to touch something in him no other woman had ever touched—a tenderness he hadn't known he possessed, and a need to take care of someone. Now there was an empty void.

In the other room, he could hear Mandy begin to sing. For a change, the saloon was silent. Well, at least Matt was happy, he thought as he poured himself a drink. He stared into the amber liquid. Hell, one woman was as good as another for what he needed from them.

Shadow moved the food around on her plate while her grandfather tried to carry on a pleasant conversation with her over breakfast.

"It's a beautiful day, Shadow."

Shadow looked up from her plate and glanced out the window. "Yes, I suppose it is."

"Toby agrees with me that this is going to be the best cotton crop we've had in several years."

"That's wonderful, Grandfather," she said, genuinely happy. "It will be a blessing after the poor crop the last couple of years."

"It certainly will. Now I can have those repairs made on the cotton gin, and Martha and Abraham can plan to make the repairs needed to the workers' cabins."

"And they need some new clothes, Grandfather," Shadow added. "The children are dressed in rags."

"I'll leave the details of that to you and Martha. Now, if you're finished pushing the food around on your plate, what do you say to walking down to the stables with me?"

"All right." She forced a smile, assuming her grandfather had purchased a horse to replace

Rapscallion. How could she tell him that nothing would replace the gray stallion she loved so much.

"I'm going to ask Doc Morgan to stop by this afternoon," Noble said as they walked toward the stables.

"Why?" Shadow asked. "I'm really fine."

"You don't act fine. You haven't eaten a thing since you've been home and you're far too quiet." He didn't mention that he hoped the doctor would be able to tell him what had happened to his grand-daughter.

"Please don't worry about me. I'm really fine, and I don't want to see Doc Morgan."

Suddenly Shadow froze in her tracks. In the field behind the stables she caught a glimpse of gray streak by. "Grandfather . . ."

"Yes." He laughed. "It's Rapscallion."

"But how . . . when . . . ?"

"That was my business last night. Josh Rawlings promised to give me a chance to win him back."

Shadow's eyes widened. "You played cards with Josh Rawlings last night?"

"Now, don't get upset, Shadow. You know I enjoyed a good card game, but I promise you I won't bet Rapscallion again. The only reason I did it in the first place was because I was sure I had the winning hand. Not too many people can beat a full house of kings over tens, but Rawlings had four threes."

"He was probably cheating," she said bitterly.

"No, I don't think so. Rawlings is an honorable man."

Oh, Grandfather, if you only knew, she thought silently.

"Go on, girl, see to your horse." He laughed. "You'll need to be getting him ready for the race on Celebration Day."

Shadow sprinted across the field toward the gray stallion. The horse lifted its head and sniffed the air.

"Come here, my beauty," she shouted. The horse danced sideways, then circled her in a playful mood. "Easy boy" — she held out her hand — "let me look at you. It looks like you were well taken care of." She ran her hand over the velvet smoothness of his neck. "I think you fared better than I did," she whispered.

"Why don't you just drop it, Josh," Matt Rawlings suggested. "The girl doesn't want to be found, and you've checked out every possibility."

"Not every possibility. I have a man going to Port Gibson to see if she was telling the truth about being from there."

"I don't understand your preoccupation with the girl. You said you didn't think she was one of the robbers." Matt watched Josh's face, trying to understand his brother's motives for going to such lengths to find the girl. "Perhaps there is some other reason you want to find her, big brother. Some other reason than wanting her for your mistress."

"Don't you have something to do, Matt?" Josh asked impatiently. "I thought you were going to take Mandy for a fitting for her wardrobe."

80

"Well, I'll be damned. The untouchable Josh Rawlings let a female get under his skin. I don't believe it," he laughed.

"I don't want to discuss this, Matt," Josh growled.

Matt wiped the smile off his face, seeing that his brother didn't find the subject amusing. Josh had never had any trouble attracting women, but none had ever been able to get close to him. *Use them and lose them,* he had once laughed when Matt had asked him why he didn't settle down. Matt knew that Josh fought the demons caused by their step-mother. Being older, Josh had been the one she sought out when she was drunk, and Josh had been there when his father put a gun to his head and killed himself. Matt was sure all this kept Josh from showing any feelings toward the opposite sex, but now, this mysterious girl seemed closer than anyone ever had. "You can talk to me, Josh. I'll understand."

"How can you understand when I don't understand it myself. All I know is there was something different about this girl. She was sweet and vulnerable, yet . . . hell, I don't know what's wrong with me," Josh said, running a hand through his touseled hair. "What do you say we get out of here and take a ride. I'd like to ride out to Middleton Place and ask Allen Middleton about that horse Noble recognized the other night."

"Sounds good. Mandy has already had her fitting. Besides, I hear Middleton breeds excellent horseflesh. Are you still planning to enter the race at

Lansing Creek, even though you let that big gray slip through your hands."

"I doubt it. Jericho is an excellent riding horse, but he doesn't stand a chance against the likes of Rapscallion."

"That's something I've been wondering about; Noble told me you practically gave the horse back to him."

"The horse belongs to his little granddaughter, and I could see it was very important for him to get it back for her."

"You're getting soft in your old age," Matt said, slapping his brother on the back. "But I must admit, I like this new Josh Rawlings."

"You don't know what you're talking about," Josh said gruffly. "And if I have to listen to this drivel all the way out to Middleton Place, then I'd rather go alone."

Matt threw up his hands in mock surrender. "I won't say another word." He laughed.

Middleton Place was a beautiful plantation with hundreds of acres of green pastures. The house was red brick with large white columns. Blacks were busy everywhere, washing windows, polishing brass and trimming hedges.

They stopped their horses before starting down the long drive. "Looks like he keeps his slaves busy," Josh commented, looking out over the place.

"He certainly seems to have enough of them,"

Matt agreed. "This place looks pretty prosperous compared to some of the others we've seen. I thought planters in this area were suffering from the effects of two years drought."

"Maybe Mr. Middleton doesn't have to rely on his cotton crop."

"Surely he couldn't make enough money robbing the likes of us to keep this place going," Matt said incredulously.

"Don't you notice something strange, Matt?"

Matt glanced around again. "No . . ."

"There are acres of pastures, but not a crop field in sight."

"I'll be damned. You're right. Then what does he need all the slaves for?"

"Breeding, if I'm not mistaken. I'd say Mr. Middleton has found a profitable way of keeping his plantation running without worrying about the weather and cotton prices."

"That's disgusting," Matt hissed. "Breeding human beings like they were animals. What is this world coming to."

"It's because of swine like Middleton that it's coming to war," Josh answered. "People up North, and a lot of people in the South, don't look favorably on slaves, much less breeding farms."

"That's putting it mildly." Matt laughed bitterly. "But none of this explains why he'd be involved in the robberies at our place, if he is involved."

"Oh, I'm sure of it, but I don't think he gives a damn about the money from the robberies; I think he's trying to run us out of town. Mr. Middleton apparently doesn't like strangers coming to town, particularly strangers who ask questions."

"Do you think he knows about your meetings with Will Gregory?"

"I'd be willing to bet on it. The last time I met Gregory on the outskirts of town, I was sure we were being watched. Knowing Allen Middleton, I doubt there is much going on around Natchez he doesn't keep informed about," Josh said before urging his horse onto the winding drive.

Two Negroes rushed down the steps to take the reins of their horses.

"Gentlemen, how nice to see you," Allen Middleton said, coming out onto the porch. He was tall and slender with thin, straight sandy hair, and piercing ice-blue eyes. Leaning against one of the columns, dressed in a rose-colored fitted jacket and cream-colored riding pants, he looked every inch the plantation gentleman who had ruled the South for generations. "What brings you to my humble home?" he asked.

"Horses, Middleton. I'm told you raise some of the best."

"Well, you heard right, sir," he drawled. "Middleton Place is producing some of the finest horseflesh in the state, maybe even in the South. Follow me, gentlemen, and I'll show you my stables," he said, leading the way around the side of the house. "I've already been approached about supplying a cavalry unit from Natchez with horses if we should go to war," he said, puffing up like a peacock. "It would be one of the best units assembled."

"Is that right?" Josh asked, hoping the pompous fool would keep talking. "Do you really think there will be a war?"

"I'm sure of it. The South will have to break away if we are to preserve our way of life. Of course, not being from the South, I don't suppose you would understand that."

"I've been in enough fights to wonder why anyone would want war," Josh said flatly.

"The North wants us to give up our slaves, sir, but slavery is necessary for the prosperity of the South, and even for the prosperity of Europe. Cotton is king, sir, and without the slaves, there would be no cotton," he said pompously.

"I noticed you have a lot of slaves, but I didn't notice any cotton, Mr. Middleton," Matt commented.

"I own hundreds and hundreds of acres, sir. You're seeing very little of Middleton Place from this point," he answered, skirting the issue.

"Ah, here we are," he said as they rounded the corner of a large brick stable. "What are you looking for, a riding horse or a horse to race?"

"I think one to race," Josh answered.

"That's right," Middleton laughed, "I understand Noble Lansing won his gray stallion back. I had heard you planned to race Rapscallion at the Lansing Creek Annual Celebration."

"Yes, I had planned to, but things don't always

work out the way you plan."

"I have a magnificent stallion I've been racing myself that may be able to beat Rapscallion, but I wouldn't guarantee it. That horse of Noble's is a remarkable animal. I've been trying to buy him myself for the past two years, but Noble won't budge. Always says it belongs to his granddaughter. That's why I was really surprised when I heard you had won it from him."

"I don't think Noble would ever have bet the horse if he hadn't thought he had the winning hand," Josh said in defense of the old man.

"Zeke, bring out Sir Scott," Middleton ordered.

"Yessir," the black man ran at his order.

"That's a beauty in your pasture," Josh said, noticing a black stallion in the field with several other fine looking horses.

"That's Black Demon," Middleton offered. "He's my hope to beat Noble Lansing. The foal over there by the fence with its mother was sired by him, and from all indications looks like he will be one of my finest one day."

The black man led out a bay horse. It was a large, muscular horse, but it didn't have the fine lines of a racer. Josh suppressed a smile, knowing this horse couldn't compete with the likes of Rapscallion or Black Demon. Did Middleton take him for a fool, he wondered, as he checked out the horse's fetlock. "You need to get some liniment on this cut before it becomes infected," Josh said, noticing a gash on the inside of the horse's hind leg.

"How the hell did this horse get hurt?" Middleton grabbed the black man by his ragged shirtfront.

"Doan no, sir," the man whined, fear in his eyes. "Doan no."

"Black bastard," Middleton swore, shoving the man away. "You can't trust any of them. I'll have your hide for this."

Matt glanced at Josh and knew his brother was trying to hold his temper. "The horse could have gotten that cut from a nail in the stable," Josh said.

"There shouldn't be anything like that in the stable. Zeke is responsible to see that my horses are kept safe and well. Isn't that right, Zeke?"

"Yessir, master. Is my fault, sir. Zeke will take care of it rightta way, sir," the old man said, backing away from Middleton.

"Thanks for the tour, Middleton, but this horse isn't really what I had in mind," Josh said.

When they mounted and were out of hearing, Matt turned to Josh. "I thought you wanted to ask him about the horse used in the holdup the other night."

"I didn't have to. It was in the pasture. It wasn't hard to spot the horse Noble described: a large bay with one white leg and a white star on its forehead."

"That wasn't very wise of Middleton to use a horse with such distinguishable marks."

"The man figures he doesn't have anything to worry about, Matt, and he may be right. I wouldn't be surprised if half the people in Natchez don't know who has been robbing our place, and the other half probably don't care. Gregory is a fool if he thinks he can stop the momentum of what's happening down here. These people are bound and determined to have a war. Did you see the look of excitement in Middleton's eyes when he talked about it?"

"Then why the hell are we sticking around?" Matt asked. "You said a few weeks ago that you thought you'd sell Yancey's. Tell Gregory what you think and let's go home."

"Soon, Matt, but not yet," Josh answered. "I don't like the idea of being run out of town, particularly by someone like Middleton."

"Nor do I, but I don't like what is going on here, either."

Suddenly Josh slowed his horse, watching a rider off in the distance. It was too far away to be able to tell if it was a man or woman, but there was something strangely familiar about the rider.

Realizing Josh had nearly stopped, Matt pulled his horse up. "What is it, Josh?"

"Why don't you go on back to Yancey's. I have something I want to look into."

Matt wondered what his brother was up to now. He was getting harder to figure out all the time, but he knew there wasn't any sense arguing with him. "All right, I'll see you later."

Shadow let Rapscallion have his head, hoping the wind in her face would clear her mind of the cobwebs — and memories. The fact that she couldn't put Josh Rawlings out of her mind was very disturbing. She should hate him for what he had done to her, yet instead she yearned for his touch. Good God, what evil demons had he released in her, she wondered.

Suddenly Shadow spotted another rider. They were separated by a fenced field; but she could tell he was heading in her direction, and she wasn't in any mood to be sociable.

"Come on, Rapscallion, run like the wind," she urged, heading the horse toward the woods near the river.

Josh pulled his horse up. He stood up in the stirrups, shielding his eyes with his hands as he scanned the field. There was no sign of the horse and rider he had seen only a few moments ago. For a minute he had thought it was the girl. My God, was he losing his mind, he wondered. He had to put the girl out of his mind.

A great flame follows a little spark.

—Dante Alighieri

Chapter Five

The sun was high in a cloudless sky, and the heat came up from the road in simmering waves. Shadow pulled her damp shirt away from her body, feeling as if she were soaked clear through. "I think it's time for you and I to cool off," she said, rubbing the sweat-glistened coat of her horse.

She followed an overgrown path where the Spanish moss trailed from the oaks, until she came upon her secret swimming hole. Removing Rapscallion's saddle, she smacked him on the rump, sending him into the water. "Cool off, boy. I'm going to be right behind you," she said as she slipped her boots off. As she had done a hundred times before, she slipped out of the rest of her garments and quickly dove into the water.

This is heaven, she thought, floating on her back. *My own private paradise.* She had never even shared it with Toby. They often swam together at the boat landing, but she had always wanted to keep this place to herself. She had discovered it shortly after she had come to live with her grandfather, and it had always been her own little retreat where she could come and think about things without Martha following around behind her.

She stared up at the cloudless sky, lost in thought. It would be the kind of place lovers would meet, she thought, and suddenly her mind wandered to Josh Rawlings. What would he look like swimming nude, she wondered. Even in the dimly lit glow of his room, she had been aware that his body had been beautiful. His arms and back had been so muscular and hard. What had he thought when he discovered her gone, she wondered. He probably called one of his whores to comfort him, and that thought made her furious. "Damn the man," she swore as she stood up and strode from the water. What in the world was wrong with her, she chastised herself. How could she even think of the disgusting man? He had ruined her life, and worse, he wouldn't stop penetrating her thoughts. She shook her head in frustration. She had to put him out of her mind.

She quickly pulled on her clothes, then resaddled Rapscallion, and took off racing toward home as if she could leave thoughts of Josh Rawlings behind her at the river.

When she rode into the stable yard, her grandfather was there working with one of the horses. She dismounted and led her horse over to him. "Something wrong with Lady Sue?"

"She has a slight limp, but I don't see any swelling," he answered. "Did you have a good ride?"

"Yes, Rapscallion doesn't seem to show any ill effects from being with . . . from his experience."

Her grandfather laughed. "I told you the man who had him appreciated good horseflesh. I knew he wouldn't do anything to harm a fine horse like Rapscallion."

Shadow rubbed Rapscallion's velvety nose, thinking that it was a shame Josh Rawlings hadn't treated her as well.

"It looks like you two took a swim," her grandfather commented as he picked up a lock of her wet hair. "It sure has been a hot one today. Thank God, it hasn't been this hot all summer, or I'm afraid we'd have another ruined crop."

"I hope it cools off by the weekend. Rapscallion runs much better if it isn't so hot."

"Do you think he's in shape for the race?" Noble asked.

"Without a doubt, but I'm still going to work with him this week. If I were to wager a bet, I'd say he'll win it going away. The best horse against him is Black Demon, and even with Toby on his back, Rapscallion beat him."

"I wanted to talk to you about that, Shadow. I think it would be better if you let Toby race Rapscallion on Saturday."

"No, Grandfather," she gasped, her eyes wide with surprise. "How could you even suggest such a thing?

I've been preparing for this race all summer."

"I want my friends to see you for the lady you are, Shadow, not some hoyden dressed in boys' clothing. You are nineteen, and it's time you started dressing and acting like a lady. If you recall, we discussed this earlier, and you agreed to take over the duties of hostess at our party this year."

"I will, Grandfather. I'll be the lady you want at the party Friday night, but please, I have to race Rapscallion Saturday. He won't run for Toby the way he runs for me, and it's important that he win so we can continue to use him for stud."

Noble ran his hand through his gray hair. "You've got to stop worrying about money, Shadow," he said in frustration. "A young lady of proper breeding shouldn't be talking about stud horses."

"But why, Grandfather? You're the one who taught me all about breeding horses."

"I know, child, and there are times I wish I hadn't."

"Grandfather, I can be a lady when I have to. Please let me race Rapscallion, and I promise as soon as the race is over, I'll change into a dress and be the very proper lady."

As always, Noble Lansing could never say no to his granddaughter when she turned her blue eyes on him. He smiled and touched her cheek. "If I have your word that you'll be the perfect hostess before and after the race, then I'll agree."

"Thank you, Grandfather." She raised up on tip-toe and kissed him. "You won't be sorry. Rapscallion will win again and bring us lots of money."

"You know, Shadow, one of these days Rapscallion may not win," her grandfather pointed out.

"I know, Grandfather, and that's why it's important that we find him the perfect mate. We're letting everyone else use him for stud when we're the ones who should be benefiting from his excellent bloodline. We need to improve our own stock."

"I'm aware of that, child, and as soon as this crop is in, I plan to look into it. We both agreed we wanted a very special horse, and I may have to look outside of Natchez for her. Leigh Thompson, the horse breeder from Port Gibson, will be here for the race. Maybe he'll have something."

"Will you have the money if he does?" she hesitantly asked.

Noble put his arm around his granddaughter. "Stop worrying about money and have a little faith in your old grandfather. Our crop will be picked by race day, and we'll have a lot to celebrate."

"It just worries me that you're spending so much money on this Celebration Day. Maybe we should skip it this year, Grandfather."

"It's a tradition, dear. Your grandmother and I started the celebration fifty years ago when we brought in our first cotton crop, and I plan to continue the tradition as long as I can."

"But there hasn't been talk of war in previous years," she persisted.

"All the more reason for a celebration now, Shadow. If this war becomes a reality, I'm afraid none of us will have anything to celebrate for a long time."

"Do you really think it will come to that, Grandfather?"

"If the way people feel around Natchez is any indication of the way the rest of the South feels, I don't see how we can avoid it."

"Why, Grandfather? Why would people want a war?"

"I don't know, child. Some people have it in their heads that it's the only way the South will survive."

"Do you believe that?"

"I know that slavery is a big issue, and Lansing Creek wouldn't be able to survive without our slaves."

Shadow fell silent for a moment. "Do you know something, Grandfather, I can understand why some people think it is wrong to own another human being."

"I know, Shadow, but unfortunately it is not something you or I can do anything about. All we can do is pray it doesn't come to war. Because if it does, we'll all suffer—black and white."

"You are such a warm, sensitive person, and I love you, Grandfather," Shadow said with tears in her eyes.

"I love you, too, child." He hugged her. "You better go get cleaned up now. Martha was looking for you a little while ago to go over the plans for the party."

"Martha could handle everything by herself even if

the whole state of Mississippi were attending." Shadow smiled.

"I know, but she wants you to know how to be mistress of a plantation."

"Oh, Grandfather, you and Martha haven't been talking about me getting married, have you?"

"You have to think about it sooner or later," he said, putting his arm around her shoulder.

"I'm very happy with things the way they are. You and I do just fine, Grandfather. Why should I need anyone else?"

"I won't be around forever, Shadow," he said, turning her to face him.

Shadow's eyes widened. "Don't talk like that, Grandfather. I couldn't bear it if anything happened to you."

Noble stared into the tear-filled eyes of his granddaughter and remembered how devastated she had been when her parents had died. He didn't know how to tell her his heart had been giving him trouble for the past few months, and Doc said there wasn't anything he could do about it. "Now what could happen to an old codger like me?" He laughed. "Besides, it would probably be impossible to find you a husband when you're always dressed in male clothing."

Shadow kissed him on the cheek. "Good, then we'll have no more talk about marriage," she said as she turned and headed toward the house.

"Not until I find a man who will love and cherish you like I do," he whispered to himself.

* * *

Shadow walked slowly up the path to the house, lost in thought. He was just being a typical grandfather, she told herself. Her parents weren't around to see that she was properly married, so he thought he had to do it. That had to be it, she thought firmly. He was too healthy and robust to be sick. A tremor shook her slim body as she remembered how quickly her parents had been taken. They were both healthy and vital one week and gone from the fever the next.

Shadow stopped and looked back toward the stables. She could see her grandfather rubbing down Lady Sue's leg. She would have to see that he took it easier, she decided.

"Shadow, wait up," Toby McAllister shouted. "I've been hoping to have a chance to talk to you," he said as he caught up with her. "I see you have Rapscallion back."

"Yes, Grandfather won him back last night," she answered as she continued to walk.

"So our trip to Yancey's was for nothing," he commented.

"I suppose you could say that," she answered in a clipped voice.

Toby glanced sideways at Shadow's frowning face. "Are you mad at me about something, Shadow?"

"No, I just have a lot on my mind."

"Is there something I can do to help?"

Shadow slowed her pace, feeling guilty for snapping at him when she had no reason to be angry

98

with him. He had been her friend since childhood. "I'm worried about my grandfather," she admitted. "He's working too hard."

"Everyone is, but we start picking the cotton tomorrow, so he should be able to slow down after that. It's going to be a real good crop, too, Shadow. My share alone will give me enough money to buy a small piece of land from your grandfather."

Shadow squeezed his hand. "I'm happy for you, Toby. You've worked so hard to keep Lansing Creek going."

"Lansing Creek has been my home, too, Shadow. My mother and father are buried on Lansing Creek Land."

"I remember," Shadow said sadly. "We've been through a lot together, haven't we."

"Shadow, you know I would do anything for you. You've always been able to talk to me before. Why won't you tell me what's troubling you?"

Shadow recognized the look in his eyes and wanted to spare him the hurt of loving her. "I know you would, Toby. I feel the same way. We will always be *best friends*," she said, hoping to spare him any hurt.

Toby shrugged, unable to think of anything to say. "I guess I better get back to work. We almost have the gin repaired."

"Oh, Toby, that's wonderful. I know Grandfather has been concerned about that."

Toby touched her arm. "I suppose I won't see much of you this week," he said.

"No, I suppose not. You and I will both be kept busy," she agreed. "Although by Friday I'll probably be ready to escape Martha's tyrany." She laughed.

"Toby picked up a stick and tossed it across the field. "Shadow, I know it probably isn't proper, but I was . . . I mean, I was wondering if . . . "

"Yes," she urged.

"Would you save me a dance Friday night?" he finally blurted out.

"I'll save you two if you promise to help me get away for a swim later this week."

"Done!" he laughed, his spirits lifting. "I'll be your knight in shining armor and save you from the wicked dragon, better known as Martha." He quickly kissed her on the cheek, then took off running across the field.

Shadow stared after him, feeling as if her whole world were suddenly in a turmoil, and it all seemed to revolve around Josh Rawlings. Oh God, why did everything have to change, she wondered. She and Toby had grown up together and had always had such good times. Now he suddenly had to get serious on her, and she couldn't even tell him she wasn't the same sweet innocent girl he had grown up with.

Shadow let the screen slam on the kitchen door as she entered, eliciting a gasp from Tilly, the cook.

"Lordy, when you gonna learn to close dat door softly?" the black woman asked. "You scared me half to death. My nerves are 'bout shot anyways."

"I'm sorry, I wasn't thinking. Why are your nerves shot, Tilly?" she asked, dipping a cup into a bucket of cool water.

"All dem people gonna be in my kitchen starting tomorrow, and I doan mind telling you, I jus' doan like it."

"I'm sorry, Tilly, but surely you must need help with the food for the party."

"I s'pose. Your grandfather said some of dem field women s'pose to help me do de cooking. Huh, I can jus' 'magine wat help deys gonna be."

"Maybe it will be better than you think," Shadow said, preoccupied.

Seeing the worried look on her young mistress's face, Tilly tilted her chin up. "Wat's bothering you, missy?"

"Just about everything." She sighed.

Tilly held out a plate of hot ginger snaps. "Maybe dis will help."

"I'm sure it will," Shadow agreed as she climbed onto a tall stool, enjoying her snack and conversation with the cook. Everyone at Lansing Creek felt they had a hand in raising her since her parents' death, but she was particularly close to Tilly. Martha always felt she had to be the disciplinarian, since her grandfather wasn't, but Tilly had always been her friend and confidante.

"Does Grandfather look all right to you?"

"Wat you talking 'bout?"

"Does he seem healthy to you? Has his appetite been good?"

"Dat man been eating jus' fine. I jus' wish he wouldn't drink so much."

"I know, but he's been doing that for so long," Shadow said, studying her cookie. "I suppose I'm just jumping to conclusions, but he said something about not always being around, and it frightened me."

"De master ain't a young man, missy," Tilly said sadly. "Nobody can live forever."

Shadow's eyes darkened with concern. "That's what he said."

"Dat doan mean someden's wrong," Tilly said.

"Maybe not, but I wish I could get him to take it easier. He's been working so hard to keep Lansing Creek going, even though the drought the past two years has nearly wiped him out."

"Your grandfather is a smart man. He knows wat he's doing," Tilly assured. "Many of the other planters lost everything, but not your grandfather. No, sir, he moves crops round, he breeds dat fine horse of yours and now things are gonna git good again. Yes, sir, he mighty smart man, and mighty good man. Not like some round here," she said, meaning Allen Middleton and his breeding farm.

"Who do you mean, Tilly?"

"I'se just talking, girl. Now I want you to stop worrying and start thinking 'bout Celebration Day. Your grandfather is real excited 'bout it. Says it gonna be best one yet."

Shadow finished her cookie and stood to leave. "I wish I could get excited about it. The last thing I

102

want right now is a house full of guests for an entire weekend."

"You always been excited before. When you wuz a little girl, you thought Celebration Day was the biggest thing in your life."

"Maybe that's the problem, Tilly. I'm not a little girl anymore."

Josh rode across the field still looking for some sign of the rider, but there was none. After riding along the river for a while, he topped a hill and could see the stables at Lansing Creek. He was about to turn back toward town when he spotted Noble Lansing rubbing down Rapscallion. He rode toward him, thinking what a difference there was between the man who owned Lansing Creek and the man who owned Middleton Place. Noble was dressed in work clothes, and from the looks of them, he had been doing just that.

"Good afternoon, Noble," he greeted.

Noble looked up in surprise. "Josh, what are you doing out here?" he asked, rubbing his hands on a rag before shaking Josh's. "I hope it's not to renege on returning Rapscallion to me."

"No, nothing like that. I was just over at Middleton Place, trying to find a horse to replace him, though." He laughed.

"I'm sorry, Josh. I know you wanted Rapscallion, but you'll find another horse as good."

"I doubt it, Noble, but I'm going to try. You have

a real nice place here," he said, looking around. You look like you have an excellent crop of cotton."

"Thank God. It's been touch and go for the past few years, and we really needed this one."

"I noticed Allen Middleton doesn't seem to have had any trouble making ends meet," Josh commented.

"Yeah, well we all have our own way of dealing with problems," Noble snorted. "I couldn't do what he's doing."

"You have slaves, Noble. Why is breeding them for profit any different?" Josh asked to see his reaction.

"I'm not saying my slaves don't breed, but I don't tell them when they can breed, and who they can breed with. In my opinion, it's just not human to breed them to sell."

"Nor in mine," Josh answered, "and I'm glad to hear you say that. Do you think there are many people around here who agree with what Middleton is doing?"

"Too many, I'm afraid. Listen, why are we standing around here talking. Come on up to the house and have a drink with me. I'd like you to meet my granddaughter."

"Thanks, Noble, but I need to get back to Yancey's. Maybe another time."

"All right, but you'll be coming to the party Friday night, won't you?"

"I thought the celebration didn't start until Saturday," Josh said.

"Saturday is the race and picnic, but we have a party the night before. Why don't you and Matt plan to come and stay the night. We have plenty of room, and there will be a lot of pretty ladies."

Josh started to decline the invitation, but then he thought better of it. Maybe it would help him get his mind off the girl if he got away for a few days. "That's very kind of you, Noble. Are you sure you have enough room?"

"Room?" Noble laughed. "The house has nine bedrooms, and there's only my granddaughter and myself. What do you think?"

"I think I'll enjoy it, Noble. Maybe we can even get a few hands of poker in."

"Sounds good, but just know beforehand that Rapscallion won't be the stakes." Noble warned goodnaturedly.

"You're a hard man," Josh smiled, "but maybe I'll have my own winner by then. I'm heading to Port Gibson tomorrow to look at some stock."

"Look up Leigh Thompson and tell him I sent you. He raises some excellent stock. He'll be here Saturday for the race."

"Thanks, Noble. I'll do that," Josh said as he mounted his horse. "By the way, who rides Rapscallion in the race?"

"My granddaughter, Shadow," Noble answered. "Best damned rider you ever saw."

Josh trotted away from the stables thinking how strange to let a little girl ride such a spirited stallion in a race.

The cotton fields were white with bursting pods. Noble Lansing worked in the field beside his Negros, day and night. After it was cleaned in the gin, the bales were stacked on the dock at the steamboat landing, ready for transport downriver. Everyone had worked with tireless energy, knowing this was a good crop and they would all benefit from it.

On Thursday the steamboat carried the bales downriver, and once again, Lansing Creek was a prosperous plantation. Noble sat atop his horse, watching the steamer disappear around the bend. Suddenly he stiffened, a sharp pain clutching his chest. "Not now," he gasped, struggling to stay in the saddle. "Please, not now. I have to make plans for Shadow . . . .

The pain subsided, leaving him drenched in sweat and chilled as the breeze blew off the river. He had to find Shadow a husband and soon, he thought with determination.

The Essence of lying is in deception
Not in words.

— John Ruskin

Chapter Six

Shortly after dawn, the household at Lansing
Creek came alive with sounds from the kitchen.
Dressed in her riding clothes, Shadow headed downstairs, grabbing a biscuit as she slipped through the
kitchen. She had to admit, the excitement of the
party had finally rubbed off on her. She smiled to
herself, thinking it was impossible not to have, since
everyone around the place was humming and sing-
ing.

She passed the long tables made to hold the food.
Tomorrow they would be covered with bright yellow
tablecloths, and have yellow and white striped cano-
pies overhead. Her grandfather had outdone himself, she thought with pride. Everything at Lansing

Creek looked so beautiful.

When Rapscallion saw Shadow approaching, he danced and kicked up his heels for her benefit. "You're feeling pretty good, huh." She laughed, standing on the bottom rung of the fence. "You better save some of that energy for the race tomorrow."

"I thought I'd find you here," Toby said, climbing up on the fence beside her.

"Good morning," Shadow greeted. "I'm sorry I never got away for that swim this week."

"I understand. Your grandfather has been keeping me hopping."

"You should see the activity up at the house this morning." Shadow laughed. "Just be glad you haven't had Martha ordering you around. She's been a tyrant."

"She's always a tyrant in my opinion." Toby laughed. "Are you getting ready to exercise Rapscallion?"

"Yes, I thought I better do it before Martha finds something for me to do," she said hopping down and heading for the stables.

Toby jumped down and followed her. "It looks like the weather is going to be beautiful for you, Shadow. Sunny and not too hot."

"I know, Grandfather says he ordered it just for this weekend."

"I heard talk in town that Allen Middleton thinks Black Demon will beat Rapscallion."

"Rapscallion and I have other plans," Shadow said, taking a saddle down from the rack. "If you're betting any money, you better put it on us."

"You know I will. You know what else I heard? They say Josh Rawlings has been looking for some girl that disappeared on him. Isn't that a lark. He's supposed to be such a womanizer." Toby slapped his knee.

Shadow froze. "Josh Rawlings? Did they say who the girl was?"

"No, that's the funny part. He doesn't know who she was."

"I've got to go, Toby."

"Wait a minute, Shadow, did I say something wrong?" Toby asked.

"No, of course not, but if I don't exercise Rapscallion now, I'm not going to have time."

Shadow saddled Rapscallion, her mind in a turmoil. He was looking for her. Oh God, what was she going to do? She would never be able to go into town again. Damn the man. He had ruined her, and now he was going to haunt her for the rest of her life.

Shadow studied her reflection in the mirror as Martha styled her hair into an elegant coiffure. The gown delivered the previous day by Madame Roget was the most beautiful dress she had ever seen. The colors seemed iridescent, changing from deep lavender to pale blue as the light caught it. The shallow bodice pressed her bosom upward until she seemed to overflow its bounds. It was a big change from her riding clothes; she smiled.

"Your mother's amethyst and diamond necklace will be beautiful with disdress," Martha suggested.

"Do you think Grandfather would mind?"

"He's de one who suggested it," Martha said, producing a black velvet box. "He said you was a woman now."

Shadow studied her flushed face in the mirror. *More woman than he knows,* she thought silently.

"De guests have started arriving," Martha mentioned. "Some very nice looken men here."

"Are you trying to marry me off, Martha?" Shadow laughed.

"Jus' wants you to be happy."

Shadow hugged the black woman who had been her mother since her own mother had died. "Thank you for being concerned about me, Martha, but I'm already very happy."

Shadow stood at the top of the stairs, listening to the gentle hum of activity spreading throughout the house. This wasn't her first party, yet she felt different; perhaps she had finally grown up, but she wasn't sure that thought really made her happy.

Hearing her grandfather's voice greeting guests, Shadow slowly descended the stairs. Conversation ceased as everyone's gaze followed her down the stairs.

"For a moment I thought it was your mother descending the stairs," her grandfather said, holding out his hand to her. "You are quite breathtaking, my child."

"Thank you, Grandfather." She curtsied.

"You're not going to tell me this is little Shadow," Allen Middleton interrupted. "What happened to the dirty-faced kid I've seen riding Rapscallion?"

"She'll be back tomorrow." Shadow held out her hand. "It's nice to see you again, Mr. Middleton."

"Please, call me Allen. We are neighbors, my dear," he said, looking her up and down appreciatively. "I must say, I regret not having been more neighborly."

Shadow thought the tall man in front of her was quite charming, and she wondered why her grandfather didn't seem pleased by the attention he was paying her.

"Will you save me a dance, Shadow?" he asked.

"Of course," she agreed.

"Are you going to give any of the rest of us a chance to introduce ourselves?" another gentleman asked, shouldering his way in front of Allen Middleton.

"I'm sorry, Leland. Let me introduce you to my lovely neighbor, Miss Shadow Lansing. Miss Lansing, may I introduce my cousin, Leland Brandon from Vicksburg."

"How do you do, Mr. Brandon. Welcome to Lansing Creek."

"Thank you, Miss Lansing," he said, kissing her hand. "My cousin has some explaining to do."

"I beg your pardon?" Shadow said in confusion.

"I won't forgive him for not telling me such a beautiful young lady was so close by, while I've been wasting away for female companionship at Middleton Place."

Shadow laughed at the absurdity of his statement.

"I admit I deserve to be horsewhipped" — Allen laughed — "but Noble is the one to blame. He's been

111

keeping this lovely flower well hidden."

"Yes, I suppose I have," Noble said. "I knew the effect she would have on the male population of Natchez." He smiled lovingly at his granddaughter.

"What is this about the male population?" a female voice asked.

A beautiful dark-haired woman several years older than Shadow wrapped her arm through Allen Middleton's arm. "Ah, so this is the attraction." She looked at Shadow as if she were no threat.

"Rose, this is my Granddaughter, Shadow."

"My, my, I had no idea your grandchild was almost grown, Noble."

Almost grown, Shadow fumed, but forced a smile at the woman's snide remark.

"She is quite lovely, Noble," she said as if Shadow wasn't standing right there. "Have you been away at finishing school, my dear?" She finally directed a question to Shadow.

"No, ma'am," Shadow drawled, "I've been right here."

"I'm surprised we haven't met before. Allen, dear, why don't you get me a glass of champagne," she suggested, dismissing Shadow as unimportant.

Allen Middleton bowed over Shadow's hand. "Don't forget that dance," he reminded.

"Miss Lansing, may I get you a glass of champagne," Leland Brandon asked.

"I've already gotten her a glass," Toby said, stepping forward.

"Thank you, Toby." Shadow smiled, appreciating the way he looked in his finery. She very seldom saw him in anything other than jeans or overalls. Tonight

112

his unruly red hair was combed neatly off his forehead, and he wore a dark blue suit with a white ruffled shirt.

"Leland, this is Toby McAllister, a very dear friend of mine."

"It's nice to meet you," Leland said, obviously upset that this rough-looking young man seemed to mean something to Shadow. "Are you from around here?" he asked.

"I live at Lansing Creek," Toby answered.

At the look of surprise on Leland's face, Shadow stepped in. "Without Toby, Lansing Creek wouldn't be having this celebration today. This year's crop was the best we've had in years."

"I don't understand."

"Toby is our overseer."

"The overseer?" Leland said, looking down his nose at Toby.

"That's right." Toby smiled, enjoying the expression on the pompous fool's face.

"If you will excuse me, I think I'll get myself a drink," he said, quickly departing.

Toby laughed. "You see how fast I can clear a room. I hope your grandfather doesn't regret inviting me."

"Don't be ridiculous. You deserve to be here more than any of these other people."

"That's nice of you to say, Shadow, but I don't mind telling you I feel a little out of place."

"There isn't any need to, Toby. You and I are friends."

"Toby, there you are." Noble joined them. "This is Walter Ryan from Iuka. He'd like to know more about how you've been rotating crops."

"Yes, sir, I'd be glad to explain." He beamed, happy that someone was interested in what he had to say. "Shadow, will you excuse me?"

"That was kind of you, Grandfather. Toby was feeling a little out of place."

"I realized that, sweet, but that wasn't my only reason. I want you to meet a friend who will be staying the weekend as our house guest."

"All right, Grandfather, but first let me greet Camille and her family," she said excitedly. "I just saw them come in."

"All right." He laughed. "My guest will wait. I'll greet the Deverauxs with you."

Shadow hurried to greet Camille Deveraux, the only young lady her age whose company she enjoyed. She and Camille had been tutored together since they were twelve, and Camille had even traveled to Europe with her when her aunt had taken her. But then her family had moved to New Orleans.

"Camille," she greeted, hugging the black-haired girl. "It's so good to see you again."

"Look at you, Cassandra," Camille's mother exclaimed, her dark eyes wide with disbelief. "You are so beautiful."

"Thank you, Mrs. Deveraux, but look at your own daughter," Shadow said, squeezing Camille's hand.

"Yes, it seems the two of you have finally grown from awkward girls into lovely young ladies," Mrs. Deveraux said proudly. "Your mother and father would be very pleased."

"Yes, they would be," Noble agreed, looking at his granddaughter lovingly. "It's good to see you again,

Patrice," he said, kissing her cheek. "Andre, I hope you brought that horse you claim can beat Rapscallion."

"Ah, do not worry, mon ami, I brought Sorcerer with me. Luke is looking after him right now."

"Good." Noble laughed, rubbing his hands together greedily. "This is going to be one hell of a race."

"I looked for Toby outside," Camille whispered to Shadow, "but I didn't see him."

"That's because he is right over there." Shadow pointed across the room. "Doesn't he look handsome?"

"Oh, my," Camille exclaimed, having had a crush on Toby McAllister for the past five years. "I thought he looked handsome in his work clothes, but seeing him dressed like that makes me want to swoon."

Shadow giggled. "Come on and say hello. He looks like he's finished talking to Mr. Ryan."

Toby turned around as Shadow and Camille came toward him. He smiled as he recognized Camille Deveraux.

"Hello, Toby," Camille shyly greeted.

"Hi, Camille. It's good to see you again. It's been a long time. Shadow tells me you live in New Orleans now."

"Yes, that's right. I miss Natchez . . . and . . . and Shadow, though."

"We've missed you, too," Shadow exclaimed. "Haven't we, Toby?"

"How could I miss being driven crazy by two females?" He laughed. "One of you is bad enough."

Shadow glanced toward the door where her grandfather was talking with guests. Suddenly her eyes met the gold eyes of Josh Rawlings. She was only dimly aware of the conversation going on around her as her heart began beating erratically. She actually felt faint and willed herself not to make a scene.

"Shadow, are you all right?" Toby asked. "You look as if you've seen a ghost."

"I . . . I have to get a breath of air," she said quickly, heading out the French doors onto the veranda. Oh, God, what was she going to do. She had never imagined her grandfather would invite him. And he had seen her. She had to find a way to escape. Heading for the back stairs, Shadow hoped to hide in her room, but it wasn't to be.

"There isn't any sense running from me, Wildcat. I know who you are."

Shadow spun around and came face to face with Josh Rawlings. "How dare you come here!" she spat.

"I've been friends with Noble since I came to Natchez."

"You have a strange way of showing your friendship," she snapped.

"Dammit, don't blame me for what happened. If you had only told me who you were, nothing would have happened between us."

"Oh, so you're going to blame your lack of self-control on me," she said in disgust.

It hadn't been Josh's intention to argue with her. He had wanted to take her in his arms and kiss her, and tell her he had been searching for her, but she was making him angry. "Lack of self-control?" he repeated in disbelief. "Lady, you have a hell of a lot

116

of nerve. You're the one who barged into my room. It wasn't the other way around."

Her eyes widened in shock. "I knew you weren't a gentleman. No gentleman would have done what you did."

"I never claimed to be a gentleman." He smiled, a mischievous twinkle in his gold eyes. "And might I add, no lady would have done what you did."

Shadow raised her hand to slap him, but he quickly seized her wrist. "I wouldn't advise it, Wildcat. I already have scars from one of your childish temper tantrums, and I don't intend to carry any more of them."

"Then stay away from me!"

"I'm afraid it's too late for me to do that," he said, still holding her wrist. "I've been searching all of Natchez for you. You and I have a lot of talking to do."

"Why?" she asked angrily. "Are you still intent on sending me to jail?"

"Of course not. I already told you if I had known you were Noble Lansing's granddaughter, none of this would have ever happened. As it is, I'm already finding it difficult to face him."

Shadow yanked her wrist away. "I don't believe for a minute that you have a conscience, Mr. Rawlings, but if you do, then you will stay away from me." Shadow turned and walked swiftly away from him.

"No way in hell, lady." He smiled.

Shadow considered telling her grandfather she didn't feel well and that she was going to her room. It wouldn't be a lie. But then she decided she wouldn't let Josh Rawlings drive her away from her own party. Instead she headed for a group of friends, hoping to avoid him the rest of the evening.

Josh entered the French doors and saw Shadow talking with Allen Middleton. As soon as she saw him, she became very animated, laughing at everything Middleton said. He stiffened as he watched them move out onto the dance floor. *Why him?* he wondered angrily. *The man is the scum of the earth.*

Seeing Josh Rawlings' expression as he watched Shadow dance with Middleton, Noble headed toward his friend. "Have you met my granddaughter yet, Josh?"

"Yes," he answered, forcing his attention away from Shadow.

"What do you think of her?"

"She's a very interesting young lady."

Noble had a strange feeling that there was something Josh was leaving out. When Josh had first seen Shadow he had asked who she was, then before even finishing his conversation, he had rushed off after her. Was it possible they had met before, he wondered.

"I would suggest you be more discriminating about who you let her associate with."

Noble looked at Shadow and Allen Middleton dancing. "Oh, you mean Middleton. It does seem like Allen discovered my granddaughter this evening, but Shadow has a lot of admirers here tonight. Perhaps even you are interested since you are concerned for her."

Realizing he'd said too much, Josh laughed. "I'm

118

sorry, Noble. I shouldn't be telling you who to let Shadow see; but Middleton is such a despicable bastard, and your granddaughter seems like a nice young lady."

"She's a very nice young lady, Josh, but she is still very innocent."

Josh couldn't think of anything to say. Damn, he cursed silently, why did she have to be Noble's granddaughter? He had wanted to make her his mistress. . . .

"I'm sorry Matt won't be able to stay over tonight. I have a card game planned for later," Noble said.

"Yes, I'm sorry, too, but he brought Mandy Cameron with him, and they have to return to Yancey's later tonight."

"I'm hoping Miss Cameron will sing for us this evening," Noble commented, smiling as he noticed Shadow had Josh's attention again.

"Yes, perhaps she will," Josh answered.

"I'm anxious to see this horse you purchased in Port Gibson," Noble changed the subject.

"She's a beauty. Even before I saw her, I was interested in her."

"Really, why was that?"

"Her name is Gambler's Lady."

"I'll be damned." Noble laughed. "Well, tomorrow we'll see if your gamble paid off."

"Is your granddaughter still going to ride Rapscallion in the race?"

"Yes, I tried to talk her out of it, but she doesn't think anyone else can win on him."

"I have to tell you, I don't feel right beating a young lady."

"Don't count Shadow out just yet, Josh." Noble laughed. "You haven't seen her on that horse."

"No, I haven't." *But I'm looking forward to it,* he thought silently.

"Darling, there you are," Rose Jardine drawled. "I heard you were already here, and I've been looking all over for you."

"I've been right here," Josh answered. "You're looking very lovely tonight."

"Just for you." She smiled seductively.

"Does that mean the rest of us can't enjoy your beauty?" Noble asked, a twinkle in his blue eyes.

"Of course not, darling. I appreciate all the admirers I have."

"Then, why don't you dance with me now," Noble suggested. "Josh can dance with you later."

"Of course," she agreed. "Now, you stay right there, Josh Rawlings. I don't want to have to go looking for you again."

"I'll be around," he answered, glancing back toward Shadow, who was now dancing with a young red-haired man. This was as good a time as any, he decided.

Toby was surprised when Josh Rawlings interrupted his dance with Shadow, and even more surprised when Shadow protested.

"You don't want to cause a scene now, do you, Miss Lansing?" Josh asked, one gold eyebrow raised.

"Listen, Mr. Rawlings, if Shadow doesn't want to—"

"It's all right, Toby," Shadow reluctantly agreed.

"Don't you have any compunction about forcing your attentions on young ladies who don't want it?"

she spat as he took her into his arms.

"I've never met one who didn't want it," he answered arrogantly, trying to keep his eyes off the creamy white breasts that threatened to tumble out of her low-cut dress.

"Well, you've met one now, Mr. Rawlings. I despise you."

His laughter surprised her, and her eyes met his. "Come, Wildcat, you and I both know better than that. I remember what you were like in my bed."

"Be quiet!" she hissed. "My God, haven't you already done enough to ruin my life?"

Josh stared down into her blue eyes. "Have I really ruined your life, little one?"

Shadow looked away. The memory of his hard body against hers made her skin flush. "My grandfather wants me to marry," she finally managed to get out. "How do I explain to my husband why I'm not a virgin?"

Josh laughed deep in his chest. He didn't know what he was going to do about this childlike woman, but he had no intention of letting her marry anyone. "There are many ways to fool a man, Wildcat. You should be an expert at it, if how you duped me is any indication."

"Duped you?" She stared at him in disbelief. "How can you . . . oh, you make me so furious. . . ."

The music stopped, but Josh didn't release Shadow. "You and I need to talk someplace private."

"The time for talking is past, Mr. Rawlings. It would have saved both of us a lot of trouble if you had suggested doing that the other evening."

"I'll take some of the blame, Wildcat, but if you had been honest with me, none of this would have happened."

"Would you please release me," Shadow insisted. "People are beginning to stare."

"Surely a little notoriety doesn't bother you." He laughed.

"Excuse me, Mr. Rawlings," she said, pulling away. "I have guests to see to."

Josh held on to her wrist for a moment longer. "Just stay away from Allen Middleton," he warned.

Shadow's blue eyes met his gold ones. "You have a lot of nerve, Mr. Rawlings."

Josh should have known what she'd do next. She immediately headed toward a group of people that included Allen Middleton.

They say best men are molded out of faults,
And, for the most, become much more the better
For being a little bad.

— Shakespeare

Chapter Seven

Shadow moved out on the dance floor with Allen Middleton, taking perverse pleasure in the fact that Josh Rawlings was watching her with a scowl on his handsome face.

"Isn't that your lady outlaw?" Matt asked as he joined his brother.

"That's her," Josh snorted. "Would you believe she's Noble's granddaughter?"

Matt let out a low whistle. "You do know how to pick 'em, big brother. I just hope Noble is an understanding fellow."

"If he's as hot-headed and stubborn as his granddaughter, then I'm in trouble."

"Have you already talked to her?"

"I guess you could call it that. She didn't exactly welcome me with open arms."

"Does that surprise you?" Matt laughed.

"No, I suppose not," Josh answered, unable to take his eyes off Shadow.

"She seems quite taken with Allen Middleton," Matt commented, watching the two of them dance around the room.

"She's only doing it to spite me."

"Now come on, Josh. Surely you don't think—"

"There you are, darling." Rose wrapped her arm through Josh's. "I do declare, I am having a hard time keeping up with you this evening."

"I can't believe how you've suddenly grown into such a beautiful young woman," Allen Middleton said, pulling Shadow closer than was proper.

Shadow realized she may have made a mistake flirting with her neighbor. She could almost feel his devouring gaze upon her low neckline, and she suddenly felt very uneasy.

"I feel like I've wasted a lot of time." He gave her a lecherous smile.

"I don't understand." Shadow smiled back.

"I mean, we're neighbors. We could have been enjoying each other's company."

"I'm sure we travel in different circles." She laughed uneasily.

"Well, we'll just have to remedy that." He smiled, tightening his hold on her waist even more.

Shadow glanced over his shoulder and could see Josh Rawlings with Rose Jardine. The woman was hanging on to him, laughing at something he said.

Shadow stiffened as unreasonable jealousy possessed her. What in the world was wrong with her, she wondered. How could she possibly be jealous of a man she hated?

She missed a step and stumbled against her partner. "I'm sorry, Allen. I suddenly seem to have two left feet."

"Perhaps you would like to have a glass of champagne and get a breath of fresh air."

"Yes, that sounds wonderful." *Anything to get away from Josh Rawlings,* she thought silently.

She laughed gayly at something Allen said as they passed Josh Rawlings and his friends. She had already had one glass of champagne, and she knew she shouldn't be accepting another so quickly on an empty stomach; but she had to look like she was having a good time.

"Now how about that fresh air," Middleton said, taking her by the arm.

When she noticed Josh watching her, she smiled up at her escort in a flirtatious manner. "The roses on the veranda are beautiful and so fragrant this time of year."

"I'm sure they will dull in your company, lovely lady."

"Why, thank you, Allen," she drawled, hoping Josh Rawlings had heard.

When they were outside, Allen Middleton took Shadow's glass and set it on a table. Then he pulled her into his arms.

"What a delightful surprise you are."

"Just a moment," she protested. "You have no

right to take such liberties. . . ."

"Come now"—he laughed—"you've been inviting me to kiss you for the past hour."

"I'm sorry if I gave that impression, but you are mistaken."

He laughed softly. "Don't play games with me, Shadow," he said, pressing his lips against her throat.

"Mr. Middleton, please!" she protested indignantly. "Let me go this instant!"

He covered her lips with a hungry kiss as his hand moved up her back to bring her closer. She struggled against him, but he held her firmly. Suddenly, to her relief, he was torn away from her.

"The lady told you she didn't want your attentions," Josh Rawlings growled.

Shadow stumbled back against a stone wall and watched in stunned disbelief as the two men faced each other. Finally Middleton turned to Shadow and smiled.

"I'm sorry if I misread your invitation, my dear."

"I'm sorry if I gave you the impression I was interested in kissing you," she said, her eyes lowered, knowing she had led him on with her flirting.

"If you will excuse me," he said, bowing over her hand, "I will return to the party. Perhaps we can dance later." He turned and faced Josh Rawlings. "I don't appreciate outsiders meddling in my affairs, Rawlings. I suggest you remember that."

"Or you'll what?" Josh asked, his gold eyes glittering dangerously.

"Just be warned," Middleton said before walking

away.

"I told you to stay away from him." Josh turned angrily on Shadow.

"You have no right telling me anything, Mr. Rawlings. I'll see who I please."

Josh grabbed her by the arm before she could walk away. His mouth captured hers, forcing her lips apart.

Again, Shadow found herself struggling to keep from losing her dignity. When he lifted his head and looked down into her eyes, Shadow slapped him hard across the face.

"You are no better than Allen Middleton," she hissed. "You are both rutting animals!"

Josh watched her run up the stairs to the upper gallerie. He started to go after her, but decided against it. She was right, he thought in disgust. He hadn't acted any better than Middleton. He touched the side of his face and smiled. There was something about her that brought out the worst in him. All he could think of was possessing her.

Shadow leaned against the door of her room, her heart pounding erratically. She touched her bruised lips, her mind a contradiction of feelings and emotions. She had been repulsed when Allen Middleton had kissed her, but with Josh Rawlings it had been different. All the memories of the night he had held her prisoner came back, and the feelings weren't unpleasant.

Shadow moved like a sleepwalker toward her mirror. It was her own fault Allen Middleton had acted the way he had. She had flirted like a cheap hussy, and all to make Josh Rawlings jealous. Why did he have this strange effect on her? she wondered as she stared at her own reflection. It was as if she had no control over her own body and mind where he was concerned.

"Well, Shadow Lansing, are you going to hide up here away from everyone all evening, or do you have the courage to go back and face . . . face Josh Rawlings?" she said aloud.

Josh stood away from the crowd where he could watch the stairs unobserved. He drew leisurely on his cheroot, wondering for the hundredth time if he should find Shadow's room and apologize to her. Suddenly he saw a lavender-blue swirl of skirt at the top of the stairs. God, but she was beautiful, he thought, and so damned desirable.

Shadow paused uncertainly. Her gaze was drawn past the gathering crowd to the gold eyes of Josh Rawlings. He was staring at her, an unreadable expression on his face. She flushed, remembering that look when he had held her prisoner. One part of her wanted to turn and run, but another part told her to move forward, to stop running from life and Josh Rawlings. He was only a man, and in another few hours, he'd be leaving Lansing Creek and she'd have peace.

Josh pushed away from the wall and put his cheroot out. He had to make another attempt to make peace with this infuriating, beautiful woman.

Before he reached Shadow, Noble Lansing was there, holding his hand out to his granddaughter.

"Josh, have you met my granddaughter?" he asked.

"We have not been formally introduced," Josh answered.

"Well, let me present my beautiful Cassandra, better known as Shadow."

Josh bowed and lifted her hand to his lips. "I am honored, *Miss Lansing*."

She knew her face turned red as he caressed her with his eyes, but there wasn't anything she could do about it. "I am pleased to meet you, Mr. Rawlings. I've heard a great deal about you."

"Josh is one of our houseguests," Noble commented.

Shadow stared at her grandfather as if he'd grown horns. "House . . . houseguest?"

"I hope you don't mind, Miss Lansing."

Shadow met his mocking smile with one of her own. "No, of course not, Mr. Rawlings."

"Josh has a horse he thinks can beat Rapscallion," Noble said.

"Really?" She forced a smile. "Well, we'll see tomorrow, won't we. If you will excuse me, I see some friends." Shadow hurried away toward Toby and Camille before either man could say anything.

"She's matchmaking." Noble laughed. "Toby is infatuated with her, and she's trying to get him interested in her friend, Camille."

"Who is Toby?" Josh asked, noticing the red-haired young man smiling at Shadow.

"He's my overseer. He and Shadow grew up together and are still very close. His father had been my overseer for years before he died."

"Overseer." Josh laughed. "Your highclass friends must love you, Noble. An overseer and a gambler as guests."

"My friends and neighbors are used to me by now, Josh. I'll tell you something, I had hoped to find a husband for my granddaughter at this gathering, but there are only a few men here I'd even let near her. You may be interested to know that you are among the few, my friend."

"Whoa, hold on, Noble." Josh held his hands up. "I'm a wanderer and a gambler. Not a likely combination for a husband."

"Love can change a man." Noble smiled.

"Not this man."

"I may be getting old, Josh, but I'm not too old to realize that there is a special look that passes between you and Shadow."

"You're imagining things, Noble. Your granddaughter is very beautiful, and I always enjoy looking at a beautiful woman. Speaking of beautiful women, I see Rose. Will you excuse me?" Josh quickly escaped.

I think you've been running too long, my friend, Noble mused as Josh hurried to the safety of Rose Jardine.

Buffet tables had been set along the length of the

huge dining room. Hams, pheasants, oysters and other seafood covered the tables, along with vegetables, fruits and desserts.

Shadow tried to eat something at the insistence of her friends, but she was too nervous to be hungry. Glancing across the room, she saw Rose Jardine pop a bite of food into Josh's mouth, and then he had the audacity to lick her fingers. *My God, what would they do next?* she wondered in disgust.

"I'm going to mingle with the guests," Shadow said, unable to stay and watch their display any longer.

Shadow moved through the crowd, smiling and speaking to different people until she reached the door. Then she quickly escaped out the back. Lifting her head toward the heavens, she took a deep breath of the fresh night air. *Will this night ever be over?* she wondered. How could she possibly expect to get any sleep with him in the same house—and she had to sleep so she'd be alert for the race tomorrow.

Thinking about the race, Shadow decided to check on Rapscallion. With the full moon to guide her, she lifted her skirts and hurried down the path toward the stable.

Able greeted her, a big smile on his face. "Dat horse of yours tells me he gonna win tomorrow."

"I hope so." Shadow laughed. "Able, where is Mr. Rawlings' horse?" She tried to sound disinterested.

"Down de other end next to Rapscallion." Able pointed. "Mighty fine horse, too."

Shadow lifted her skirt and climbed up on the broad crossbar of the stall. "Oh, you are beautiful," she exclaimed, stroking the nose of the silver horse. "Where did he find you?"

"Port Gibson," Josh said from behind her, his voice lazy and amused.

Shadow turned around to find him casually leaning against the stable door.

"I hope you don't mind me following you. I saw you leave and was concerned Middleton might bother you again."

"That's very kind of you, Mr. Rawlings, but I can take care of myself. Besides, I'm sure Mrs. Jardine will be looking for you," she said, turning back to his horse.

Josh moved to stand beside her. "Do I detect a hint of jealousy, Wildcat?"

"You flatter yourself, Mr. Rawlings."

"Don't you think after what we've been through, that you could call me Josh?"

"You are a stranger to me," she said, her face turning a bright pink.

Josh ran a finger down her arm. "You are no stranger to me, love. I know every inch of you by heart."

His touch made her tremble, and she quickly moved away. "What is your horse's name?"

"Gambler's Lady." He smiled at her obvious attempt to change the subject.

"How appropriate."

"It was her name before I bought her."

"She'd make a beautiful match for Rapscallion."

"We'll have to talk about that" — he smiled — "after we talk about you and me."

132

"I'll make a deal with you, Mr. Rawlings," she said, quickly moving toward Rapscallion's stall. "If Rapscallion beats Gambler's Lady tomorrow, you breed her to my horse and I get the foal. If your horse wins, we'll give you stud rights for three seasons, and I keep the foal the third season."

"That means you win either way," he said, following her to Rapscallion's stall.

She couldn't think straight with him so close. "You haven't answered me," she said, looking up into his gold eyes.

"I'd rather make a different wager, Wildcat," he said, pulling her into his arms. "If I win, you come to my bed. If you win, I'll come to yours. Don't look so shocked." He laughed. "I've been able to think of little else but you since that night you spent with me. You invade my thoughts during the day and my dreams at night."

Shadow stared at him in disbelief. "I must return to the party," she said breathlessly.

"Not so fast." He stopped her. "I think I know why you were at my place that night. It was to win back your horse, wasn't it?"

A liquid weakness assailed her as he continued to hold her wrist in his grasp. "Yes," she whispered.

"Why didn't you just tell me that?"

"I couldn't let my grandfather know what I was doing."

Josh smiled. "You have an odd way of looking at things, Wildcat."

"I must go." She tried to pull away.

"Not yet. This time we will finish what I started

133

on the veranda." His hand grasped her chin, and he gently lowered his head and kissed her. After the first moment, she lost all desire to struggle. She had no will to resist the urgent demand of his lips, nor could she escape the hard strength of his body.

When he raised his head, he stared down into Shadow's face, struggling with the bewitchment she presented. "I can't seem to keep my hands off you, Shadow Lansing."

Shadow didn't know what to say. "I must go."

Josh stepped aside and bowed. "Go, Wildcat." He smiled. "Go before I make love to you on the stable floor."

Shadow ran back up the path, her mind in turmoil. It wasn't natural to react to a man the way she reacted to Josh Rawlings. Neither Allen Middleton nor Toby affected her the way he did. Oh God, why was her heart pounding a mile a minute?

When she reached the back door, her grandfather was sitting on the step smoking a cigar.

"Checking on Rapscallion?" he asked casually, knowing that Josh Rawlings had followed her.

Shadow took a deep breath and sat down next to him. "Yes, it was getting a little stuffy inside for me."

"I agree." He drew deeply on his cigar. "Did you see Josh Rawlings' horse?"

"Yes. She's a beautiful animal. She'd make a good match for Rapscallion."

"Yes, I agree, but I doubt Josh would agree."

"You never know," she said. They sat in silence for a few minutes.

"Have you been having a good time this evening?" he asked.

"Yes, it's been a wonderful party."

"Have you met anyone you like?"

Shadow glanced at her grandfather. "I like everyone I've met. Well, maybe there is one exception. I don't care for Rose Jardine. She treats me like a child."

Noble laughed. "She probably sees you as a threat."

"I doubt that. She's a very beautiful woman."

Noble put his arm around his granddaughter's shoulder. "I don't think you realize it, sweet, but you have also turned into a beautiful woman. I don't think I realized just how beautiful until this past week."

"This past week?" she repeated hesitantly.

"Yes, there's been a change in you. Maybe it's just growing up. Your father was like that. He seemed like a gangly, immature boy; then he met your mother, and suddenly he was a virile young man."

"I miss them, Grandfather," Shadow said after a few moments silence.

"I know, Shadow. I miss them, too. But as long as you remember them, they'll always be with you in spirit."

"Yes, but there are times I need to talk to my mother."

"This old grandfather can listen."

"I know you can," she hugged him, "but I'm talking about woman talk, Grandfather."

"I know something has been bothering you,

135

Shadow. I wish you would talk to me about it. You might be surprised that I can help."

"I appreciate the offer, Grandfather, and I'll keep it in mind. Well, I suppose I should get back inside to our guests." She rose and stretched.

Noble tossed his cigar out into the yard. "Shadow, what do you think about Josh Rawlings?"

Shadow froze. "Josh Rawlings?" she repeated.

"Yes, I like the young man. I wondered what you thought of him."

I haven't thought one way or the other about him," she said, hurrying inside.

Noble smiled to himself. "Why don't I believe that?" he said aloud.

Josh stood in the shadows thinking about the conversation he had just overheard. What was Noble Lansing up to, he wondered.

Shadow rejoined the party, but she felt restless and alone. She watched Toby and Camille dance by, each smiling at the other in a special way. Well, at least something had gone right, she thought. Then she noticed Josh enter the room, and immediately he was surrounded by women. He glanced her way, and for a moment it seemed she could feel the intimate caress in his eyes.

"We wondered where you had disappeared to," Camille said as they joined her.

Shadow tore her eyes away from Josh Rawlings. "I walked down to the stables," she answered.

"Toby said you had probably gone down there."

Camille laughed.

"He knows me too well," Shadow agreed.

"Camille, would you mind if I danced with Shadow?" Toby asked.

"No, of course not. I see Mother talking with Noble, so I'll just join them. But Shadow—" she clutched her friend's hand and whispered, "I want him back."

"I'm so glad to see you and Camille enjoying each other," Shadow said as she moved into Toby's arms.

"She always seemed like such a kid to me before, but tonight she is different. She has really grown into a beautiful young woman."

"I suppose we are all growing up," Shadow said sadly.

"Shadow, are you all right?" Toby asked, concern in his voice. "You just haven't seemed yourself tonight. As a matter of fact, you've been acting strange since our escapade at Yancey's."

"You're imagining that." She forced gaiety in her voice. "I'm just fine."

Josh watched Shadow from where he stood. Noble must have been right, he thought. From the way the young red-haired boy was looking at her, he was quite smitten with Shadow. As he considered excusing himself from the group he was with and dancing with Shadow, another gentleman cut in. Josh thought he recognized the man as Allen Middleton's cousin.

"If you're going to dance with her again, you better ask her before the evening is over," Matt said at his side.

"What makes you think I want to dance with her again?"

"Who are you trying to fool, big brother. You haven't let her out of your sight this entire evening."

"Maybe she brings out the protective instincts in me," Josh replied dryly.

"There is one problem with that, big brother. Who's going to protect her from you?"

Josh stared at his brother for a long moment. "It's funny you should ask. That's exactly what I have been wondering. Excuse me, Matt. I need something stronger to drink than this champagne," he said, leaving the group.

Shadow moved to join Camille and her family when Allen Middleton approached her. "Miss Lansing, I hope you will do me the honor of this dance so I can make amends for my earlier transgression."

Shadow was about to refuse, but then she saw Josh dancing with Rose Jardine. "Of course," she agreed.

When they reached the dance floor, this time he held her very properly. "I have no excuse for my earlier actions, other than I was overwhelmed by your beauty. I hope you will forgive me."

Knowing that it had been partly her fault, Shadow nodded. "Of course, Allen."

"If you have no objections, I'd like to ask your grandfather for permission to call upon you."

Shadow didn't know what to say. She wasn't sure she wanted his attention, but she didn't want to seem rude. "You have always been welcome at Lansing Creek, Allen," she smiled.

"Is that a polite way of telling me you're not interested, Shadow?" He smiled down at her.

"At this point in my life I'm not sure what I want," she admitted. The music stopped, and Shadow moved off to the side, coming face to face with Josh Rawlings, Rose and her grandfather.

"We were discussing the race tomorrow," Noble said as Shadow moved to stand beside him. "Josh thinks he has a winner."

"What do you think about that, Shadow?" Allen Middleton asked.

Josh stiffened at Middleton's familiar use of her name.

"I'd say we'll know tomorrow." Shadow forced a smile.

"My dear child, I can't believe you mean to ride that great beast," Rose said in her usual condescending tone.

Shadow felt laughter bubble up inside her at the absurdity of the woman's statement. She glanced at Josh and saw the smile in his eyes. "My dear Mrs. Jardine, I not only mean to ride him, I mean to win the race," Shadow retorted, trying to keep a straight face.

"Your granddaughter and I have already made our own wager," Josh announced in a lazy drawl.

"Really?" Noble laughed, enjoying the look of surprise on Allen Middleton's face. "And just what is the wager?"

Shadow looked at Josh, defying him to say anything. "It has to do with breeding." Josh smiled at her. "If Rapscallion beats Gambler's Lady tomorrow, I breed her to your horse and I get the foal. If my horse wins, I'll have stud rights for three seasons, but Shadow keeps the foal that is dropped in the third season."

"It sounds like we win either way." Noble laughed.

A smile curved Josh's mouth. "Yes, your granddaughter is a very shrewd woman."

Shadow's eyes met his, daring him to say more.

"There are still a few details we have to work out," he continued, staring back at Shadow. "Perhaps you would honor me with this waltz and we can discuss it," he smiled.

"You have more nerve than anyone I've ever met," she hissed as they spun around the room.

"Thank you," he smiled. "You are the most intriguing female I've ever met."

Shadow bit back a retort, keeping her eyes fastened on the diamond stickpin in his neckscarf. She was extremely aware of his hand on her waist, and of his warm breath against her temple. He held her at just the proper distance, but his grip on her other hand was warm and tight.

She's a nice height, he thought to himself. *She fits perfectly in my arms.*

"Why are you here, Mr. Rawlings?"

"It's not to torment you, if that's what you think, Wildcat," he assured her. "As I said, your grandfather and I are friends."

"If he knew what kind of man you are—"

"What kind of man am I?" he asked, a smile

140

glittering in his gold eyes.

"You know very well what I mean," she hissed.

"I'm a man who takes what is offered, Wildcat."

"Are you insinuating that I was in agreement with what happened?" she asked, her eyes wide with disbelief.

"Maybe not entirely, but you could have stopped me with the truth."

"Really? Are you trying to convince me now that you're an honorable man, Mr. Rawlings?"

"I wouldn't go so far as to say that"—he smiled—"and it's Josh."

"*Mr. Rawlings*, I find this a very awkward situation."

"To say the least," he agreed. "I think we could clear the air if we went someplace private and talked about our situation."

"Oh, no, that wouldn't be wise," she exclaimed, afraid to be alone with him again.

A faint smile tugged at his firm lips. "Your grandfather and I are good friends, Shadow, and I'm sure we'll be thrown together often, particularly since we plan to breed . . . our horses."

She glanced quickly at him, then away. "Perhaps tomorrow after the race," she agreed.

"Ah, yes, the race. I must admit, I feel very strange racing against you."

Shadow met his mocking smile with one of her own. "You're going to feel even stranger after I beat you."

"Is that a challenge, Wildcat?"

"Please don't call me that," she begged, looking

around to see if anyone overheard him. The music stopped, but he still held her. "Some of our guests are leaving," she said breathlessly. "I must go."

Reluctantly he released her. "Until later, then." He bowed over her hand.

After Shadow had departed, Josh glanced around the room to find his brother. He was surprised when he saw Mandy engrossed in a serious conversation with Allen Middleton. She looked distressed, and he noticed Middleton had hold of her wrist.

When Mandy saw Josh heading in their direction, she quickly said something to Allen and he walked away.

"Is he giving you trouble?" Josh asked.

"No, of course not. We were just talking about the race tomorrow."

Josh wasn't sure he believed her, but he didn't have any reason not to. "Would you like to dance?"

"I thought you'd never ask." She smiled as they moved onto the dance floor. "It was so nice of you to bring me along."

"You can thank Matt," he replied. "You know he's quite taken with you."

"Matt is very sweet," she smiled up at him, "but I'd prefer the company of his brother."

One gold eyebrow raised. "I'm flattered, Mandy, but I'm not interested," he said bluntly.

"Now, Josh, how do you know until you give me a chance?" she persisted.

Knowing how his brother felt about this girl, Josh became suddenly angry. "Just take my word for it," he said in a tone that made it very clear how he felt.

"I understand you will be staying as Mr. Lansing's houseguest," she changed to a safer subject. "When will you be returning to Yancey's?"

"I don't really know."

The music finally stopped. "There's Matt now," Josh said, relieved to see his brother.

Shadow had been dancing with Leland Brandon, but she hadn't been able to keep her eyes off of Josh Rawlings. Nor had the woman he'd been dancing with, she thought bitterly. She remembered the woman called Mandy Cameron had come with Matt Rawlings, but it was obvious who she was interested in. *What is it about the man?* she wondered. *Listen to me. I'm as helpless under his spell as the rest of them, yet I should hate him.* She glanced at Matt Rawlings. He was as handsome as his brother. Why weren't the women clamoring all over him?

"He is very handsome, isn't he?" Camille said as she joined her friend.

"Who?" Shadow laughed, embarrassed to be caught staring at Josh Rawlings.

"The man you haven't been able to take your eyes off all evening."

"Has it been that obvious?"

"Only to me. Who is he?"

"He's just a gambler." Shadow pretended disgust. "He won Yancey's in a card game while on a steamboat, and he and Grandfather have become good friends."

"He's probably the most handsome man I've ever

143

seen." Camille sighed.

"Not you, too," Shadow exclaimed. "Why, Camille? What is there about him that makes you say that? The man standing next to him is his brother. Isn't he just as handsome?"

"Yes, I suppose so, but there is an animal magnetism that the blond-haired man possesses. He exudes masculinity. I can feel it all the way over here. He seems cool and arrogant, yet beneath the surface is a wild animal waiting to pounce."

Suddenly Shadow began to laugh, and moments later both women were in such a fit of giggles that they had to escape to the veranda, shrieking with mirth.

"How would you know about such things?" Shadow was scarcely able to ask.

"I read it somewhere," Camille answered, tears streaming down her face. "But you know, every word of it seems to fit him. Can you imagine being held in his arms and being kissed by him?"

Oh yes, I could imagine.

> Love bade me welcome,
> yet my soul drew back.

— George Herbert

Chapter Eight

Shadow woke slowly the next morning, a soft lingering smile on her lips as she remembered Josh Rawlings was in a room down the hall. She stretched luxuriously, wondering what the day would bring. He had been charming and attentive to her at the party, almost making her forget their previous encounter—almost. The look he had given her when she had said goodnight had brought it all flooding back. She had spent hours lying awake remembering the feelings and emotions his touch had evoked, and the way her body had reacted to him.

Would he be as sweet today after she and Rapscallion beat him, she wondered with a smug smile on her face as she swung her legs off the side of the bed. The race was the first event of the day. After that there would be a picnic with games and challenging events.

Suddenly Shadow's door flew open, and Martha came bustling in. "Child, ain't you outta dat bed yet? Your grandfather and dat nice Mr. Rawlings done already gone to de stables."

"The stables?" Shadow exclaimed, jumping off the bed. "My heavens, what time is it?"

"Still early. People jus' started arriving, but you better git a move on." Martha removed a beautiful white silk gown, embroidered with flowers of blue, lavender and green, from the armoire. A green ribbon trimmed the waist and cuffs.

"I'm not ready for that yet, and you know it." Shadow laughed. "I need my riding clothes."

Martha clucked disapprovingly as Shadow pulled on a pair of fawn-colored riding pants. "Why your grandfather lets you ride dat big animal I'll never know; and against men!"

"And I'm going to beat them all," Shadow proclaimed.

"You sure in a good mood dis morning." Martha smiled knowingly. "Doan suppose it has nothing to do with dat nice Mr. Rawlings."

"Maybe," Shadow said, buttoning up a soft, yellow silk blouse. "Or it could be Mr. Middleton. He's very nice, too," she said, hoping to hide her real feelings.

Martha snorted in indignation, handing Shadow her shiny brown riding boots. "Dat one's a bad one."

"Why do you say that?" Shadow asked. "What's wrong with him?"

"He doan treat people good, black or white. You'd do best to stay way from him."

"That's strange, he told me the same thing," she mused.

"Who told you dat?"

"Nobody," Shadow said, brushing her long, strawberry-blond hair.

"Here, let me do dat," Martha said, pulling all of Shadow's luxurious hair back as she braided it into one long braid with yellow ribbon entwined through it. "Least we'll keep you looking like a lady." She hugged Shadow when she was finished. "You jus' be careful, child."

"I will." Shadow returned the hug.

She tried to eat some breakfast, at Tilly's insistence, but she was too excited to get down more than a biscuit. Promising she would eat later, Shadow headed for the stables, passing Vern, the black servant who was in charge of the whole hog that had been roasting in a pit most of the night.

"Good morning, Vern." She waved. "It sure smells good."

"I'll save you de best piece as always." He waved back.

As Shadow neared the stables, she spotted Josh

riding his silver mare across the field. Several of the other people who planned to race were also exercising their horses, but Shadow only had eyes for Josh and Gambler's Lady. They looked good together, she thought in admiration.

"Well, there you are, sleepyhead. I wondered if you were going to get up today." Her grandfather hugged her.

"Someone should have woken me earlier," Shadow admonished, kissing him on the cheek.

"You needed your rest. Besides, I thought Toby could exercise Rapscallion this morning. He should have him back in a few minutes."

"Oh," Shadow said in disappointment. "I hope he doesn't overdo it with him."

Noble laughed. "Toby knows better than to do anything to Rapscallion that you wouldn't approve of. He's a smart boy, and you have him thoroughly intimidated."

"Oh, Grandfather, you make me sound like a tyrant." She laughed. "Surely I'm not that bad."

"You are when it comes to that horse," he teased. "I thought you were going to disown me when I lost him to Josh. If the man hadn't practically given him back to me, I'd probably be living in that shack by the river."

"Given him back to you?" Shadow asked in surprise. "What do you mean, Grandfather?"

"The night I went to play to win Rapscallion back, Josh was in a foul mood. You remember, it

148

was the night after you had your accident. Anyway, Matt said something about a woman walking out on Josh, and he was having a hard time dealing with it. When I walked into his dark room, he told me he didn't feel like playing cards, and he wanted to know if I'd come back another time. I explained to him that my granddaughter was furious with me, and I couldn't face you without that horse another night, so he agreed. We played one game of five card stud in his room, and I won Rapscallion back with an ace. Not even a pair, Shadow. Can you believe that?"

"Do you know what he had?"

"No, he barely looked at his cards, but I had the distinct impression that he had the winning hand."

Shadow stared at her grandfather in disbelief. "Josh Rawlings doesn't seem like the type of man to let something he wants slip through his fingers."

"I agree, but apparently he wanted the lady more than he wanted my horse. I really felt sorry for him that night. He was alone in his dark room, drinking. I always thought he was immune to the attention of the ladies around Natchez, but I guess I was wrong."

Shadow couldn't believe what her grandfather was saying. Why would he have been upset about her disappearance? She had just been another conquest to him. Hadn't she seen him with Rose Jardine and also the new singer at his club. Come to think of it, the night she walked in on him he was with the girl he called Patience. She looked past her grandfather and saw Josh heading in their direction.

"What you say doesn't make any sense, Grandfather. Josh Rawlings is a gambler, and from what I hear, a money-hungry one at that—"

"He's also an honorable man, Shadow."

"Good morning," Josh greeted as he dismounted. "You are certainly a ray of sunshine," he said, referring to Shadow's yellow silk blouse.

"Sunshine is it?" She laughed, trying not to dwell on what her grandfather had just disclosed. "That isn't what my grandfather says. He just told me I intimidate most people."

"I don't believe that for a moment," Josh smiled. She looked so beautiful to him, so fresh and natural. Her color was gloriously high, and her eyes sparkled with excitement. He had spent a restless night knowing that she was so close by, yet he couldn't in all good conscience, go to her. When he woke up, he had felt surly and irritable, but now seeing her bright smile and hearing her infectious laughter made his mood suddenly brighten.

"Is it your intention to win by taking everyone's mind off the race?" he asked.

"I don't need to use any high-handed tricks, Mr. Rawlings," she warned, "as you will soon find out."

"Why don't you join Josh and me for breakfast, Shadow," Noble suggested. "You two can discuss who is going to win, over some of Tilly's hot cakes."

"All right. Let me check with Toby on Rapscallion's condition, and then I'll join you."

"Why don't you go on, Noble? I'll wait and walk up with Shadow. If that's all right with you?" He smiled a disarming smile.

Shadow nodded, suddenly feeling very apprehensive about being alone with him. "I need to check Rapscallion to make sure Toby hasn't tired him," Shadow said nervously, walking toward the stable. "Then I need to check my gear, and . . ."

"Hold it," Josh interrupted bitterly. "I don't have to be hit over the head with the truth. If you're looking for excuses to avoid me, just say so and I'll leave you alone."

"I'm sorry. She smiled tentatively. "I suppose I do feel, well, strange being alone around you. I mean after what happened . . ."

"I suppose that's understandable. Why don't you pretend we just met last night," he suggested.

It would be impossible to forget what happened, she thought. "I'll try," she agreed.

I'll try too, he thought, *but I'll never forget that night and the way you felt in my arms.*

"I suppose Toby can take care of things," Shadow admitted. "Why don't we go have breakfast? I'm suddenly very hungry."

"So am I," Josh said, taking her hand, "but I'll settle for breakfast." He laughed at the puzzled expression on her face. "Come on, sunshine, I need

151

a good breakfast if I'm to beat you in this horse race."

"Beat me?" She laughed. "You are going to be in for a rude awakening, Josh Rawlings."

By the time they finished breakfast, Lansing Creek was crowded with people gathered in the yard, many placing bets on the upcoming race.

"I'll be damned," Josh exclaimed as he walked out the door with Noble. "I had no idea half of the county turned out for this event."

"Word gets around," Noble replied. "They've come to see some of the finest horseflesh in the state race here today."

"I'd be willing to bet they've also come to see your beautiful granddaughter race," Josh said, noticing Shadow talking with her friends.

"So, you agree she's beautiful," Noble said, pleased.

"Of course I agree." Josh laughed. "How could anyone in his right mind not think she's beautiful."

"Shadow is very headstrong and spirited," Noble commented. "Some men don't like that in a woman, but in my opinion these are qualities that a special man will appreciate."

"I agree. The man who Shadow chooses will be lucky," Josh said very seriously.

"My sentiments exactly." Noble gave Josh a very odd smile and slapped him on the back.

"Noble, I don't know what you're getting at, but you certainly couldn't want your granddaughter to marry me. I have a rotten reputation, as you well know."

"Did I say anything about you marrying Shadow?" Noble laughed. "Excuse me, Josh, I see someone I need to talk to."

Josh watched Noble head across the yard. The man was up to something, he thought suspiciously. Before he had time to think about Noble's intentions any further, Matt joined him with Rose and Mandy.

"It looks like the odds are on Miss Lansing. Are you sure you can beat her?" Mat asked, a twinkle in his brown eyes.

"I'm not sure of anything where Miss Lansing is concerned," he admitted, "particularly this race. I've never seen her ride, but I would be willing to bet she is an expert."

"That doesn't sound like a very confident man to me." Mandy laughed.

"Oh, Josh is a very confident man," Rose stated, wrapping her arm through his possessively. "At least in most things." She smiled up at him seductively.

"We were discussing the race," Matt said irritably. "Most people think Noble's granddaughter can win," he continued, ignoring her.

"That child?" Rose laughed in a condescending tone. "Surely you don't think Josh or Allen are

153

going to allow that."

Josh glanced across the lawn toward Shadow and noticed Allen Middleton and his cousin in conversation with her. "There may not be a whole lot we can do about it," he said. "Excuse me."

"Ah, Mr. Rawlings, I hope you have the two thousand dollars ready. I plan to collect soon," Allen Middleton said in an insulting tone.

"You have to win the race first, Middleton."

"It's only a matter of time," he answered.

"You gentlemen are forgetting about me," Shadow interrupted.

"That would be impossible, lovely lady," Allen Middleton gushed.

"Well, I plan to win this race, gentlemen, so be prepared to follow me across the finish line."

"I'd follow you just about anywhere," Leland said with a lovesick expression on his face. "I'm just sorry I don't have a horse in the race."

Josh felt an uncontrollable urge to laugh at the look on the young man's face. "Miss Lansing, do you have a spare bridle I could borrow?" Josh asked. "Gambler's Lady broke hers this morning."

"Yes, of course," she agreed, wondering why he hadn't said something sooner. "We better see to it now."

As they walked toward the stable, Shadow commented, "You should have said something before we went to breakfast."

"I didn't know I needed one."

Shadow gave him a sideways glance, freezing in her tracks as she saw the lazy, devilish grin on his handsome face. "You don't need a bridle. . . ."

"No," he admitted. "I wanted to be alone with you for a few minutes before the race."

"Why?" she asked, innocence written all over her face.

"I was hoping you'd give me a kiss for good luck." *Who sounds like a school boy now?*

"You can't be serious?" Shadow laughed. "Why would I want to wish you good luck when I'm racing against you."

"Why let a small matter like that stand in the way?" he taunted, grinning down at her.

Shadow couldn't help but laugh. "As I've said before, you have a lot of nerve, Mr. Rawlings." She resumed walking toward the stables.

"Don't you think it's a little ridiculous to keep calling me Mr. Rawlings?"

"I feel safer calling you that," She said, uncomfortably aware of the magnetic charm he was exuding.

Suddenly Josh pulled her around to face him. "Why are you afraid of me, Wildcat?"

"That's a stupid question." She tried to pull away. "You should know why better than anybody."

"I think you're afraid to admit you are attracted to me."

"That's . . . that's ridiculous—" Before Shadow realized his intent, Josh pulled her into his arms

155

and slowly captured her mouth, cutting off her retort. Shadow's traitorous body responded immediately as his warm lips moved on hers. Her legs became weak, and a gnawing feeling grew in the pit of her stomach.

"Please no," she begged against his mouth.

He brushed a warm kiss against her temple. "I'm sorry, Wildcat. It seems I can't keep my hands off you."

"But you must," she said softly.

"Why must I, Shadow?"

She started to tell him that she couldn't trust herself around him, but she didn't. "My reputation . . . I mean . . ."

What a fool he was, he thought. She had been brought up a lady with morals and breeding, not like the women he was used to. He gently touched her cheek. "Your grandfather told me he is looking for a husband for you."

Shadow blushed. "My grandfather talks too much," she said, walking away from him.

"Wait a minute, Shadow," he called, hurrying to catch up with her.

"I have to get ready for a race, Mr. Rawlings. Something you should think about if you don't want to get beaten by the whole pack," she warned.

"It's Josh," he said, grabbing her arm again.

"What?" she asked, one eyebrow raised.

"You promised to call me Josh."

"I don't recall—"

"There is one more wager I want to make," he persisted.

"You are a glutton for punishment." She laughed. "Well, what is it?"

"If I beat you, you have to be my companion at the picnic all afternoon."

"If I lose the race, I may not be fit company."

"I'll chance it," he smiled. "Well, is it a bet?"

"What do I get if I win?" she asked.

"Anything you want." His smile was devastating.

"I'll have to think about that," she said, walking toward the stables.

The race at Lansing Creek was a combination of obstacles and flat racing. The course was contrived to test the rider's judgment and nerve, and the horse's stamina and speed. There were six horses in the race, but most of the bets had been placed on only three: Shadow's Rapscallion, Allen Middleton's Black Demon, and Josh Rawlings' Gambler's Lady.

Everyone who had attended the party, and probably a hundred more, gathered at the starting point. Wagers were still being made, and everyone was in a festive mood.

Josh was tightening the girth on Gambler's Lady when Shadow trotted past him. She stopped and turned in the saddle. "I'll be waiting at the finish line." She waved.

"We'll see." He laughed. "Don't forget our wager." Noble smiled to himself as he saw Shadow blush. He was sure Josh wasn't just talking about the bet of breeding their horses.

At the sound of the starting gun, the horses broke away. Shadow rode low in the saddle, leaning forward over Rapscallion's neck. Any notion that she might not be experienced enough to ride the big stallion quickly left Josh's mind. She looked magnificent on the big gray, and as she had predicted, she was in the lead over the first three fences. Josh and Allen Middleton were side by side, just a short distance behind her.

They thundered across the field toward the last obstacle, a slope that dropped into a water hole. The horses had to wade across a pond, then climb a steep bank to get to flat land and the finish line.

Shadow was still in the lead, but Josh was closing fast. Middleton had faded back, but was still ahead of the other three horses. Rapscallion managed the downhill obstacle with no trouble, but as he prepared to climb out on the steep bank, a snake dropped from a tree and slithered across their path. Rap stopped so abruptly that Shadow was tossed over the stallion's head and landed hard on the bank, half in, half out of the water.

Josh had just cleared the water when he saw what happened. While the other horses continued past her toward the finish line, he turned back to help Shadow. He dropped to his knee and began to feel for broken bones.

Shadow opened her eyes. "Just what do you think you're doing?" she asked in a breathless whisper.

His concerned expression turned to a smile. "I'm not trying to molest you, if that's what you're worried about. I was feeling for broken bones. Do you hurt anyplace?"

Shadow struggled to sit up. "Only my pride."

Josh picked her up and carried her to dry grass. "Just lie still for a few minutes," he gently ordered as he stretched out next to her.

Shadow couldn't argue with that. The wind had been knocked from her when she hit the bank, and she wasn't feeling very energetic at the moment. "Is Rapscallion all right?"

"He's fine. He's grazing over there by the trees."

For a few moments there was silence between them. Shadow studied his face as he chewed on a blade of grass. "I don't understand you," she said. "You could have won. Now you owe Allen Middleton all that money."

"That's not important."

"Not important?" she exclaimed. "How can you say that?"

Suddenly he had a very strange expression on his face, as if he had just realized the truth of his statement. "Because it's true. When I saw you go over Rapscallion's head, all I could think about was getting to you."

Shadow stared into his eyes. "I'm . . . I'm grateful."

Josh touched an errant curl. "Grateful enough to still spend the afternoon with me?"

His touch made her pulse race. "There are so many beautiful women here today. Why would you want to spend the entire afternoon with me?"

Captivated by the look of naiveté on her face, Josh smiled. "Sweet Shadow, don't you realize you are the most beautiful woman here? Besides being beautiful and spirited, you also have a good heart. Everything a man could want in a woman."

Shadow blushed at the way he was looking at her. She laid back on the grass and stared up at the sky. "Allen said you have several mistresses, including Rose Jardine."

"Did he?"

"Is it true?" she asked, looking searchingly into his gold eyes.

A constricting knot of tenderness and desire tightened in his throat. He leaned over Shadow, his face only inches from hers. "Would it bother you if it was true?"

Shadow lifted her hand to touch his face, but quickly drew it back.

"Tell me, Wildcat. Would it bother you?"

"Yes," she whispered.

Her words struck some strange chord deep within him. "Wildcat," he moaned before capturing

160

her mouth with a sudden, urgent hunger. She answered his passion, parting her lips beneath his.

The thunder of horses' hooves penetrated Josh's mind, and reluctantly he released her. Shadow surfaced more slowly from the passion of his kiss. It wasn't until she heard her grandfather's voice that she sat up.

"Are you all right, Shadow?" Noble shouted, jumping from his horse.

"Yes, I think so," she answered, still staring at Josh. "A snake . . . Rapscallion. . . ." She couldn't seem to think of what to say.

"Shadow was thrown over Rapscallion's head when a snake startled him," Josh informed him. "She was stunned for a few minutes, but nothing seems to be broken."

"She still looks stunned to me," Noble said with concern.

Shadow quickly lowered her eyes. "I'm fine, Grandfather. I just want to get back to the house and soak in a hot bath before I dress for the picnic."

Noble helped her to her feet while Josh rounded up their horses. "Are you sure you're all right?"

"I've never been better," she sighed, forgetting all about losing the race.

Where more is meant than meets the ear.

— John Milton

Chapter Nine

The picnic was in full swing by the time Shadow finished bathing and dressing. She stood at the doorway of the front porch for a moment, suddenly feeling very awkward as she glanced around to see where Josh might me. His voice startled her as he stepped up behind her.

"You look beautiful."

She smiled at him, her heart pounding wildly. "Martha insisted on the hat," she said, touching the wide brim of the straw hat decorated with lavender flowers.

"She was right to." He smiled. "The sun is getting hot." He was unable to take his eyes off her, feeling intense pleasure just looking at her. She was tall and slim, yet she appeared almost fragile. His eyes moved unwillingly to her small waist.

163

"Your dress is beautiful."

"It's one of Madam Roget's creations." She twirled around, then suddenly met his smiling eyes and realized what he was thinking. "Oh," she said, dropping her gaze from his laughing eyes.

"That wouldn't be why you got so upset about me having her come to make you a wardrobe, would it?" he teased.

Shadow couldn't hold back her laughter. "It all seems so funny now."

He felt his whole being drawn to this girl, to her sweetness and innocence. "I'm glad you don't hate me, Wildcat. I don't think I could stand that."

Her tongue moistened her suddenly dry lips. "I don't hate you," she whispered. *Far from it,* she thought.

If they hadn't been standing there in the open, he would have pulled her into his arms and kissed her. Instead he settled for offering her his arm to lead her out into the yard. "Are you hungry?"

"Famished," she admitted with enthusiasm.

"Now that's refreshing," he said. "A woman who isn't ashamed to admit she's hungry."

Shadow blushed. "I suppose it's considered unladylike to admit it?"

"Not in my opinion. I like a woman who enjoys good food." Josh said, grabbing them each a plate.

Shadow went down the table, piling her plate

164

full. When they came to Vern, he told her to take a seat and he'd bring them a plate of roast pork and some wine. "Your grandfather is keeping a place for you over there." He pointed toward the oak trees.

"It's nice to be with someone who gets preferential treatment." Josh laughed.

As they neared the table where Rose Jardine and Allen Middleton sat, Shadow wasn't sure who glared at them the most, but she felt very uneasy at the way Rose was looking at her.

"Do you have my money, Rawlings?" Middleton called after them.

"I didn't realize you needed the money so bad, Middleton," Josh replied. "Would you hold my plate for a moment, Shadow?" He took out a roll of money and threw some bills on the table in front of Middleton. "I think that takes care of our bet."

"It's not that I need the money, but I always feel when you're dealing with strangers, you shouldn't let them get too far before they pay up their debts," he said nastily. "It's been my experience that gamblers are not the most trustworthy lot to deal with."

"Is that what you've found?"

Shadow saw the muscle tighten in Josh's jaw, and she knew he was trying to control his anger. "Josh, Vern has our drinks over there."

"All right." He smiled at her.

"Why don't you join us," Rose suggested, giving Josh a seductive look. "We have plenty of room."

"Thanks, but Noble is waiting for us," Josh replied. He started to walk away, but then turned back. "You know, Middleton, Shadow would have put you and I both in our places if that snake hadn't startled Rapscallion. She was beating us soundly."

"I didn't see it that way, Rawlings. I was just holding back until the right moment. It was just a coincidence that Rapscallion bolted at the same time I made my move."

"I tell you what, Middleton, I think we should run another race in the near future. Then we'll really see who has the fastest horse."

"I know who has the fastest horse," Middleton said snidely. "I proved it this morning."

"You didn't prove anything this morning, Middleton, unless it was to show that you're not much of a man," Josh baited him.

Middleton stood up and faced Josh, his eyes blazing with anger. "Those are dangerous words, my friend."

"Don't call me your friend, Middleton. That's the last thing I want to be. What do you say; do you want to challenge me? It can be on horses or any other way you choose."

Middleton glanced around to see how many people overheard their conversation. This wasn't the way he liked to take care of unpleasant business. "I'm a gentleman, Rawlings. I don't brawl like some ruffian from out West," he said, sitting back down.

"That figures," Josh said, taking his plate from Shadow. "If you change your mind, just let me know."

"Josh, from what I hear, Allen Middleton isn't a man you want to anger," Shadow whispered as they continued toward their table. "Particularly if you plan to stay in Natchez."

"I don't like the man," Josh answered. "Everything about him makes my skin crawl."

"What was that all about?" Matt asked as Shadow and Josh sat down. "I thought you and Middleton were going to start throwing punches."

"It was nothing," Josh answered.

Matt turned his attention to Shadow. "I haven't had a chance to tell you what a great race you and Rapscallion ran. It's too bad that snake had to make an appearance when it did."

"Isn't it?" Shadow agreed, smiling warmly at Josh's brother for not saying anything about meeting her before. "It was very kind of Josh to give up winning to help me."

"That's my brother." He laughed. "Always the gallant."

"Are you two trying to ruin my bad reputation?" he asked, a twinkle in his gold eyes.

"I doubt that's possible," Shadow retorted, her face glowing with merriment as she took a bite of her food.

"I've always heard a good woman could change a man," Matt threw in.

Shadow raised her eyes to meet Josh's smiling face. "Have you tried the pork?" she asked, quickly stabbing another piece on her fork. "It really is delicious."

Josh took a bite of the roasted pork. "It is excellent," he agreed, "and the oysters are incredible. Noble, you certainly know how to throw a party."

"You can thank Shadow and Martha for arranging everything." Noble smiled.

"Don't you have parties like this in California?" Shadow asked.

"Yes, I suppose they do, but I was always too busy to participate."

"Too busy? Just what did you do in California, Josh?"

Before Shadow could get an answer, Mandy Cameron joined them. "I talked with the musicians, and I think we have agreed on a song," she said to Noble.

"Wonderful," Noble exclaimed. "My guests have all been asking if you were going to entertain us."

Mandy glanced at Shadow and Josh sitting across from each other. "It's a shame you lost the race, Miss Lansing. I'm sure a lot of people who bet on you were upset about losing their money." Her voice dripped icicles.

Shadow hadn't been surprised when Rose Jardine had treated her rudely, but she hadn't expected it from this woman.

"I'm sure Miss Lansing didn't plan it that way, Mandy," Matt said, embarrassed. "It was just a freak accident."

"No, I certainly didn't plan it that way," Shadow said, her eyes flashing defiantly. "My grandfather and I are the losers since we will not get the business in stud fees we would have if Rapscallion had won."

"Well, I'm sure when you have all this," she said with a flourish of her hands, "a few stud fees couldn't matter much."

"Oh, you are very wrong, Miss Cameron. A planter is at the mercy of mother nature, cotton prices and half a dozen other obstacles. We are just getting back on our feet after losing everything to two seasons of drought. This is the first good year we've had, so a few lost stud fees do matter."

Josh watched Shadow, impressed, but not surprised at her spirit as she put Mandy in her place.

"Mandy, I think I see one of the musicians trying to catch your eye," Matt lied. "I'll walk you over," he said, helping her up before she could argue.

"I"ll go with you," Noble volunteered.

"Was it something I said?" Shadow asked.

"No." Josh grinned. "I was very impressed."

"Were you now?" She laughed. "So you enjoy

seeing a woman lose control?"

"You're beautiful when you're angry, but then I already knew that."

"Oh come now," she protested, embarrassed. "I wasn't really angry, just annoyed. And what I said was the truth. We have had a hard time keeping things together the past couple of years. That is why I wanted to be sure to get Rapscallion back after Grandfather lost him to you."

"I understand that, Shadow. I apologize for Mandy's behavior. I'm not quite sure what her problem is."

"I think I know, but you needn't apologize for her, unless you're responsible for what she said."

"I'm responsible for no one's actions but my own," he laughed, "and sometimes I'd rather not claim those."

Shadow stared at him in stunned silence.

"Now, just a minute, Wildcat. I know exactly what you're thinking."

"Do you?"

"Yes, and it is something we need to talk about, but not here or now."

"I'd rather not talk about it anytime."

Seeing the look of hurt on her face, Josh wanted to take her in his arms and tell her that he would never let any harm come to her. My God, what was happening to him, he wondered. He was a gambler and a wanderer. He had nothing to offer this girl. If she hadn't been Noble's granddaughter, he would have made her his mistress, but he couldn't even do that now.

Shadow watched the changing expressions on Josh's face, then reluctantly turned her attention back to the food on her plate. "The pheasant is very good," she commented.

"Shadow, give me a chance . . ." he asked, turmoil in his voice.

"A chance to what?" she asked.

"I don't know. A chance to figure out what to do about you, I suppose." As soon as he said it, he knew how cold it sounded.

Shadow's eyes widened in surprise and anger. "Do about me? What makes you think you have the choice to do anything about me?" she asked in disbelief as she stood up.

"You misunderstood . . ."

"I don't think so," she said, leaning her hands on the table as she glared at him. "You misunderstood, *Mr. Rawlings,* but let me make it perfectly clear; stay away from me!" she spat before storming away.

Josh started after her, then decided against it. He'd let her calm down, then he'd try to explain. He shook his head in disgust. He couldn't explain to her until he figured out why he was acting like such a fool.

"Trouble, darling?" Rose asked, taking the seat Shadow had just vacated. "What in the world did you say to the child to make her so upset?"

"It's none of your damned business, Rose."

"Why don't you let Allen Middleton have her, darling. He's more her type," she persisted, then cringed at the look Josh gave her. "Well, it's true. Noble isn't going to let her become involved with a gambler."

"As I said, it's none of your business."

"Oh, but it is, darling. You mean a great deal to me, and I don't want to see you making a fool of yourself over that child."

Damn the man, Shadow thought silently. What was this power he had to keep her in such a turmoil? She wished that she understood her feelings for him. One moment she was sure she was in love with him, then the next she hated him.

"Hey, Shadow, wait up a minute," Toby called. "Are you gaving a good time?"

When Shadow looked at him, there were tears in her eyes. "I'm having a wonderful time," she lied.

"Shadow—" he pulled her around to face him— "I know you better than anyone. Tell me what's wrong."

"I don't know, Toby. Nothing is simple anymore. My feelings are . . . I mean I'm confused about what I feel. . . ."

"Does it have something to do with Josh Rawlings?" Mutely she took his arm and began to walk. "Your silence answers my question, Shadow.

Are you in love with him?"

"I don't know, Toby. I don't know anything," she cried miserably.

His voice seemed to break as he hugged her. "Tell me what I can do to help," he said.

"There isn't anything anyone can do." She smiled up at him. "This is something I have to work out myself. Where is Camille? I haven't seen her since this morning." She forced herself to sound gay.

"She's talking with Middleton's cousin."

Shadow looked toward where Toby was staring. "Well, let's go save her. That young man is a terrible bore."

Josh watched the tender scene between Shadow and the young overseer. Even though he was sure Shadow only felt friendship for the young man, he felt a gripping pang of jealousy that she should be comforted by him. And dammit, he was the bastard who had caused her pain. The whole situation had gotten completely out of hand. It seemed everytime he opened his mouth he made it worse. He had to remember she wasn't a sophisticate. She was a sweet, guileless innocent who took everything he said literally. Damn, what was he going to do about her. It was all getting too complicated. The smartest thing he could do would be to stay away from her.

His gaze wandered across the lawn to where Shadow stood with her friends. Loose tendrils of reddish-gold curls framed her face, and her blue eyes seemed to sparkle more than usual. She had a radiant look about her, a look that intoxicated and aroused his senses. God, how he wanted her. But at the expense of his freedom?

A horn sounded and someone shouted. "Come on everybody, the joust is about to start."

Josh hung back as everybody started toward the field.

"Come on, Josh, aren't you going to participate?" Noble asked as he joined him.

"I don't care for children's games," he answered.

Noble laughed. "When you see some of the cuts, bruises and wounded pride that come out of this, you'll see it isn't a child's game. This event is a jousting contest, and the winner gets to choose the queen of the games."

"That should be interesting to watch," Josh said, falling into step with Noble.

A flag-draped square had been set up, and two horses draped with silk stood side by side, looking like something out of medieval times.

Two young men, probably in their late teens, Josh assessed, started the tournament. Instead of using lances, they used long sticks with large padded heads. The first to be knocked off balance was the loser.

The contest started off tame enough, but by the fifth match it was getting rough. Toby McAllister had been the winner through the last two matches, and now he was calling for challengers.

Leland Brandon accepted the challenge, a sneer on his face as he said something to Toby that the others couldn't hear. The previous matches had been in good sport, but this time the two men had determined, angry looks on their faces.

"It isn't going to take much to beat an overseer," Leland taunted for everyone's benefit. "He just hasn't had any real competition yet."

The crowd suddenly fell silent. Then, as the two men made a run at each other, they started cheering Toby.

"It seems the crowd prefers the hometown overseer to a loudmouth from Vicksburg," Toby announced.

Leland kicked his horse to a gallop and charged. Toby ducked the charge, laughing as he turned his horse around.

"You bastard!" Leland swore, charging again before they were set.

This time Toby lifted his weapon just as Leland reached him, knocking him sideways out of the saddle.

The crowd cheered as Toby bowed in the saddle, loving every second of his momentary glory.

"It wasn't a fair fight," Leland claimed. "Besides, what's an overseer doing in these games anyway. It's beneath my dignity—"

"He's here as my guest"—Shadow stepped forward—"and he won fair and square."

"Listen here—" Leland faced her angrily.

"Take it easy, cousin, Allen Middleton interrupted. "We're not going to let this young upstart off so easy." He turned to Toby. "Let's see what you can do against a man," he challenged.

"These are supposed to be games," Noble pointed out as Allen mounted.

"Your boy has overstepped his bounds, Noble."

"Toby McAllister is not *my boy*," Noble growled. "Though God knows I'd be proud to call him son. The fact is he deserves to be here more than you or your cousin."

Middleton smiled patiently at Noble. "If you'll step aside, we'll get on with the games."

The two men charged toward each other. Instead of aiming at Toby with the padded end of the stick, Middleton used the handle to land a blow to the side of Toby's head, knocking him from the saddle. The crowd gasped in shock.

"Well, so much for boys," Middleton said as Shadow and Camille rushed to help Toby up. "And now to choose my queen."

"Just a minute, Middleton," Josh said, rolling up his sleeves. "You did say all challengers were welcome?"

"You intend to challenge me, Rawlings." He laughed. "I didn't think you had it in you."

Noble held Josh's horse as he mounted. "I thought you didn't like children's games." He smiled knowingly.

176

"They just ceased being games." Josh winked.

Suddenly the rules didn't matter, and the crowd sensed it. This wouldn't be a match that was decided on who was knocked off balance. Josh and Allen faced each other like knights of old. After two passes, it was obvious Josh was the stronger of the two. He was playing cat and mouse with Middleton, landing blows in the stomach and chest, but not hard enough to knock him off his mount.

Shadow couldn't take her eyes off Josh. His shirt, damp with perspiration, clung to his chest, and his rolled-up sleeves revealed muscular arms. His blond hair curled riotously, making him look rakishly handsome and masculine, bringing unbidden memories of the time he had held her against her will.

Her attention was brought back to the present as the crowd cheered. Josh lifted Middleton out of the saddle and dumped him on the ground with a blow square to the stomach.

With hatred in his eyes, Middleton got up and brushed his clothes off. "You've make a bad mistake, Rawlings. A mistake you'll live to regret."

Josh leaned forward in the saddle and smiled. "I don't think so, Middleton."

"Pick the queen," someone shouted.

Noble smiled at Josh. "It's your honor, Josh."

"Just what does this queen do for me?" Josh asked, his gaze on Shadow.

"She'll be your companion for the day," Noble replied.

"It seems I've heard that before," Josh said, trotting toward Shadow and her friends.

Josh was looking straight at Camille, and for a moment Shadow thought he was going to pick her friend. Her heart nearly stopped beating before he turned and lifted her easily into the saddle before him. Shadow struggled to keep her skirts down as everyone cheered.

"Are there any more games?" Josh whispered in Shadow's ear. "I'm beginning to like being the conquering hero."

She turned her face to look at him. "No more games." She smiled, forgetting about their earlier argument.

"I need to cool off." He smiled down at her. "I must smell like a horse."

"I happen to like the way horses smell." She laughed, then added, "I do know a place along the river where you can cool off, but I have to swear you to secrecy about it."

Josh felt his heart do a flip-flop. He wasn't the conquering hero, he thought with a smile on his face. This lovely angel in his arms was the conqueror, and suddenly he didn't care.

"I'm proud of you, Toby." Noble slapped the young overseer on the back. "You did very well—"

178

Suddenly Noble gasped in pain, grabbing Toby's arm for support.

"Mr. Lansing, what's wrong?" Toby exclaimed.

"It's all right," Noble assured, clinging to him for a long moment. "Walk back to the house with me, Toby?" Noble asked, white as a ghost. "I hope after today I won't have to worry about Shadow. . . ." he said in gasping breaths.

"Well I'll be damned," Allen Middleton swore, watching the scene between Noble and his young overseer. "Now that's an interesting development."

"What are you talking about?" Leland asked, still smarting from his defeat.

"I was just thinking that Miss Shadow Lansing would make a lovely bride."

The wrong way always seems the more reasonable.

—George Moore

Chapter Ten

Allen caught up with Noble and Toby before they reached the house. "Noble, I wanted to talk to you about—" Pretending to suddenly notice Noble's pallor, Allen exclaimed, "My God, are you all right, Noble? You're as pale as a ghost."

"I'm just tired," Noble said, sinking into a rocking chair on the porch. "Toby, would you ask Abraham to bring me a bourbon? As a matter of fact, tell him to bring me the bottle." Turning his attention back to Allen when they were alone, he asked, "All right, Allen, what did you want to talk to me about?"

"I find your granddaughter refreshing and lovely."

"That's nice to hear," Noble answered coolly,

"but I'm sure that isn't the reason for this conversation."

"No, not entirely. I wanted to ask your permisson to call on Shadow."

Noble's knuckles turned white as he clutched the arm of the chair. "That will have to be Shadow's decision."

"But you're her guardian . . ."

"That's true, but I want Shadow to marry whomever she wishes. If she wants you to come courting, then so be it. You may have waited too long to offer for her, though. I think she may have already found someone else she's interested in."

"You don't mean Josh Rawlings?" Middleton exclaimed. "Surely you wouldn't permit that. My God, the man is a gambler and a drifter, and worse, he isn't even a Southerner."

"Better a gambler than a man who would breed human beings for profit, Southerner or not," Noble growled.

"Dammit, Noble, we've been through all this before. I did what I had to do to keep from losing Middleton Place. You're just damned lucky you got a good crop this year, or you may have had to resort to the same thing."

"Never!" Noble answered angrily.

Allen could see his chance of gaining Lansing Creek slipping through his fingers, and all because of the damned gambler. "Listen to me, my friend. We're neighbors. You must know I could give Shadow everything a woman could possibly want. She'd live like a queen as my wife."

Noble was still suffering some discomfort, and he wished Middleton would leave him alone. "I don't want to argue with you, Allen. As I said, you'll have to take this up with Shadow. The decision is hers to make."

"All right, Noble, but may I make one suggestion. Check out Rawlings before you let Shadow get too serious about him. I've heard rumors that he's in Natchez to spy on us."

"Spy?" Noble laughed incredulously. "What the hell are you talking about, Middleton?"

"If you'd get more involved in our activities, Noble, you'd know that there are people up North who are very interested in knowing our strengths and weaknesses. If you don't believe me, ask Rawlings what brought him to Natchez. I'm only suggesting this for Shadow's welfare. I'd really hate to see her get hurt."

"I appreciate your concern," Noble answered, taking his drink from Abraham. "I'll take your suggestion under consideration."

Josh's arm felt good around her waist as they rode toward her secret place. She could feel his warm breath against her temple.

"Where is this place?" he asked softly in her ear as they stopped before what looked like an impenetrable mass of foliage.

"You must promise never to tell anyone about this place," she insisted, smiling up at him.

"Hmmm, another secret we share. I like that."

Shadow blushed. "Go through there." She

pointed to a large weeping willow.

He urged his horse through the long tendrils of the weeping willow and the sweet-smelling pines until they came out of the trees to a natural swimming hole the river had carved into the land. A bird took off in flight, screeching its displeasure at being disturbed.

"It's beautiful," Josh said in awe as he dismounted on the moss green ground. The place was hidden from view by ancient live oaks covered with lacy Spanish moss. Even someone boating on the river wouldn't notice it.

"It's where I come to think and just be alone," she said sadly.

Josh held his hands out to her, slowly lowering her to the ground. "What do you think about, Wildcat?"

"About what the future will bring," she answered before walking toward the water.

"And just what do you want the future to hold for you?" He walked beside her.

"I don't know," she answered, embarrassed. "Didn't you say you wanted to cool off?"

"I did, didn't I?"

To Shadow's surprise, he started to remove his shirt. "I'll wait over there," she mumbled quickly moving away.

"It's all right." He laughed. "I don't plan to take off anything else."

Shadow still moved away a few yards, but she couldn't keep her eyes off his rippling muscles as he leaned over and splashed water on his face and chest. She felt a sudden twinge of fear—or was it

184

anticipation? They were totally alone for the first time since he had held her prisoner.

Josh straightened up and glanced toward her. "Are you all right?" he asked, noticing the odd expression on her face.

"Yes. Yes, of course. I was just thinking Grandfather might be wondering where we've disappeared to. I probably should have said something to him before we rode away."

Josh laughed softly as he moved toward her. "Are you afraid of me, Wildcat?"

Shadow lowered her eyes. How could she tell him she was afraid of herself, of the strange feelings he evoked. "I have this strange feeling like I'm standing too near a fire when I'm near you," she admitted softly.

"I admit you stand in dangerous company"—he smiled warmly—"but I would never knowingly hurt you, sweet. I'd like for you to trust me."

Shadow met his smile. "Grandfather always said to beware of a man who says trust me."

"Your grandfather is a very wise man." He laughed, taking her hand.

"It was very kind of you to challenge Allen Middleton after he humiliated Toby," she said, quickly changing the subject.

"Come sit with me," he said, indicating a rock in the sun, "and I'll tell you why I challenged Middleton."

She moved with him, her eyes never leaving his face. God, but she was beautiful, he thought. So sweet and innocent looking, yet he knew the passion that lay just beneath the surface.

Shadow spread her skirt out around her as she sat down. "Why did you challenge Middleton?" she asked.

Josh tossed a stone into the water, then picked up another. "It was to impress you," he answered.

"Surely you jest." Her blue eyes lit up with laughter.

"Afraid not." He grinned. "I couldn't let Middleton have all the glory."

"Men!" she laughed. "You are all still fighting dragons."

"I suppose you're right. Did I mention that I thought you were magnificent on Rapscallion this morning? If he hadn't spooked, you would have put us all to shame."

"That's very kind of you to admit," she smiled. "Most people think it is very unladylike for me to be riding, including your friend, Rose Jardine."

"I think she envies you," he commented, leaning back on one elbow so he could watch her. "You were going to tell me what you wanted the future to hold for you, Shadow."

"I don't know." She sighed. "I suppose eventually marriage. But I want a man who will respect my intelligence and not want me to stay hidden away doing needlepoint and taking care of children. I don't understand why when a man marries a woman he wraps her in layers of dullness, pretending she doesn't have a brain in her head."

"Only a fool would do that to you, Wildcat." he said lazily.

Shadow glanced at him, wondering if he was teasing her.

186

After a few moment's silence Josh said, "You still haven't told me what you think about when you come here alone."

"I think a lot about my mother and father," she admitted. "Grandfather has been wonderful, but sometimes I miss them so much."

"How did they die, Shadow?"

She kept her eyes on the water. "The fever. One day they were both alive and vital; three days later we were burying them on the hillside overlooking the river."

"I'm sorry, little one," he said, gazing at her face.

"Are your parents alive?" she asked.

Josh was silent for a moment, and she was sure she saw pain cross his face. "No, they are both dead," he said.

"Then you know the pain," she said, tears in her eyes.

Emotion he had never experienced surfaced. He pulled her into his arms and cradled her, wanting to protect her from ever knowing another moment's unhappiness. He stared at the river over her head, reminding himself that the first time he had taken her, he didn't know who she was, or that she was a virgin. Now, despite the throbbing pain he felt in his loins, he couldn't do anything about it. She was Noble Lansing's granddaughter.

He lifted her chin, forcing her to meet his gaze. "I should get you back," he said, turmoil evident in his voice.

"You said we needed to talk," Shadow said, reluctant to leave the comfort of his arms.

"At the moment, talking is the last thing on my mind."

"What is on your mind?" she asked with heart-rending innocence.

"I want to kiss you, to hold you against me and feel your velvet skin," he said in a soft caressing voice. "To enjoy your body the way I did when you were with me at Yancey's. That's all I've thought about since I met you. But I can't, Wildcat. Not now—not like this. Your grandfather is my friend."

"I understand. But there is something I want to tell you, too," she confessed shyly. "I haven't been able to put you out of my mind, either."

He was touched by the innocence in her liquid blue eyes. "Sweet Shadow," he whispered. "You are like no other woman I've ever met."

"Oh," she murmured, assuming the wrong thing. "I suppose I seem like a child to you after all the women you've had."

He touched her face gently. "That isn't what I meant, sweet. You are open and honest, a trait I haven't found in too many women."

Shadow had to smile. "A few days ago you didn't feel that way about me."

"No, I suppose I didn't," he admitted warmly. Cradling her face between his palms, Josh touched his lips to hers. "A man can be wrong about a lot of things," he whispered against her mouth. His tongue traced the line between her lips, coaxing her mouth to open.

Shadow wrapped her arms around his neck and answered his urgent hunger with a passion of her own. His hands tangled in her hair, pulling her closer.

Suddenly he pulled back. Dazed with desire, Shadow stared at him. "What's wrong, Josh?"

"We have to go back," he said, standing up and pulling her along with him. "Your reputation will be ruined if we stay away any longer."

"When did you start worrying about my reputation?" she asked as he lifted her into the saddle.

"Just believe me, this is for your benefit, not mine. If I had my way . . . well, never mind."

When Josh and Shadow returned to the picnic, the fiddle players had just started up a tune, and everyone was gathering around them.

"Are you up to a spirited dance, m'lady," he bowed, a challenging expression on his handsome face.

"To this music?" she laughed.

"Of course to this music. You don't mean to tell me the waltz is the only dance you know," he feighed disbelief.

"No," she grinned, accepting his arm. "Just don't step on my skirt."

"I can dance with the best of them, love, and I have never been known to step on a toe or a skirt," he promised.

Shadow's heart skipped a beat at his term of endearment. "We shall see."

The fast-paced dance was exhilarating and took a great deal of stamina. Shadow felt giddy and light headed as Josh twirled her around to the cheer and taunts of the crowd. When the music finally stopped she was exhausted and breathing heavily.

"You are full of surprises, Wildcat. I haven't met too many women who could dance like that."

"Is that a compliment?" She laughed. "Or are you saying a lady wouldn't dance like that?"

"It was a compliment," he said, taking her hand. "I find I like everything about you, Shadow Lansing."

"Careful, you'll turn my head," she warned, a pink flush rising to her cheeks.

Josh gave her a devilish grin. "That was my intention, Wildcat."

Abraham touched Josh's sleeve. " 'Cuse me, Mr. Rawlings," he drawled, "but Mr. Lansing would like a word with you."

"It seems our absence didn't go unnoticed," Josh said, accepting Noble's invitation. "I fear I'm going to have some explaining to do to your grandfather."

"Grandfather likes you," she assured, "but if he gets too rough, just call." She winked as she walked away.

Josh threw back his head and laughed, as he went to join Noble. "Little hellion."

"Sit down, Josh," Noble said. "Abraham has fixed you a drink. I hope brandy is agreeable."

"Most agreeable," Josh accepted the drink.

"I'll get right to the point, Josh. I'd like to know what your intentions are toward my granddaughter."

Josh took a long, slow drink. "I'm not quite sure what you mean, Noble."

"You're acting like a man who is interested in

marriage, my friend. Particularly when you take her off alone. You must realize I can't allow behavior like that unless you intend to marry her."

"Now hold on minute, Noble. I'm very fond—"

"You better make up your mind, Josh," Noble cut him off, "because Allen Middleton has already asked my permission to court Shadow."

Josh slammed his glass down on the wrought iron table. "I can't believe you'd allow that!"

"Dammit, Josh, either make a commitment or stay the hell away from her!" Noble shouted. Suddenly sweat broke out on his head, and he clutched the arms of his chair. "Jesus," he hissed between gritted teeth.

"Noble, what's wrong?" Josh asked, concerned.

"It's nothing. Don't change the subject, Josh. I like you, but I can't let you ruin my granddaughter's reputation," he said in short, painful breaths.

"I'm sorry, Noble. I wouldn't knowingly do that."

"I swore to Shadow's mother and father that I would look after her until she married. Allen Middleton is certainly wealthy enough to take care of her, but you're right, I would prefer leaving Lansing Creek to someone I trust and admire, and someone I think Shadow cares for."

Josh ran his hand through his hair in a frustrated gesture. "God, Noble, I don't know what to say. I've never been able to stay in one place or with one woman longer than a month or so: so it wouldn't be fair for me to make a commitment to Shadow.

"Look around you, Josh. Lansing Creek is a

prosperous plantation. Marry my granddaughter and everything I have will be yours."

"No, dammit! If I married Shadow, it wouldn't be for what you offer me, Noble. It would be because I love her."

Noble smiled. "Then you're saying you do love her."

"I didn't say that. To be honest with you, I'm not sure what I feel," he said as he stared across the lawn toward Shadow. Would it be so bad being married, he wondered. He had to admit, it drove him crazy to think of her with anyone else. No, he couldn't do it. It wouldn't be fair. . . .

Shadow watched Josh and her grandfather from across the yard. What was her grandfather up to now, she wondered. They both looked so serious. Surely he wouldn't take Josh to task for riding off alone with her.

"You look like you could use a cool drink," Allen said beside Shadow. "Did you enjoy your ride with the conquering hero?" he asked sarcastically.

"Yes, very much," she answered, staring him straight in the eye.

"The widow Jardine was looking for her escort," he said snidely.

"Josh isn't her escort," Shadow snapped.

"Listen, my dear, I don't want to see you hurt, but you must realize Josh Rawlings is unsuitable for you. The man is a gambler and womanizer."

"You have overstepped your bounds, Mr.

ACCEPT YOUR **FREE GIFT** AND EXPERIENCE MORE OF THE PASSION AND ADVENTURE YOU LIKE IN A HISTORICAL ROMANCE

Zebra Romances are the finest novels of their kind and are written with the adult woman in mind. All of our books are written by authors who really know how to weave tales of romantic adventure in the historical settings you love.

Because our readers tell us these books sell out very fast in the stores, Zebra has made arrangements for you to receive at home the four newest titles published each month. You'll never miss a title and home delivery is so convenient. With your first shipment we'll even send you a FREE Zebra Historical Romance as our gift just for trying our home subscription service. No obligation.

BIG SAVINGS AND **FREE** HOME DELIVERY

Each month, the Zebra Home Subscription Service will send you the four newest titles as soon as they are published. (We ship these books to our subscribers even before we send them to the stores.) You may preview them *Free* for 10 days. If you like them as much as we think you will, you'll pay just $3.50 each and *save $1.80 each month* off the cover price. *AND you'll also get FREE HOME DELIVERY.* There is never a charge for shipping, handling or postage and there is no minimum you must buy. If you decide not to keep any shipment, simply return it within 10 days, no questions asked, and owe nothing.

Get a Free
Zebra
Historical
Romance

*a $3.95
value*

ZEBRA HOME SUBSCRIPTION SERVICES, INC.
P.O. BOX 5214
120 BRIGHTON ROAD
CLIFTON, NEW JERSEY 07015-5214

Middleton. My friendship with Mr. Rawlings is none of your business."

"I feel it necessary to make it my business, my dear, because I care about you."

"That's ridiculous," Shadow snapped. "We hardly know each other."

"We are neighbors and Southerners, and we must stick together, particularly in times like these," he persisted.

Shadow couldn't believe her ears as he continued on about how important it was to guard against outsiders. As she stared at him, she realized how plain and weak looking he was compared to Josh. Josh was so arrogantly alive and intense, while this man . . .

"As you can see, you don't have a lot of time, my friend." Noble pointed out Shadow and Middleton deep in conversation. "If Shadow accepts Middleton's proposal, I'll have to go along with her decision."

Watching Shadow with Middleton, Josh felt an odd mixture of anger and jealousy. What the hell was he going to do? He didn't want to lose her, but marriage—could he stop being a wanderer? There would be no more gambling halls and no more women. Fear suddenly clutched at him. He remembered his mother dying in childbirth, and the sweet young girl his father had brought home to raise them . . . the sweet young girl who had caused his father's death. No, he couldn't do it. Marriage wasn't for him.

"Noble, I'm sorry. You'll have to do what you think best for Shadow. I'm not going to be around Natchez much longer, so you see my problem."

"Yes, I see your problem," Noble answered, surprised that his friend had such a fear of commitment.

Josh searched for Shadow, knowing he couldn't leave without saying good-bye to her. He found her talking with Camille and her family.

"Shadow, I'm going to have to leave, but I'd like to talk with you alone for a moment."

Shadow's heart beat wildly, hoping that he was going to tell her he'd be back to court her. He took her hand and led her toward the deserted picnic tables.

"I've enjoyed these two days with you, Wildcat."

"I've enjoyed them, too," she answered, suddenly feeling shy.

"Then you've forgiven me for our first meeting?"

"I suppose I was partly to blame," she admitted softly. "I think there is an expression about being in the wrong place at the wrong time."

"It would be very difficult for me to leave Natchez knowing you hated me."

Shadow stared at him in shock, her blue eyes filling with tears. "You are leaving Natchez?"

"I think it best," he said, feeling strangely empty.

"Are you going back to California?"

"Eventually. I'm a wanderer, Wildcat. I'd make a lousy husband."

Shadow felt humiliated. "I never said anything about marriage," she said defensively.

"I know you didn't, but your grandfather won't tolerate my attention to you if it isn't honorable."

"No, I suppose he wouldn't, but you don't have to leave Natchez, Josh. I won't pressure you." She wanted to cry. She felt as if her heart were breaking. There was something special between them, yet he wouldn't admit it. He was going to leave Natchez. . . .

"I'm sorry, Shadow. I never meant to hurt you."

"It looks like your boyfriend has other interests," Allen said to Rose.

"Nonsense," Rose said, eyeing Josh across the lawn. "He is just being kind to the child for Noble's benefit."

Allen laughed in a sarcastic manner. "You can't be that big a fool, Rose. Shadow is a stunning beauty, and she has Josh Rawlings wrapped around her little finger."

"I've noticed you've been very attentive to the chit yourself."

"That's true. I intend to marry her," he answered bluntly.

"Really?" She laughed. "And of course, Noble's extensive lands wouldn't hurt the bargain."

"I won't deny I've had my eye on Lansing Creek for a long time. I thought I would have it when Noble went bankrupt, but as you can see, he's brought it back to life with a good crop."

"Poor darling." She patted him on the cheek. "Perhaps we can help each other."

"My thoughts exactly." He smiled.

There is no greater sorrow
Than to be mindful of the happy time
In misery.

— Dante Alighieri

Chapter Eleven

Josh stared into space, his mind tortured as he remembered his parting conversation with Shadow, and the look of hurt in her eyes. Damn him for a fool! Why had he ever gotten mixed up with the girl? When he found out who she was, he should have run like hell.

He grabbed the empty whiskey bottle on the table. After spending a sleepless night, he had turned to the bottle to help him forget, yet still she invaded his thoughts. Maybe he needed another bottle, he decided.

It was early and the place was still empty as he made his way behind the bar. He knocked over several glasses, searching for a bottle of his good stock.

"Do you really think you need any more to

drink?" Matt asked.

Josh started to tell his brother to mind his own business, but seeing the concern on his face, he changed his mind. "No, I suppose I don't."

"Do you mind a bit of brotherly advice?"

"If I did, would it matter?"

"No," Matt admitted. "I hate to see you doing this to yourself, Josh. Why don't you just admit you're in love with Shadow, and then do something about it."

Josh was silent a long moment. "You know me better than anyone, Matt. What kind of husband do you think I'd make?"

"Maybe better than you think. You'll never know until you try, Josh."

"There's a lot more to it than just being in love. War is coming to the South. A war I don't want any part of."

"Have you asked Shadow how she would feel about leaving the South?"

"No, the subject has never come up."

"Why don't you talk to her about it?"

Josh ran his hand through his hair. "That brings us back to the subject of marriage."

Matt felt a twinge of sympathy at the suffering in his brother's voice. He knew their stepmother's behavior had left a mark on Josh. He had never trusted any woman after seeing the way she had cheated on his father and eventually even caused him to take his own life.

"You know, Josh, we've never really talked

about it, but we both know Stella had a lot to do with your . . . your hesitation about getting involved."

"I think fear is the word you were looking for," Josh said bitterly.

"Not all women are like Stella, Josh."

"Most of the ones I've met have been. They'd lie and cheat in a second if it served their purpose."

"Do you think Shadow is like that?"

Josh poured himself a cup of coffee. "No. I don't think so. She seems innocent of the games most women play."

"Not most women, Josh. You've just had some bad experiences. You must admit, when you look for the worst in people, you can usually find it."

"Yeah, I seem to have a knack for finding whores and rich widows." He laughed bitterly.

"Maybe you've never given a woman a chance," Matt suggested.

"Listen to my little brother." Josh laughed. "He sounds like a man who has had a lot of experience with women."

"No, far from it. As a matter of fact, I'm probably the last person who should be giving advice."

"Why do you say that?"

"I think you know I was interested in Mandy."

"*Was* interested?"

"Yes, unfortunately Mandy seems more interested in your comings and goings than she is in me. I got tired of getting the third degree from her."

"That's very strange," Josh mused. "At the party I saw her arguing with Allen Middleton, yet she denied it. She said it was the first time she'd met him."

"I'll tell you something even stranger. I saw Middleton come out of Mandy's dressing room last night just before she went on."

"I think we better keep a close eye on our Miss Cameron," Josh suggested.

"Do you think there could be a connection between her and Middleton?"

"I wouldn't be surprised at anything."

"We've gotten off the subject here, big brother. You still haven't said what you're going to do about Shadow."

"I suppose I should talk to her. Hell, I could be all wrong about how she feels about me. She may just laugh in my face."

"I doubt it. How could any woman in her right mind refuse you?" Matt laughed.

"Thanks for the vote of confidence." Josh slapped him on the back. "How would you feel about being best man at my wedding?"

"I'd be honored. But Josh, I want you to know, no matter what happens, I'm going to be moving on."

"Moving on? What are you talking about?"

"I'm going to head back to California. This area is a tinder box and could go up in flames at any time. Besides, you know I've wanted to go back for a long time. California is my home, Josh, no matter what the memories are."

"I know, Matt. I guess I've always felt the same way. As a matter of fact, I've often dreamed about building a mansion overlooking the bay in San Francisco," Josh mused. "Maybe Shadow would like to help me plan it."

"You'll never know until you ask."

Shadow sipped her tea and tried to be attentive as Allen Middleton bored her with talk about a horse he was purchasing from a breeder in Jackson. The last thing she wanted to do today was entertain Allen Middleton. She had spent a sleepless night cursing herself for having been such a fool about Josh Rawlings. If only she hadn't been so obvious about her feelings. The man had practically run from her.

"So what do you think, Shadow?" Allen asked, an annoyed look on his face.

"I'm sorry, what were you saying?"

"I was saying that I'd like to court you."

Shadow's eyes widened in surprise, and she quickly stood up and began pacing. "Oh, no, Allen. Please, I need some time. I'm not ready to get married."

"Not ready?" He laughed. "My dear, if you wait much longer, you'll be considered a spinster."

"And if I am, that's my business," Shadow retorted angrily.

Allen had started out wanting to marry Shadow

to get his hands on Lansing Creek, but her reluctance intrigued him. Now he considered it a challenge to win her.

"My dear, I didn't mean to sound insulting. It's just that you're so lovely that I don't want to see your beauty go to waste."

"That's very kind of you to be concerned, but I can take care of myself."

Allen pulled Shadow into his arms. "I can give you everything you could ever want, Shadow. Nothing would be too good for my wife."

"I'm flattered, but—" He cut off her protests with a kiss. All she could think about was how different his kiss affected her. When Josh kissed her her knees would go weak—

"I'm sorry to interrupt such a tender scene," a cold voice said from the doorway. "I can see the lady is compliant this time. I guess persistence does pay off."

"Josh . . ." Shadow stared at his forbidden face. "What are you doing here?"

Staring at her in Middleton's arms, he didn't understand any of the emotions he was experiencing. He wanted to hurt her, to lash out. He couldn't tell her he'd come to ask her to marry him. By God, wouldn't the two of them get a good laugh about that. What a fool he'd been to think she was different.

"I came to discuss some business with your grandfather," he lied. "Would you mind telling me where I can find him."

"I'll get him for you," Shadow volunteered, eager to escape the tension in the room, but Allen didn't release her.

"I'll say good-bye for now, my dear," Allen said, kissing her hand. "We'll discuss our plans later."

"Don't let me run you off," Josh said caustically.

"You're not, Rawlings. I have some important business to take care of, or I wouldn't be leaving."

"Lining up the troops, no doubt," Josh sneered.

Shadow could feel the hatred between the two men; the tension in the air was palpable.

"Our troops are ready and willing to protect their loved ones, Rawlings. Which side will you be on when the time comes."

"I won't be on any side," Josh growled. "War is for fools and boys who want to play games."

"A typical excuse of a coward," Allen said in an insulting drawl.

"I think we both know who the coward is." Josh smiled, his gold eyes glittering dangerously.

Middleton returned the smile, but it didn't reach his eyes. He wasn't about to be drawn into a fight wiht this uncivilized bastard. He had other ways of dealing with the likes of Josh Rawlings.

"I'll be going now, Shadow. If it is agreeable with you, I'll pick you up for a ride tomorrow morning around eleven. We can talk further then."

"Yes, yes, of course," she said, anxious for him to leave.

"Rawlings, until we meet again." Allen clicked

203

his heels as he gave an insulting bow.

"Well, you didn't waste any time," Josh said when they were alone. "That sounded like marriage plans to me."

"I'll get my grandfather for you," Shadow said, realizing Josh wasn't in any mood to be rational.

Josh grabbed her by the arm as she walked past him. "Not just yet," he growled.

Shadow stared at him, shaken by the violence she could feel in his touch. "Why are you so angry?" she whispered. "You're the one who said good-bye."

He stared down at her, shaken by the innocence of her question. But he couldn't soften. She had shown her true colors by running to Allen Middleton. "And like a whore you made sure you had a man waiting in the wings."

Dumbfounded, Shadow stared at him. "Like a whore?" she gasped in disbelief. She drew a shuttered breath and, without thought to the consequence, raised her free hand and slapped him soundly across the face.

A faint smile curved his firm lips. Before she guessed his intention, he pulled her hard against him. His gold eyes held hers, then bending his head, he captured her soft lips. His mouth searched hers with an almost desperate urgency.

Mindless, Shadow returned his kiss, too wrapped up in the fierce pleasure of being with him again to remember his harsh words and accusation.

Suddenly he released her and he gave her an evil smile. "As I said, every woman is a whore, and you're no different, love. It doesn't make any difference to you who the man is in your life, just so long as there is one to fall under your spell."

Shadow jerked away. "You were too busy running away to get to know me, so how do you have the nerve to make such judgment? You call me a whore," she spat. "Well, I think you're a coward. The worst kind of coward. You're afraid to face your own feelings."

"Shut up, Shadow," he warned between gritted teeth.

"Have I hit a nerve?" she asked sarcastically. "The great Josh Rawlings is afraid of a mere girl?"

"If you're so brave, come away with me," he challenged.

"As your mistress?" She laughed bitterly.

"That's right. No ties. We'll just enjoy each other for the moment."

Tears glistened in her blue eyes as she stared at this too-handsome, arrogant man who had taken her heart and then thrown it back at her. "That's what I mean, Josh. If you loved me, you'd make a commitment. But you're afraid to."

"Sure, you want me to make a commitment, and then I'll come home and find you in bed with someone else." His laugh was wry and short. "No, thanks, lady."

"You call yourself a gambler, but you're not willing to take a gamble on life. I really feel sorry for you, Josh. You have the chance to know love, but you don't have the courage to accept it. Goodbye, Josh, she said, walking from the room.

She passed her grandfather as she left the room. "Mr. Rawlings has business with you. I'm going to change and go for a ride."

Noble shook his head. He had hoped Josh had come to his senses, but from the expression on Shadow's face, apparently he hadn't.

"Hello, Josh. Shadow said you wanted to see me."

Josh walked past him toward the door. "She was wrong, dammit. The same way she's wrong about a lot of things."

Josh kicked Gambler's Lady to a gallop, leaving a cloud of dust as he left the drive of Lansing Creek. She wasn't going to give him ultimatums. Dammit, if she loved him, she'd go with him any way he wanted her. He wasn't a coward. Hell, maybe he was when it came to women, but he had good reason. He remembered how sweet and innocent Stella had seemed when his father had married her. It didn't take long for her to bed every man in the mining camp—and most of the time he and Matt had been in the next room. Matt had been too young to really know what was going on, but he hadn't been. He knew only too well the shame and humiliation his father had felt before taking his own life.

"Damn women!" he cursed aloud. "Damn them all for the calculating, demanding bitches they are."

And Shadow wasn't any different. Hadn't he heard her making wedding plans with Allen Middleton. God, how could she be so unfeeling?

So lost in thought was Josh that he didn't see the three hooded men coming toward him until it was too late.

Shadow rode Rapscallion hard across the field, trying to outrun the hateful words Josh had said. Whore indeed, she fumed. He forgot that she had been a virgin until he raped her. If she had had any sense, she would have told her grandfather what he did and let him have the bastard hung. How dare the man suggest she go away with him as his mistress. That just proved what a despicable cad he was, she told herself.

She pulled her horse to a halt and laid her head againt his soft neck. "I really thought he cared for me, Rapscallion. I should have known things were happening too fast. You don't just fall in love over night. That's only in fairy tales. Oh, Rapscallion, why does it hurt so bad?"

She rode across the field in the opposite direction of the river, deciding she didn't want to go to her secret place just now. There would be too many memories of her last visit there. She urged Rapscallion to a full gallop again, hoping to clear the cobwebs in her mind. They cleared a fence and raced down the river road toward town. As she rounded a bend in the road, she came upon Gambler's Lady grazing along the side of the road. A knot of fear clutched her stomach. Josh's valuable horse wouldn't be roaming around loose unless something was wrong.

Examining Gambler's Lady, Shadow couldn't find any sign of injury. She began to search the roadside and the edge of the woods. Something must have happened to him, she thought in a panic. She remounted and began to look for tracks. She had only gone a short distance when she noticed the brush trampled down. It looked like a lot of horses had gone into the woods at that point. She followed the path, her heart pounding rapidly. *Please let him be all right,* she prayed.

Rapscallion snorted and reared back. The trees and brush were thick, but she spotted a flash of color just ahead. "Josh! Oh God, Josh," she cried out in fear as she flung herself from the saddle. He had been badly beaten, but what scared her the most was the amount of blood on his clothes.

"Josh, please speak to me," she begged, placing her ear to his chest. "Thank God," she whispered, finding a heartbeat. "Please wake up, Josh. It's me, Shadow."

Josh moaned and turned his head away.

"Oh, Josh, who did this to you?" she cried as she took off her scarf and touched his mouth.

"I've got to get you back to Lansing Creek. Grandfather will know what to do. Please, Josh, can you sit up? You must help me. I have to get you on Rapscallion."

Josh opened his eyes and stared at her. "So beautiful," he whispered in a raspy voice.

"Josh, I've to get you on Rapscallion."

"I don't . . . don't think I can."

"You must. You're bleeding bad, Josh. There isn't time to go for help. We'll do this slowly . . . try to get to your knees."

With strength born out of fear and desperation, Shadow somehow got Josh into the saddle. He sat doubled over in pain, and she knew galloping back to Lansing Creek was out of the question.

"Just hold on," she pleaded. "It won't be long."

By the time they reached the house, Josh had lost consciousness. "Grandfather! Somebody, help me!" Shadow screamed.

Noble and several servants arrived on the scene in a matter of minutes. "Shadow, my God, what happened?" Noble asked.

"I found him like this, Grandfather. Someone tried to kill him. He's bleeding real bad. I don't know if he's been shot or stabbed."

"Get him upstairs," Noble ordered one of his servants. "Abraham, send one of the boys for Doc Morgan. Tell him to hurry."

"Also tell one of them to go out on the river road and bring Josh's horse back here," Shadow asked.

When Shadow reached the room where they had taken Josh, Martha was already stripping his bloody clothes from his body. "You shouldn't be in here," she said, noticing Shadow standing in the doorway.

"He's going to be all right, isn't he?"

"I'se no doctor, but he looks strong to me. Why doan you git me some hot water, and we'll see how much is injuries and how much is jus' blood."

Glad to have something to do, Shadow hurried downstairs to find Tilly. "Water is already on," Tilly announced, "but it will boil faster if you'd stop pacing and causing such a breeze."

Shadow sank into a chair. "He looks so terrible. Whoever did this meant to kill him." She jumped up and started pacing again. "Oh, God, why would anyone do this? Matt . . . I forgot Matt," she exclaimed.

"You think someone named Matt did this?"

"No, no. Matt is Josh's brother," she explained. "I have to send someone with a message to him. I'll be in the library. Call me as soon as the water boils."

Shadow hovered in the doorway, out of sight, but not out of hearing, as Doc Morgan examined Josh. "Looks like you made some enemies, Mr. Rawlings."

"It does look that way," Josh gasped as Doc

treated one of his wounds.

"I don't think they meant you to live, young man. Besides the lumps and bruises, you have two knife woulds. You're damed lucky you didn't bleed to death before someone found you."

A shiver of fear ran down Shadow's backbone. If she hadn't gone riding . . .

"It wasn't robbery," Noble said. "He still had his money and a gold pocket watch on him."

"I suggest you notify the sheriff, though I doubt it will do much good. In the meantime, you're not to move from this bed for the next couple of days. I'll come back tomorrow to check on you."

"I can't stay here," Josh feebly protested.

"Of course you can." Noble quickly stepped in. "You'll stay here as long as it takes to get you well."

"Listen to me, young man," Doc said, "you've lost a lot of blood, and you're still not out of the woods. If you're not careful, infection can set in, and then we'll have our hands full. Right now I'd suggest complete rest and some good food."

"All right, if you're sure you don't mind, Noble."

Doc laughed. "Have you seen Noble's granddaughter? Now that's the kind of nurse men would kill for."

Josh tried to smile, but he grimaced in pain. "She is beautiful, and I have her to thank for getting me here."

"In that case, you're a lucky man in more ways

than one, my friend," Doc said as he closed his black bag. "Noble, I'm leaving this bottle of laudanum. I've already given him a strong dose, and he should begin to feel it soon."

Hearing Abraham greet Matt, Shadow hurried downstairs to meet him.

"Shadow, is he all right?" Matt asked, concern etched on his face.

"The doctor is with him now, Matt. I'll show you up to his room."

"Is it bad?" he asked as he followed her.

Shadow stopped at the top of the stairs. "Someone tried to kill him," she said, tears in her eyes.

"Damn! I was afraid of this," Matt exclaimed.

Shadow stared at him in shock. "You mean you're not surprised that this happened?"

"I warned—" Matt broke off in midsentence. "I'd like to see him now, Shadow."

"I'd like to hear what you were going to say."

"Shadow, I'm very concerned about my brother."

"All right, but I want to talk to you before you leave."

Shadow waited patiently for Matt to come back downstairs. She was anxious to know what he meant when he said he had warned Josh. What could he be involved in that someone would try to kill him.

She swallowed convulsively, remembering how Josh had looked when she found him. How could anyone do such a thing?

Voices interrupted her thoughts. She rushed to

212

the stairs to find her grandfather and the doctor.

"I think he'll make it, Shadow." Doc patted her hand. "Our main concern is for infection and fever. For the first forty-eight hours, he'll need someone with him constantly."

"Don't worry, Dr. Morgan, we'll take care of him," Shadow assured, "but do you think you should leave so soon?"

"He's going to sleep for a while," Doc answered. "I gave him enough laudanum to knock out a horse. Don't worry, I'll be back tomorrow."

"Is Matt still with him?"

"Yes, Josh wanted to talk to him privately," Noble said.

The fire which seems extinguished
often slumbers beneath the ashed.

—Pierre Corneille

Chapter Twelve

Shadow sat in a chair next to Josh's bed and studied his sleeping profile. He was so pale and lifeless that it frightened her. She kept checking his pulse and each time was relieved to find it strong.

Matthew hadn't supplied her with any reason for his statement about warning Josh that something like this was going to happen, so she still had no idea why anyone would want to kill Josh. Maybe it had something to do with his gambling, she pondered. Someone could have lost big to him and decided to take revenge. But kill a man? That just didn't make sense.

She jumped when he whispered her name. "Shadow, is that you?" he asked in a slurred voice.

"Yes, I'm here," she said, sitting on the side of

the bed. "Would you like some water."

"Yes . . ."

Shadow put her hand at the back of his neck while he sipped the cool water. "Stay with me, Shadow," he said, taking her hand.

"I'll be here," she promised.

"I'm surprised you helped me—" he licked his dry lips before continuing—"after the things I said."

"Josh, do you know who did this to you?"

When he didn't answer her, she realized he was asleep again. She gently pried his fingers loose from her hand. "I am going to have some answers sooner of later," she said in determination.

"Shadow, you shouldn't still be in here," Noble said as he entered the room.

"Please, Grandfather, let me stay. He may need me."

"If he needs anyone, Martha can help him."

"But I promised him I'd be here while he slept. Please don't make me go back on my word."

Noble's eyes softened, knowing how she felt about Josh Rawlings. "Child, it just isn't proper."

"No one has to know."

"All right, Shadow, but Martha is to take care of his personal needs, and as soon as he is conscious, you are to leave this room. Is that understood?"

Shadow kissed her grandfather on the cheek. "There is something I think you should know. I'm in love with Josh."

"I thought so, child. I could see it in your eyes

216

the night of the party."

"I think he loves me, too, Grandfather, but he's afraid to admit it. But I don't intend to let him leave this house until I know the reason for his reluctance."

Remembering his conversation with Josh, Noble wasn't sure Shadow would find out. "Don't get your hopes up, Shadow. Josh is a hard man to figure, and he may not be the marrying kind."

"I realize that, Grandfather, but you've always taught me if something was worth having, it was worth fighting for."

"I'm not sure that applies in this case, Shadow."

"You wouldn't be opposed to me marrying Josh, would you, Grandfather?"

"No, child. I like Josh Rawlings, but I don't want to see you hurt."

"I don't want to be hurt; but I'm vulnerable because I love him, so it has to be this way. If he can't accept my love, then I'll go on with my life from there."

"All right, Shadow. I'll trust you to use good judgment in this matter, as you always do." He kissed the top of her head, then left her alone with Josh.

Josh woke up some time during the night and was surprised to find Shadow sleeping in a chair next to his bed. He smiled, thinking what an enigma she was. He didn't deserve the attention she was giving him after the way he had treated her.

Suddenly Shadow's eyes opened, and she stared at Josh. "Are you all right?" she asked, turning up the lamp.

"How could I not be with an angel guarding over me?"

"You must be feverish," she said, feeling his forehead.

"No, I don't think so," he replied, grabbing her hand, "but whatever that doctor gave me makes me feel like I'm floating."

"It's supposed to ease the pain," Shadow said.

"Shadow, if you insist on watching over me, why don't you lie down next to me. You'd be more comfortable."

"Don't worry about me. I'm just fine."

"There really isn't any reason for you to give up your sleep for me. I'm doing pretty well. If you won't lie with me, why don't you go to your own bed."

"Doctor Morgan said you could become feverish and someone should stay with you for the first forty-eight hours."

"I'm amazed you volunteered."

"I'm just taking my turn. Martha will be relieving me soon."

"Martha? Isn't that the black woman who watches over you like a mother hen?"

"One in the same." Shadow chuckled.

"I don't think she likes me."

"Martha is very perceptive."

Josh laughed softly. "I suppose she is." He closed his eyes and slept again.

The next time Shadow woke, it was to Josh's cursing.

"Damn heartless, bitch," he swore, tossing and turning on the bed. "You killed him, Stella, sure as you pulled the trigger," Josh shouted out.

Shadow felt his head; he was burning up. "Josh, drink some of this," she encouraged, holding the glass of water to his lips. His teeth chattered against the edge of the glass.

"Cold . . . so damned cold." He shivered.

Shadow opened a chest at the foot of the bed and took out a pile of quilts.

"Lie still and let me put these on you," she said, piling the quilts on top of him.

"Lie with me," he mumbled thickly.

"Josh . . ."

"If I'm going to die, I want you in my arms."

"You're not going to die," she insisted, crawling in beside him. As she cuddled up to him his trembling seemed to subside. "I won't let you die, Josh Rawlings," she said as tears ran down her face. "I'm not going to let you off that easy."

"Shadow, git outta dat bed 'fore your grandfather sees you," Martha said, shaking Shadow awake.

Shadow bolted upright. "Is he up yet?"

"He is."

Shadow stood up and tried to straighten the

wrinkles out of her skirt. "Josh was feverish and had chills. I was only trying to keep him warm."

"He's still hot," Martha said, feeling his forehead. "Go git cleaned up, and I'll sit with him."

Shadow knew she must look a mess, and she certainly didn't want her grandfather to see her that way. "All right, but I'll be right back. Dr. Morgan said he'd be here this morning, and I want to talk to him."

Shadow took great care with her toilette, but she was sure she must look dreadful. She really hadn't fallen asleep until almost dawn. Lying in Josh's arms was too unsettling to sleep.

She ran a comb through her long hair and pulled it back with a ribbon. He had said if he was going to die he wanted her in his arms. Weren't those the words of a man in love, she asked herself as she stared into the mirror.

"The poor man was delirious, you fool. He would have said the same thing to any woman who'd been close by," she chastised herself.

When Shadow returned to Josh's room, Martha was struggling to keep him in the bed and covered. She rushed in to help.

"Josh, please lie still. You'll start bleeding again."

"Tell her to stay away from me and Matt," he shouted in anguish.

"Who, Josh? Who do you want to stay away from you?"

"That lying, cheating whore. We're leaving, Matt

. . . we're getting out of here," he shouted in his delirium.

"It's all right, Josh. You're safe." Shadow touched a cool, wet cloth to his head.

"Shadow . . . where am I?" he asked, suddenly lucid.

"You're at Lansing Creek. Remember, someone attacked you, and I'm taking care of you now."

"Why are you doing this?" he asked, staring at her, his gold eyes glittering with fever. "Why would you take care of me?"

"You claim to be a smart man, Josh Rawlings. You figure it out."

"Lie with me, Wildcat. . . ."

"Not this time." She squeezed his hand. "Dr. Morgan should be here soon."

"I don't need a doctor," he insisted in a slurred voice as he grabbed her. "I need you."

"Josh—" she glanced at Martha to see if she had heard him—"please just lie still so you don't start bleeding again."

"You better listen to the young lady," the doctor said from the door. "You're in bad enough shape without aggravating those wounds," Doc added, sitting on the side of the bed. "And I suggest you be careful how you treat Shadow Lansing, my friend, or I'm afraid Noble will put you out of your misery before I have a chance to heal you."

"He's delirious, Dr. Morgan," Shadow quickly made excuses for him. "He's been feverish since the middle of the night."

"I was afraid that might happen. It's the body's way of fighting infection, but we'll just have to be sure it doesn't last too long. The quilts are good. Keep them on and try to sweat the fever out of him."

"I don't need to be putting Noble and his family to this much trouble," Josh said, lucid once again. "If he'll just lend me a carriage, I'll go back to Yancey's," he said, trying to sit up.

"Go right ahead, young man," the doctor said, moving aside.

"Dr. Morgan . . ." Shadow pleaded.

"See if you can stand up, Mr. Rawlings." He put out a hand to stop Shadow from assisting Josh.

Josh leaned up on one elbow, then fell back unconscious.

"He's a stubborn man, Shadow. I thought we'd have peace a little quicker if he saw for himself that he isn't up to going anyplace."

"He's going to be all right, isn't he?" she asked, concerned.

"I don't like the turn he's taken, but he's a strong man. I think he'll make it."

"There must be something we can do to help," Shadow said.

"Just keep the quilts on him, and give him plenty of fluids. I'll leave more laudanum. That should help keep him calm."

Shadow glanced at Martha as the black woman shook her head and clucked her tongue while she moved around the room pretending to straighten

222

up. Shadow knew Martha had her own ways of healing people, but she had always had reservations about the strange potions she treated the other blacks with.

"I'll come back by tomorrow morning," Dr. Morgan said. "If he isn't better, I'll let some blood."

"Hasn't he already lost enough blood?" Shadow exclaimed.

"I just don't know what else to suggest, my dear."

"Huh," Martha snorted.

"Now, Martha, I know you have your own ways of dealing with sickness," Dr. Morgan said, "but if you start doctoring my patient, I won't be responsible for him."

"You ain't responsible for him no how," Martha said, tucking the quilts around Josh. "God decides whose medicine makes him well—if he's meant to live."

Shadow had completely forgotten that Allen Middleton was coming to take her for a ride, and she was surprised to find him pulling up in the drive as Dr. Morgan left.

"Allen, I'm so sorry. I should have sent a message to you. I'm afraid I won't be able to take that ride today."

"I saw Dr. Morgan leave. Is your grandfather ill?" he asked, taking her hand.

"No, Grandfather is fine, but Josh Rawlings was

223

attacked yesterday. Someone tried to kill him."

Allen's pale blue eyes widened in surprise, then turned cold. "He's here?"

"Yes. I found him on the road between our place and yours. I just barely managed to get him back here."

"Is he going to live?"

Shadow didn't notice the cold tone of his voice. "I don't know, Allen. He's been delirious since early this morning. We had to fight to keep him in bed."

"My God, surely you haven't been playing nurse-maid to him."

Shadow stared at Allen in disbelief. "The man is fighting for his life. Of course I've been there doing what I could for him."

"I won't have it, Shadow. We have to think about your reputation."

Shadow was getting angrier by the moment. "You let me worry about my reputation."

"But if we're to be married—" he protested.

"I never said anything about marrying you," she retorted in disbelief.

Allen, seeing that he wasn't getting anyplace with Shadow, decided on a new tack. "I have a solution." He patted her hand. "I'll take Rawlings back to my place. He'll get the best of care, and your reputation won't be ruined."

"You needn't worry about Shadow's reputation," Noble said as he stepped out onto the porch. "I'll be the one to see that her reputation isn't dam-

224

aged."

"Of course, Noble," he said sheepishly. "I was just concerned after hearing the gambler was here."

"Josh Rawlings is a friend, and he'll stay here until he fully recuperates."

"Do you really think he will recuperate. Shadow said it was bad."

"It's bad, but I think he'll make it," Noble said, putting an arm around Shadow. "And when he's well, I pity the fools who tried to kill him."

"Does he have any idea who did it?" Allen asked, fidgeting with a large diamond ring on his finger.

"He said there were three of them and they wore masks. Sounds like the same fellows who've been robbing him."

"Probably someone who doesn't approve of gambling," Allen commented. "Well, I better be on my way. Shadow, I'll check back with you tomorrow to see if there is anything I can do. Perhaps we can take that ride another time."

"Perhaps," Shadow said, still annoyed that he assumed so much just because she had agreed to take a carriage ride with him.

"It's a shame he isn't more like his father," Noble said as Allen left. "Colter was a good man."

"All Allen cares about are money and possessions," Shadow said in disgust. "The only reason he's interested in me is for Lansing Creek."

Noble laughed. "I didn't realize you were that perceptive. I don't know why I was worried about you."

"I don't know why, either," she said, kissing him on the cheek. "I'm going back to see if I can help Martha."

"Have you had breakfast yet?"

"No, but I'm not hungry, Grandfather. I'll eat something a little later."

By late afternoon, Shadow feared for Josh's life. His fever rose and with it his agitation. He cursed and continually threatened someone named Stella. Then he'd cry out for his father not to do it . . . please, not to do it. . . .

During one of his more lucid moments, he clasped Shadow's hand and stared at her, his gold eyes brilliant with fever. "Wildcat, if I don't make it . . . want you to know . . . I love you. . . ."

Tears ran down Shadow's face. "You don't think I'm going to let anything happen to you after you made that declaration, do you?"

Josh didn't answer as he lapsed into unconsciousness again.

"Doan look good," Martha said, feeling his forehead. "Fever gitting higher."

"Is there something you can do to help, Martha," Shadow asked in tears. "We can't let him die."

"I'll get my potions," she said, hurrying from the room.

Shadow clutched Josh's hand and prayed silently.

226

She couldn't let him die, she thought staunchly. Somehow she would pass her strength to him.

There was a tap at the door and Matt entered. "How is he, Shadow?"

"Not very good, Matt. His fever is so high."

Matt felt Josh's flushed face and quickly pulled away. "My God, can't Dr. Morgan do something?"

Shadow wiped a tear away with the back of her hand. "He doesn't know what to do, but Martha thinks she may have something to help Josh."

"Martha . . . your servant?"

"Yes. She's always treated our people when they've been ill, and quite successfully, I might add. Her methods are a little primitive, using herbs and roots, but I just don't know what else to do."

"If there is a chance she can help him, then by all means, tell her to do whatever she can."

Josh shouted out in a tortured voice. Then he began to thrash about. Matt knelt next to the bed, trying to calm him down. After Shadow bathed his face in cool water, he seemed to relax.

"Matt, who is Stella?" Shadow asked.

"Stella? Has he been talking about her?" he asked in surprise.

"Yes. He's been cursing her since early this morning."

"I don't doubt it. She was our stepmother, although saying it leaves a bitter taste in my mouth."

"Then you hate her, too?"

"Most definitely. Our mother died when Josh was thirteen and I was ten. Father decided he

227

needed help raising two boys, so he sprung this sweet, innocent girl on us. Sweet and innocent," he laughed bitterly. "It didn't take more than three months to find out otherwise. For more than a year, Pa drank himself into a stupor while Stella turned our home into her own personal bordello."

"Is that why Josh doesn't trust women?"

"There's a little more to it," Matt said. "One night Stella went to Josh's room. He was a big, strong youth even at fourteen. I had noticed Stella looking at Josh in a peculiar way; and she was always touching him, but I wasn't sure why. Anyway, Pa caught her before she did anything with Josh, but the nightmare still wasn't over. Stella left after Pa threatened to kill her. Josh and I thought our lives would get back to normal, but it wasn't to be. That night Josh walked in on Pa as he blew his brains out."

"Oh, no!" Shadow gasped, "That's terrible . . ."

"I suppose because Josh was older, and actually witnessed Father killing himself, it made an indelible impression on him. He made up his mind that he would take care of the two of us without anyone's help."

"At fourteen?" she asked in disbelief.

"At fourteen." He sighed. "Until I was seventeen he took care of both of us, financially and physically. It's always been that way, Shadow. Over the years I've watched him keep everyone at arm's length to insure that he didn't get hurt. From the day our father died, Josh swore no woman would ever get close enough to do that to him."

"I had no idea. . . ." Shadow said staring at Josh's flushed face.

"I don't think Josh ever planned on meeting someone like you, Shadow. He's been fighting his feelings ever since he met you. Then when he finally decided to see if you'd have him, this had to happen."

Shadow's eyes widened in disbelief. "He decided what?"

"He was coming here to see if you'd consider marrying him and leaving the South," Matt explained.

"Oh, he came her all right," Shadow said bitterly, "but it was to ask if I'd leave here with him as his mistress."

"I don't understand," Matt said, running his hand through his hair much like Josh often did. "He was going to ask you to marry him."

Shadow touched Josh's parched lips. "I think I understand," she said, remembering the scene with Allen Middleton that Josh walked in on. "This morning he admitted he loved me."

"That's wonderful," Matt exclaimed.

"Yes, it is wonderful. The only problem is, he was delirious."

Martha came into the room with a steaming bowl of an odorous concoction.

"My God, the smell of that stuff alone could raise the dead," Matt exclaimed, holding his nose.

"It does many things," Martha grinned, "but it

ain't raised de dead yet."

"Just so it breaks Josh's fever," Shadow said.

For a little while Josh was quiet. Shadow and Matt sat by his bedside and talked. Suddenly Josh sat straight up, startling them both. He looked straight at Shadow. "You're a heartless bitch."

"Lie back down, Josh," she said soothingly. "Everything is going to be all right."

Josh tossed the covers aside and tried to get out of bed. "No, Josh," Matt said firmly. "You're not going anywhere."

"I've got to get out of here," he said, fighting both of them. "It's too hot in here . . . too damned hot. . . ."

"Dat's a good sign," Martha said, smiling.

"How can you say that?" Shadow turned on her servant. "He's out of his head and still burning up with fever."

"You'll see," Martha assured. "You'll see."

The rest of the afternoon Shadow and Matt took turns trying to keep Josh in the bed. Shadow's back and arms ached from the struggle. Suddenly she realized he was no longer fighting them.

"Oh, my God," she cried, fearing the worst.

"It's all right, Shadow. The fever has broken," Matt assured her.

Tears ran down her face. "Thank God. I thought . . . I mean . . ."

Matt put his arm around her shoulder. "I know what you thought, Shadow, but he's going to make it now."

Martha touched Josh's head. "He gonna wake up hungry as a bear. I better have Tilly fix him somdin special."

"He's really going to be all right," Shadow whispered aloud.

If thou must love me, let it be for naught
Except for love's sake only.

—Elizabeth Barrett Browning

Chapter Thirteen

Josh was a worse patient on the mend than he had been sick. He didn't want to be in bed, yet he was too weak to be up and about for long.

"I can't just lie here. I want to find out who my assailants were," he growled.

"Put it right out of your mind, Josh Rawlings. You're not going anywhere yet," Shadow insisted, tucking the blankets in around him.

"For God's sake, Shadow, it must be eighty degrees in here. Would you please stop covering me up."

Shadow tossed the blanket aside. "I liked you better when you were unconscious," she snapped.

"I'm sorry," he apologized, a ghost of a smile on his face. "I shouldn't take my frustrations out on you."

"No, you certainly shouldn't," she agreed.

Josh leaned his head back and studied her. She looked good enough to eat dressed in pale blue, the color of her eyes. Noble would certainly have no trouble finding a husband for her, he thought bitterly. That thought reminded him. . . . "Did you take your ride with Middleton while I was on my deathbed?"

Shadow tried to keep from smiling. "What I do is my own business, *Mr. Rawlings*," she drawled.

"I can't imagine why you'd even let that slime in your house," he said in a clipped voice.

Shadow picked up her needlepoint and pretended to work on it. "Allen is a fine man," she said, enjoying baiting him. "He spends most of his time putting together a unit of men to protect our fair city."

"Ha," Josh snorted. "If he spent half as much time working to keep the South from going to war, he'd be a hell of a lot better off, and so would everyone else."

Shadow had to agree, but she wouldn't tell Josh that. "Allen is doing what he believes to be right and honorable."

Josh stared at her in disbelief. "My God, I can't believe you can sit there with a straight face and say that!"

It is hard, she thought silently. "You talked a lot while you were delirious," she casually changed the subject as she stitched.

"Did I?" When Shadow didn't say anything he laughed. "Well, are you going to tell me what I said?"

"You said a lot of things, but you talked mostly about someone named Stella."

His face suddenly looked very tired and strained. "What did I say about her?"

"You kept telling her to stay away from you and Matt, but mostly you just cursed her."

Josh was silent for a long moment. "Stella was my father's second wife."

"Your stepmother."

"I prefer not to think of her that way."

Shadow knew the story from Matt, but she was hopeful that Josh could talk to her about it.

"Why do you hate her so much?"

"It's a long story."

"We have nothing but time," she persisted.

Josh closed his eyes, and for a moment Shadow thought he had drifted off to sleep. Then he began to speak softly. "Father claimed he needed help raising his two sons. God knows why, we were both able to take care of ourselves, and had been doing it for nearly a year. I suppose what he really wanted was a woman for his bed. We would have all been better off if he'd just visited some whorehouse."

Shadow moved to sit on the bed, taking his hand. "I'm so sorry, Josh," she sympathized, seeing the pain in his eyes.

"Oh, I'm not through yet," he said in disgust. "Stella was supposed to teach Matt and me our lessons, but she was more interested in teaching us the facts of life. It was about this time that our father discovered what she was really like. He threatened to kill her if she didn't leave. Unfortunately just kicking her out didn't end the torture for my father. He put a gun to his head and killed himself."

Shadow trembled at the hatred in his voice. "And you and Matt have been on your own ever since?"

"That's right, and we've made it just fine," he said, pride in his voice.

"Grandfather says when something like that happens it sometimes makes you a stronger person."

"It can also make you a very bitter person. I'm a good example of that. My brother is the only person I've ever been close to."

Shadow stared into his gold eyes. "Surely that isn't the way you want it?"

"It's safer that way."

"I think you're wrong, Josh. You can't go through life with strangers. Sometimes you have to let down your guard and trust someone."

Josh laughed. "Noble said you were stubborn and hardheaded, but he didn't say anything about you being so blunt."

"I'm sorry, but I feel this is too important not to be blunt. You said some things in your delirium . . . things about me . . ." Shadow took a deep breath. "Never mind," she said, standing up. "I'm going to get some tea."

"Shadow, wait."

"I'll be back in a few minutes," she said, hurrying from the room.

Shadow leaned against the door, fighting back the tears. Why should she have expected him to have remembered that he said he loved her?

Josh leaned his head back against the headboard and tried to remember what he'd said. Was it possible he had admitted his feelings for her? Dammit, if he were honest with himself—

Before he had a chance to think any more about it, the door opened and Shadow came back in, a strange look on her face.

"You have a visitor," she said curtly.

Rose Jardine, dressed in emerald-green silk, followed Shadow into the room, a bouquet of flowers in her hand.

"Darling," she exclaimed, kissing him. "I just had to come to see how you are doing."

"I'm doing fine, considering," he answered, glancing at Shadow.

"Matt has been keeping me up to date on your progress." She smiled.

Josh had to smile, knowing how Matt felt about Rose. "That was good of Matt."

"Miss Lansing, would you be a dear and put these in water for Josh," Rose said, hoping to get rid of Shadow.

Shadow took the flowers and dropped them in the pitcher of drinking water beside the bed. "How's that?"

Rose's eyes widened in surprise. "That's fine, I suppose, unless Josh wants a drink of water."

"If I do, I'll just remove the flowers first," he said, a twinkle in his gold eyes. "That is what you had intended, wasn't it, Shadow?"

"Yes, but I suggest you watch out for thorns," she said, giving him a plucky smile. "Roses have

237

thorns, you know."

His eyes gleamed with laughter, but Rose seemed oblivious to the banter between the two of them.

"When will you be going back to Yancey's?" Rose asked, pulling her gloves off.

"I don't know. I'm getting such excellent care here," he said, smiling at Shadow.

"You know, darling, I would be glad to take care of you," Rose volunteered.

"You're welcome to him," Shadow mumbled as she rearranged the books on a shelf.

"What did you say, Shadow?" Josh asked, trying to keep a straight face. "Did you say you didn't think I was ready to move back to Yancey's?"

Shadow feigned a sweet smile. "It's up to you, *darling*," she drawled.

What a little hellion, he thought. *My God, I've never met anyone like her.*

"There is a drive going on to raise money to outfit an elite group of soldiers from Natchez," Rose babbled on. "That's all everyone is talking about. Pamela Damaris is having a lawn party and auction next Sunday to raise money. Everyone has been wonderful about donating items, and some very expensive ones I might add."

"It sounds like the people of Natchez are itching for a war," Josh said.

"Oh, no, it isn't anything like that. We just want to be prepared if the worst comes. I do hope you'll be up to going with me to the party. Everyone has been asking about you."

"Really?" Josh smiled politely, knowing no one in Rose's group would be concerned about him.

238

"How very kind of them, but I'm afraid I won't be up to partying for sometime to come."

"Oh, darling, are you sure?" She pouted.

"I'm positive," he answered, annoyed.

My God, why does the woman think he is lying in bed? Shadow wondered furiously. *Doesn't she realize or care that he nearly died?*

"Allen Middleton has told everyone about winning the race Saturday," she chattered away. "He now claims he has the fastest race horse in the country."

"Allen Middleton is going to be in for a rude awakening one day soon," Josh snarled.

"Now, darling, don't get yourself worked up." Rose patted his hand.

Josh leaned his head back against the pillows and closed his eyes. *If she doesn't leave soon . . .*

"Well, darling, I don't want to tire you out, so I better go now," Rose said, finally taking the hint. "I'll try to get back another day this week"—she glanced at Shadow—"unless you're home by then."

"Thanks for coming by, Rose. I appreciate the concern, and the flowers."

"Yes, of course." She leaned over and kissed him again. "I look forward to you coming back to Yancey's." She glanced at Shadow, who stood staring out the window. "Good day, Miss Lansing. Thank you for taking such good care of Josh."

Sending her a dubious look, Shadow nodded. "Someone had to do it."

When they were alone, Shadow again stared out the window at nothing in particular.

"That was nice of her to bring me flowers," he

said, purposely baiting Shadow.

"She's a saint," Shadow commented dryly.

"Do I detect a hint of jealousy, Wildcat?" He grinned.

"Of course you do, you fool!" she snapped as she headed for the door.

"Shadow, don't walk out on me again, or I swear I'll get out of this bed and come after you."

Shadow's hand froze on the doorknob. "You'd only be hurting yourself."

"Please, come sit down and talk with me."

"You need to rest, Josh. You've had a busy day, and I don't want you having a relapse."

"Shadow, come sit down," he gently ordered.

When she did, he took her hand. "Feeling jealousy is foreign to me, but that day I came here and saw you with Allen Middleton, I wanted to kill the bastard."

Shadow stared at him, amazed that he would admit such strong feelings.

"Was that what you were feeling with Rose here?" he asked.

"No, nothing quite so intense." She smiled. "I just wanted to scratch her eyes out."

"You are such a delight." He laughed, captivated by her wit and charm. She looked so adorable sitting on the side of his bed, loose tendrils of her strawberry-blond hair curling around her face. Even in his weakened state, he felt a strong impulse to pull her down beside him and make love to her.

Shadow stared into his eyes. Suddenly she could feel the heat rise from his body—and this time it

240

wasn't fever. She quickly stood up. "I should see if Tilly has your tray ready."

"You don't have to run. I'm no threat to you at the moment." He chuckled.

Seeing the sultry look in his gold eyes, Shadow wasn't so sure. "I'm not so sure of that," she said over her shoulder as she left the room.

Josh closed his eyes, a smile on his face. She was an innocent temptress, he thought, and he was afraid she had ruined him for every other woman. He used to think Rose was beautiful, but today he couldn't help noticing how she paled in Shadow's company. But there was one fact he couldn't overlook. He could have Rose with no strings attached, no commitment. When he got tired of her, he'd move on to someone else.

Josh slammed his fist on the bed. Dammit, who was he kidding? He didn't want Rose. He wanted Shadow; Shadow who meant commitment, family, permanence. But could it ever work, he wondered. He was a cynic; she was an innocent, still believing everything and everyone was beautiful. Maybe she could teach him to love and trust. God knows, he'd like to believe in something.

On that thought he drifted off to sleep dreaming about Shadow with children running around her — his children.

Shadow had made herself scarce since their discussion about him being a threat. Josh couldn't stand being cooped up in the room, only seeing her when she chose to come to him. He tried to talk the doctor into letting him go downstairs, but Morgan would only agree to letting him sit on the balcony outside his bedroom.

Martha brought Josh his breakfast as he sat enjoying the fresh air. "I can see you feel better," she smiled. "Color coming back in de cheeks."

"I certainly am, and I understand it's thanks to your medicine."

"It is old family potion my great, great grandmother concocted," she said proudly.

"Well, I'm grateful. By the way, Martha, do you know where Shadow has been keeping herself?"

Martha smiled. "If you weren't such a terrible patient, she wouldn't run away."

Josh laughed. "You're avoiding my question, Martha. Do you know where she is?"

"She'll be around," she said, pouring his coffee.

After he had finished breakfast, Josh stood at the railing and looked out over the green fields toward Middleton Place. Dammit, if she was with Allen Middleton . . .

"Good morning, Josh," Noble greeted. "I'm glad to see you're feeling better."

"A lot better," Josh agreed. "I was just enjoying the magnificent view. Lansing Creek is a beautiful place, Noble. The view of the river from here is incredible."

"It's a working plantation. That's what makes it beautiful. When you're up to it, I'll give you a tour of the place."

"I'd like that," Josh agreed.

"Who knows," Noble smiled, "maybe you'll see the benefits that would come if you married my granddaughter."

"Don't start that again, Noble."

"Well, it's a fact. This would all be yours, Josh. You really should think about it."

"Are you still interested in breeding Rapscallion to Gambler's Lady?" Josh asked, changing the subject.

"I certainly am, but you'll have to talk to Shadow about it. Rapscallion is her horse."

"I'd be glad to discuss it with her, but I think she's avoiding me."

"Maybe she's testing the theory that absence makes the heart grow fonder." Noble laughed.

Josh smiled. *If she is, it's working.* "She tells me I did a lot of talking when I was delirious," Josh said, hoping Noble knew what he'd said.

"That's a fact. I heard her talking to Matt about it."

"Do you know what I said?"

"No. I didn't figure it was any of my business. Did you ask Shadow?"

"She would only tell me part of what I said, and I must admit, it has my curiosity peaked."

"Why don't you ask your brother. He was here most of the time."

"I think I will. Martha tells me he's coming by this morning."

"That's right. He'll be surprised to see you up and about."

"You know, Noble, there isn't any way I can ever repay you and Shadow for your kindness and hospitality. Not many people would have gone to so much trouble."

"I haven't done much for you, son. Shadow and Martha are the ones who took care of you."

"I guess the best way I can repay all of you is to get out of your hair as soon as possible."

"Now don't be in a hurry," Noble protested, still hoping Shadow and Josh would work things out. "There isn't any sense leaving here until you can ride a horse."

"I could borrow a carriage."

"Now listen, Josh, to be honest with you, I've been looking forward to your company while you recuperate. I have all kinds of things I'd like to show you. Besides, why the hell are you in such a damn hurry to get back to Yancey's. Matt is handling things just fine. I can understand you going crazy being cooped up in this room, but in a day or so you can be up and about. In the meantime, you can enjoy Tilly's fine cooking and Shadow's fine companionship. Nothing will make you feel better faster, I promise."

The prospect of spending time with Shadow was very appealing, even though he knew it was probably a mistake. It was only going to make it harder to say good-bye.

"I don't know if it would be wise, Noble."

"Always doing what's wise can be mighty dull," Noble persisted.

Josh laughed. "I suppose you're right. Thank you, Noble. I'll accept your offer and look forward to enjoying more of your hospitality—particularly if I don't have to stay cooped up in this room all day."

* * *

Josh wasn't the only one with mixed emotions about his staying there for a few more days. Shadow told herself just to enjoy his company and forget that he was planning to leave Natchez. Hadn't he been the one to say live for the moment. Well, that was what she was going to do. She'd be so damned sweet and charming he wouldn't know what hit him. Who could tell, she mused, maybe he'd decide he couldn't live without her.

For of all sad words of tongue or pen,
The saddest are these: It might have
   been.

— John Greenleaf Whittier

Chapter Fourteen

"Good morning, Josh," Shadow greeted brightly as she bustled into the room with an armful of clothes. "I understand Dr. Morgan has given you permission to come downstairs today, so I had Matt send you some clothes."

"Thank you," he said absently, his mind fully occupied by the tempting picture she presented in a lemon yellow dress. Her hair was beguilingly tousled. The soft tendrils that he longed to touch framed her lovely face.

"I've missed you," he smiled.

"Have you now?" she grinned. "I've been busy helping Martha outfit our people in new clothes."

"I'm glad to hear that. I was afraid you were off with Allen Middleton."

"Oh, he's been here several times, always asking

about you, I might add."

"I'm sure he did," Josh said bitterly. "He was probably hoping to have another chance to finish the job."

Shadow stared at Josh, a puzzled look on her face. "Finish the job? What do you mean?"

He flashed her a quick boyish grin. "I just meant he'd probably like to see me out of the way."

"Oh, he knows he doesn't have to feel threatened by your presence," she drawled sweetly.

"Give me the damn clothes," he growled.

"Why, Josh, did I say something to make you angry?" She pretended innocence.

"Just mentioning Allen Middleton is enough to make my blood boil, and you damn well know it."

"I can't imagine why. You've made it very clear that there is nothing between us."

Josh slowly got up from the chair. "Come here, Wildcat."

"Now, Josh, I suggest you sit back down before you hurt yourself," she warned as he moved closer.

Taking her in his arms, Josh smiled down at her. She was so soft and appealing. Her eyes reminded him of the color of a robin's egg, and her lips were soft and pink and inviting. "I never said there wasn't anything between us. I don't think either of us can deny the feelings that are there. When you're in the same room with me, I can hardly think of anything but possessing you."

She stared at him, not saying a word, but her eyes spoke volumes. Suddenly she shook her head as if coming to her senses. "Why don't you dress and join me for breakfast? Tilly said she's fixed a special one since it's your first morning up."

Josh laughed. "All right, but I may need you to help me."

"Nice try, Josh Rawlings." Shadow laughed. "Martha already told me that you've dressed yourself the past two mornings."

"That woman talks too much," he grinned sheepishly.

"That woman saved your life," Shadow reprimanded.

"I know, and I appreciate it. Will you at least wait outside the room and help me downstairs?"

"I'll be glad to," she smiled up at him, "if you would kindly release me."

Josh moaned, but reluctantly let her go. "I'll only be a minute."

Josh leaned more heavily on Shadow than was really necessary as they descended the stairs. She smelled so sweet and natural to him that it made his senses reel.

"I hope Dr. Morgan knew what he was doing when he said you could already be up and about."

"He knew it was that or put locks on the door to keep me in," he chuckled. "If I had to stay in that room alone one more day, I'd probably go crazy."

"Are you complaining about the hospitality

you've received at Lansing Creek, sir?" Shadow feigned indignation.

"No, no, I could never find fault with that. I'm just not used to being confined. It would have been easier if you hadn't been ignoring me of late."

"I have been doing no such thing," she protested as they entered the dining room. "Sit down and I'll serve your plate," she instructed. "Let's see," she said, lifting tops off the plates on the sideboard. "There are eggs, ham, bacon, fried apples and biscuits. What appeals to you?"

"Some of everything," he laughed. "Pile it on. And I'd love a cup of Tilly's excellent coffee, please."

"It's flavored with chicory," Shadow commented. "Tilly is originally from New Orleans and apparently learned to make it there."

"All I know is it's delicious."

"Here you are," she said, placing the heaping platter in front of him, then filling her own plate. "Grandfather was telling me last night that you may still be interested in breeding Gambler's Lady to Rapscallion," she said as she sat down beside him.

"I'm very interested," he replied, taking a bite of eggs. "She should be coming into season soon, according to Leigh Thompson, the breeder I bought her from. Why don't we walk down to the stables after breakfast."

"Absolutely not, Josh Rawlings," Shadow exclaimed. "Dr. Morgan said you could come downstairs. He said nothing about you leaving the house."

"Now, Shadow, believe me, I appreciate everything you've done for me; but I'm on the mend now, so you can stop worrying and fussing over me."

Shadow pointed a finger at him, a warning in her eyes. "Mr. Rawlings, if you step one foot off the porch today, you will answer to me."

A wicked, masculine smile curved his lips. "I might just do it to see what the consequences would be."

"Do you like the idea of starving?" she asked, one eyebrow raised.

"Now that's not playing fair. I'm a sick man, and I need sustenance."

"Exactly. So you will enjoy sitting on the porch and watching the flowers grow."

"Sounds exciting." He grimaced.

"Who knows, maybe you'll be lucky and have Mrs. Jardine visit again," Shadow said, spreading jam on a biscuit. "Oh," she exclaimed as the jam dripped down on the palm of her hand. "I seem to be very clumsy this morning."

"Here, let me get that for you," Josh said, lifting her hand to his mouth.

Shadow sat immobilized as his tongue moved sensuously over the palm of her hand.

"Umm, it tastes much sweeter that way," he said seductively.

Shadow pulled her hand back, blushing to the

roots of her hair. "As I said, perhaps Mrs. Jardine will visit today. She did say she was coming back."

"I can't help it if she misses me. Women just find me irresistible," he grinned.

"So I've noticed," Shadow said in disgust. "My friend Camille said you possessed animal magnetism."

Josh threw back his head and laughed. "I *think* I'm flattered, but tell me more." His grin broadened.

"You're arrogant enough, Josh Rawlings," she admonished. "I'm not saying another word."

"Now that's not fair, Wildcat. At least tell me what your opinion is," he persisted.

"I'm afraid I just don't see the attraction," she said as haughtily as she knew how.

"Is that right, Wildcat?" he asked, his face only inches from hers. "I remember a time—"

"Ah, there you two are," Noble interrupted. "I thought you'd be up early since Dr. Morgan gave you a little more freedom."

"Yes, he has eased up on the restrictions, and now I have your granddaughter to contend with," Josh laughed. "She'd have me tied to the bed if she had her way."

Shadow choked on a bite of food, and the color rose in her cheeks.

"Shadow can be a worrier," Noble agreed as he piled food on his plate.

Josh smiled at Shadow. He had to admit, it was rather nice having someone worry about him. He couldn't recall anyone doing that since his mother died.

"I'd like to show you around the place, Josh, but I have a meeting with my banker this morning."

"Please don't worry about me, Noble. Shadow has promised to keep me company today," he said, sure that Shadow wouldn't argue the point in front of her grandfather.

"Shadow glared at him. "Yes, I plan to give him a tour of the porch, because that's as far as he's going today."

"You see what I mean, Noble. It's like being in prison." He gave Shadow a devastating smile.

"I could leave you in Martha's company," Shadow warned, "but she may feel it's necessary to fix you up with some more of her special potions."

"The porch tour sounds fine," Josh quickly agreed as Noble laughed.

Shadow finally relented to a walk in the rose garden. She was careful not to overtire Josh, walking very slowly and insisting that they sit each time they came to one of the many marble or wrought iron benches.

As they sat down on the fourth bench, Josh took Shadow's hand. "Not that I don't enjoy sitting with you, Wildcat, but do you realize we've sat on four benches in a space of thirty feet."

Shadow had to laugh. "I'm sorry, but I don't want you to have a relapse."

"If I promise not to, will you relax your vigil just a little?"

"Maybe just a little," she agreed. "Isn't this garden lovely?"

"Yes it is. Was it your mother's?"

"Originally it was my grandmother's, but my mother did enjoy it."

"I remember my mother loved roses," Josh said, a faraway look in his eyes. "She had this one bush she kept in an old barrel, and every day she'd water and tend it. It would get beautiful red roses on it."

"I had wondered if you remembered your mother," Shadow said.

"Oh, yes, I remember her. She was a real sweet woman. Unfortunately she married a man who didn't have enough money to have a wife, let alone raise a family. Instead of using a little bit of sense, he kept her pregnant almost the entire time they were married. After she had me, she lost a baby in the sixth month, then a few months later she was pregnant with Matt. After he was born, she lost three more babies, before eventually dying with the fourth one. You'd think people would learn, wouldn't you?" he said bitterly.

"Did a doctor ever tell her why he thought she was having so much trouble carrying a child."

Josh laughed bitterly. "We couldn't afford a doctor, but I think I know why. She was undernourished. She'd feed us and go without when times were hard, and they were usually hard. She would get so thin it would look like the wind could blow her over, yet still Pa wouldn't keep his hands off her. There were many times I wanted to kill him just to keep her safe, and I nearly did when she died trying to give birth to another of his offspring. If Matt hadn't pulled me off, I probably would have. I hated him for a long time after she died, but then eventually I saw that he was hurting, too."

"I'm so sorry, Josh."

"It's all past." He shrugged. "It doesn't matter now."

"I think it does, or it wouldn't have affected your life so much."

"Why? Because I don't ever want to be poor again?"

"That, and you're afraid to trust people."

"I suppose you're right," he agreed before falling silent.

"Do you think your mother ever told your father how she felt?" Shadow asked.

"I doubt it. Who knows, maybe she didn't discourage him. She had a lot of love in her for Matt and me, and I suppose she loved him, too. All I know is when she died I wanted to die with her."

"I remember feeling the same way when my mother and father died. If it hadn't been for my grandfather, I don't know what I would have done."

"You were lucky. I never knew my grandparents. My father's parents died when he was a young boy, and my mother came over from Ireland. I could still have family there, but I don't suppose I'll ever know."

"I understand now why you and Matt are so close. I always wished I had a brother or sister. I guess that's why I've always been so close to Toby. He has been like a brother to me."

"Until he fell in love with you?" Josh questioned.

"How did you know that?"

"All I had to do was see him around you. Then when your grandfather told me you were trying to play matchmaker with him and Camille, I figured you were trying to salve his feelings."

Shadow was startled by his perception. "I could never hurt Toby, yet I couldn't return his love. Not the same kind of love, anyway. As I said, I've always felt like he was a brother."

"You are very special, Shadow Lansing," Josh said, his hand caressing the back of her neck.

"Why do you say that?" She laughed, a little embarrassed.

"Because you really care about people."

"Of course I do. That isn't unusual."

"I think it is." Josh broke off a deep pink rose from a bush behind her and handed it to her. "For my guardian angel."

"Thank you, kind sir," she said, taking a deep whiff of the fragrant rose. "How did you know pink was my favorite?"

"I didn't, but it matches the color of your beautiful lips."

"Oh," Shadow said, giving the rose her full attention.

"I have been dreaming about tasting your sweet

mouth again, Wildcat," Josh said, his face only inches from hers.

She had been dreaming about his kisses, too, but she couldn't tell him. "Perhaps we should have that lemonade now," she said, quickly standing. "I'll have Abraham serve it on the front porch."

"Coward." He laughed.

As Abraham was serving them lemonade, a carriage came up the drive.

"It looks like more of your admirers," Shadow commented as Mandy Cameron and the girl called Patience stepped down from the carriage. Remembering the girl from Yancey's who had been in bed with Josh, she felt as if her blood was boiling. "I'd appreciate it if you wouldn't use Lansing Creek as a place to—" she stumbled over her words—"oh, you know what I mean, Josh Rawlings."

"I love it when you're jealous, my love," he teased.

"Do you, *my sweet*," she answered in turn. "Well, just remember, two can play at this game."

Shadow watched in disgust as both women kissed and fawned over Josh. She was sure Patience was going to fall out of the low-cut red dress she wore. Really, what did he see in a woman like that, she wondered.

"Mandy told me she was coming to visit you, so I just invited myself along." Patience bubbled with enthusiasm. "I've been so worried about you, honey."

"We all have been," Mandy said softly. "I couldn't believe something like this could happen. If you had been killed . . ."

Shadow noticed Josh staring strangely at Mandy and wondered why. Another of his conquests probably, she thought bitterly.

"I'll have Abraham bring some more lemonade," Shadow said, anxious to escape the scene.

"Oh, that would be wonderful," Patience exclaimed. "The trip out here was so dusty, I'm just fairly parched."

As Shadow went inside, she heard Mandy Cameron ask Josh if he needed anything. She hurried on to the kitchen not wanting to hear his reply. When she returned a few minutes later, Patience was standing behind Josh massaging his shoulders and neck.

"Abraham will be right out with your drinks. If you will excuse me, I'm going to check on my horse. I trust I'm leaving you in good hands," she said snidely. "Ladies, he isn't to leave the porch," Shadow instructed.

"Oh, we'll take good care of him," Patience drawled.

"Shadow, wait —"

"Don't overdo it, Josh," she said over her shoulder. "I know you're anxious to get back to Yancey's."

* * *

When Shadow came back to the house later, Allen Middleton walked with her, leading his horse. Josh was still sitting on the porch, but he was alone.

"Shadow said you were improving, Rawlings," Middleton said. "Glad to hear it."

Josh glared at Shadow, fighting the urge to wring both their necks. "I've had excellent care," he replied.

"How long will you be here?"

"I don't know. A few more days I guess," he said, perversely enjoying the fact that Middleton was worried about him being there.

"Would you care for some lemonade, Allen?" Shadow asked. "It's been a very popular drink today."

"No thanks. I have to be on my way. I'm glad I ran into you, Shadow. Don't forget we still have that ride to take."

"I won't." She smiled sweetly.

"Glad you're doing so well, Rawlings," Allen said, mounting his black stallion.

"Where did you find him?" Josh asked angrily as Middleton rode down the drive.

"He was coming to visit and saw me at the stables," she answered. "Did you enjoy your harem?" she asked sarcastically as she reached for the door.

Josh stepped in front of her before she could open it. "Why did you leave like that? They only stayed a few minutes."

"You didn't need me around with all your admirers here," she said tartly.

259

"They are friends, Shadow. Just the way you and Toby are friends."

"I don't sleep with Toby," she hissed.

Gold eyes blazed into hers. "What do you mean by that?"

"You forget, I walked in on you and Patience that night."

"No, I haven't forgotten. As a matter of fact, there is nothing about that night I've forgotten."

Josh was staring down at her, a tender smile curling his lip. He pulled her gently against him. "I think about that night every waking moment."

"Let me go!" she demanded. "Didn't you get enough affection from your two women friends?"

"Don't fight me, Wildcat. You'll open my wounds."

"That isn't fair," she protested.

"I know, but it gives me a chance to hold you."

"Well, you've held me. Now let me go."

"Not until I kiss you."

Shadow pulled away, leaving Josh gasping in pain. "What the hell is the matter with you?" he gasped.

"I'm not one of your whores," she spat.

"All I wanted to do was kiss you. But maybe you're saving your precious kisses for someone else," he growled.

"I may be. It's really none of your business."

"I'm making it my business, dammit. What's going on between you and Middleton?"

Shadow smiled perversely. "Does it bother your

delicate male ego that I would be interested in someone else? For your information, Allen wants to marry me."

"Just shut up, Shadow."

"Oh, I've hit a nerve, haven't I? You can't stand to think of me with someone else, yet you don't want me."

"Dammit, that's not true."

All Shadow's resolve to live for the moment flew out the window. "Of course it's true." She drew a long unsteady breath. "You'd rather have Rose Jardine or one of your saloon girls. You don't have to make a commitment to them. They give you what you want without it," she cried, rushing past him into the house.

Dammit, she was going to drive him absolutely crazy. "Come back here, Shadow!" he shouted as he followed her.

"Go to hell, Josh Rawlings," she shouted back.

Josh started up the stairs after her, then he doubled over, moaning in pain.

"Oh, God! Josh, are you all right?" She rushed back down the steps. "Here, let me help you sit down," she said, leading him into the library.

"I'm relieved to know you're still concerned," he said, taking hold of her wrist so she couldn't escape.

"You're not hurt!" she said indignantly.

He smiled and touched a finger under her chin. "No, I'm not, but I will be if I have to keep fighting with you. Let's call a truce, Wildcat. I had

261

hoped to enjoy a few days with you before Noble's patience ran out."

She wanted to resist the look in his eyes and the effect of his touch, but she couldn't. "I don't want to fight, either," she admitted softly.

He touched her cheek, caressing her jawline with his thumb. "God, how I want you, Wildcat." He nibbled gently at her lower lip, first teasing one corner, then the other with light tantalizing kisses.

The effect on Shadow was nothing short of devastating. She had never had a man look at her with such a mixture of passion and tenderness. A sensual ache filled her body. She responded to his kiss, her arms going up around his neck.

Josh deepened the kiss, groaning her name as his ache for her became a burning desire.

"Wildcat," he whispered, tracing her lips with his tongue, "you're so beautiful . . . so desirable . . . I can't bear being so close yet unable to have you. . . ."

Suddenly Josh was aware of the sound of a horse approaching. "Damn," he swore, releasing Shadow to glance out the window. "Your grandfather has the damndest timing."

Shadow smiled shyly. "Maybe he has a sixth sense about you and me."

"I don't doubt that," he said, heading for the French doors to the garden. "I need to walk out here for a moment before I face him."

"Whatever for?" she asked innocently.

"I'll explain it to you another time." He grinned.

262

"Just believe me when I say your grandfather would kill me if he saw me at this moment."

Shadow's gaze went to the bulge in his pants, then quickly back to his face. "Go—" She shooed him with her hand as she realized exactly what he meant.

Pain of love be sweeter far
Than all other pleasures are.

— John Dryden

Chapter Fifteen

A full harvest moon cast shadows on Josh's brooding face as he stood on the gallery. He lit up a cheroot and stared out over the lawn that lead toward the river. It was late and the house was dark, but he couldn't sleep. His thoughts were jumbled and confused. He was well enough to leave to find the men who had attacked him, yet he couldn't bring himself to part from Shadow. In the past few days he had finally admitted there was no use denying his love for her. In a matter of a few days she had brought happiness and content-ment into his life.

He drew deeply on the cheroot, then slowly ex-haled the smoke. He still wasn't sure how she'd feel about going to San Francisco with him. He supposed he should talk to her about it before proposing. He smiled to himself. Hell, it didn't make any difference at this point where they lived. If she wanted to stay there he'd fight Yankees, Indians and anything else that came along. Still, he hoped it wouldn't come to that. If he was going to fight, he would at least like it to be a cause he believed in. He didn't think the North had any right demanding that the South change its way of life, but then again he didn't think the South should talk about secession. And it was bound to come to that according to Gregory's note that Matt had brought him. He had been a fool to think spying would change anything. The situation had been out of hand for too long. Now Mr. Lincoln's election as president would be excuse enough for war.

Josh threw his cheroot over the railing, thinking if all the politicians had to fight in a war they may have second thoughts about declaring one.

As he turned to go back into his room, he glanced down the gallery toward Shadow's bedroom doors. God, he'd like to go to her. It was killing him having her so close, yet not being able to make love to her. Slowly he walked back into his room and laid across the bed.

"One of these days," he said before drifting off to sleep.

Shadow lay in her bed staring at the moon out her French doors. The last few days had been the happiest of her life. Josh hadn't mentioned finding the men who had attacked him. Instead he spent every waking moment making her feel alive and wonderful. She had made up her mind she wouldn't think about his leaving, but at night it was difficult not to. She couldn't imagine being without him or ever marrying anyone else. She melted when his eyes caressed her across the dining table. Surely she would never feel that way with anyone else—or want to. If she didn't think it would break her grandfather's heart, she'd do with Josh as his mistress. At least that way she would be with him.

She suddenly sat up with the intention of going to him to tell him that, but then she laid back down. No, she couldn't do that, as much as she wanted to.

"If only," she whispered before drifting off to sleep.

The next day was a warm and beautiful fall day. Over breakfast they planned a ride and a picnic. It was to be Josh's first time on a horse since the day he had been attacked, and Shadow was already setting the limitations of no more than a thirty minute ride.

They walked hand in hand down the path with Josh carrying an overloaded picnic basket which Tilly had prepared for them. As they neared the stables, Shadow noticed Toby leading Rapscallion to a fenced area on the other side of the building.

"Is everything all right, Toby?" she hollered.

Toby put Rapscallion in the corral, then headed toward them. "I think Mr. Rawlings' horse has come into season. Rapscallion was going crazy."

"Wonderful," Josh exclaimed. "That's what we were hoping for."

Toby glared at Josh, then turned and started to walk away.

"What's wrong with him?" Shadow asked.

"Why don't you give me a few minutes before you join us? I think Toby and I need to talk." Shadow nodded and headed in the opposite direction.

"Toby, can I talk with you a moment?" Josh said, drawing alongside the young man. "I sense there is a problem here. Do you mind telling me what it is?"

"I would think you'd know. I care about Shadow, and I don't want to see her hurt," he said as he continued to walk.

"I don't, either."

Toby turned on Josh, anger in his eyes. "She tells me you're leaving Natchez. Do you really think that won't hurt her when she loves you?"

"I'm not leaving."

Toby stared at him. "Just what do you mean?"

"I plan to propose to Shadow today."

A pleased smile crept over Toby's freckled face. "It's about time you wised up, Mr. Rawlings."

"Call me Josh," he said, holding out his hand. "I hope we can be friends, Toby. I know Shadow cares for you very much."

"Yeah, we've been close since we were kids. I

don't mind telling you, I'm damned jealous: but I want what's best for Shadow, and I know she loves you. You'll have me to deal with, though, if you ever hurt her."

"You have my word I won't," Josh said.

Josh noticed Shadow coming toward them. "Don't say anything to her yet, Toby. Not until we come back from our ride."

"Yes sir." Toby smiled.

"Do you think we should stay here and see to details?" Shadow asked. "Rapscallion will need to be teased so we can gauge what precautions are needed to protect the mare."

"I think it can wait a few hours." Josh laughed. "If Gambler's Lady is ready to be covered, she will be for a few more days."

"I know, but to be sure it takes, I'd like to have the opportunity to mate them more than once."

"We'll do all that," Josh agreed, a smile on his handsome face, "but we can take the time for our ride now. We'll leave Rapscallion and Gambler's Lady in Toby's capable hands and take a couple of other horses."

Shadow was surprised he was so insistent about the ride, but she supposed it was because he had been cooped up so long. "All right," she agreed, "but I'm sure the only reason you want to go on this picnic is so you can get your hands on Tilly's fried chicken." She laughed.

"And her blackberry turnovers," Josh added rubbing his hands together.

"I'll have a couple of horses saddled," Toby said,

smiling.

"What did you say to him?" Shadow asked when Toby was out of hearing. "He suddenly seems to like you."

"I just used my irresistible charm on him."

"Oh, and here I thought you only used that on all the women," she said sarcastically. "Now tell me what you said to him," she persisted.

"I just told him I wouldn't hurt you."

Shadow stared at him for a long moment, then shook her head and started walking.

"What's wrong?" he asked.

"Can you really guarantee that, Josh?" she asked.

"I don't suppose any of us can guarantee another's happiness, but I would never knowingly hurt you."

She wanted to tell him he was a fool if he thought she wouldn't be hurt when he left. "I'm glad to hear that," she replied. "Ah, here's Toby."

Josh and Shadow rode along the river for a while. Shadow knew he was looking for *her* place, and she had to smile at the frustration on his face.

"All right, Wildcat, where is it?" he finally asked in exasperation.

"Where is what?" she asked innocently.

"You know. That beautiful place you took me to . . ."

"Oh, you must mean my secret place," she said,

a twinkle in her blue eyes.

"I'd like to see it again." He smiled.

"I would love to take you to it, but we'll have to backtrack. We passed it a few minutes ago."

"You're a devil, Shadow Lansing. You knew very well I was looking for it."

"I know." She grinned mischievously.

"When I get you there I'm going to teach you not to play tricks on me," he warned.

"I'm not afraid of you, Josh Rawlings." She giggled, urging her horse to turn around and head back toward the path.

Josh followed her, the picnic basket bouncing on the back of his horse.

"Now do you recognize it?" she asked.

Josh glanced around, still not sure this was the place. "There was a weeping willow . . . there it is." He laughed.

"You're so observant," she teased. "I'd hate to have you leading me out of the forest."

It was even more beautiful than Josh had remembered. The sky overhead was a vivid blue with a few white whispy clouds. Even the usually muddy Mississippi River looked green.

"I think this must be the most beautiful spot in Mississippi."

"I agree," she said, spreading out a blanket on a mossy slope. We could stay hidden here forever, if we wanted to."

"Shall we do that?" He grinned. "Just you and me and the birds."

"I'm willing." She smiled, settling on the blanket

271

and leaning back on her elbows. "We could fish for our food."

"Do you fish?" he asked in surprise.

"Of course. Don't you?"

"Unfortunately I've never had the opportunity."

"Then, I will teach you." Suddenly her smile faded. *If there is time,* she thought sadly.

After untying the picnic basket, Josh dropped to the blanket beside her. "I'd like that." He grinned. "Do you even bait your own hook?"

"Of course," she said proudly. "And have been since I was twelve."

"Sounds to me like if I'm going to learn you're the one to teach me."

"The fish I've caught here have been especially big. Why, one time I caught one this big," she said, holding her arms wide. "Only problem was he got away before I got him on the bank."

"I've heard about fishermen and their stories." Josh laughed.

"It's true." She pushed at him.

Josh grabbed her and pulled her down to lean on his chest. "I'd believe anything you told me, Wildcat."

"Would you believe me if I told you this was a very special place? Magical things happen here."

"I know they do," he said, putting a hand on each side of her face. "Oh yes, I know they do." His lips touched hers, gently urging a response. When he released her he smiled. "My sweet Wildcat, I do believe you are purring."

"Nonsense." She laughed as she sat up.

Josh leaned up on one elbow. "Do you ever swim here?"

"Often."

He laughed. "Somehow I knew you'd say that. Is there anything you can't do?"

"Not that I've found," she answered smugly.

"Why don't we take a swim now? he said, a mischievous grin on his face.

"Now?" she asked, her eyes wide with surprise. "You can't be serious."

"Of course I am. It's warm enough."

"I know it is, but I don't think it would be good for you," she protested.

"Oh, it would be very good for me, particularly if you swim in the nude." He grinned.

Shadow's face turned pink. "I can't, Josh. It just wouldn't be right."

"I've seen your beautiful body, Wildcat. As a matter of fact, I have it indelibly printed on my brain, but if it makes you uncomfortable—"

"It does," she said, picking a wild flower.

Josh caressed her cheek. "Maybe another time."

"Yes, another time," she agreed softly. *Oh, God, will there be another time for us,* she thought silently.

Josh leaned back, his hands behind his head as he studied the sky. "I suppose I'll just have to imagine what you'd look like coming out of the water," he mused aloud. "First you'd swim a bit, cutting a graceful swath through the water. Then you'd rise in all your glory, with drops of water cascading over your velvet skin. The sun would catch a drop that lingered on one breast and turn it into a shining diamond waiting to be plucked — or kissed."

"Josh, please," Shadow moaned. "Can we talk about something else?"

Josh closed his eyes and smiled. When she was his wife, all his fantasies would come true.

"That's a very wicked smile," she said, touching his nose with the flower.

"It was a very wicked thought," he said without opening his eyes.

Shadow ran the flower down his nose and across his chin.

"What were you thinking?"

He opened his eyes and smiled at her. "I don't think you want to know."

"Oh," she pushed at him, "you have a one track mind, Josh Rawlings."

"I know," he laughed, "particularly where you're concerned."

"I don't know about you, but I'm starving," Shadow said.

Josh laughed as he reached for the picnic basket. "Would you look at this. Chicken, cheese, bread, blackberry tarts and even a bottle of wine. I'll have to remember to kiss Tilly for this."

"You better watch out for Jake if you do," Shadow warned.

"Jake?"

"Yes, that's Tilly's husband. He's about seven feet tall and probably weighs three hundred pounds. I've seen him lift a horse off the ground."

"Maybe I'll just verbally thank her."

"Smart man," Shadow laughed, accepting a crystal goblet. "How did you keep from breaking these?"

"Tilly had the good sense to wrap each one carefully. I suppose when she insisted on me putting the basket on my horse that she knew I wouldn't be racing or jumping."

"She has a lot more faith in you than I do." Shadow laughed. "If you want to go swimming, I wouldn't put it past you to race your horse."

Josh poured them each a glass of wine. "Wait, don't drink it yet. I want to make a toast."

"All right," she said hesitantly, wondering if it was going to be about his leaving.

"To the future," he said, surprising her.

Shadow touched her glass to his. "To the future," she repeated. *How bleak it will be without you,* she thought as she took a sip.

They enjoyed their feast, sprawled on the blanket. Shadow tried to keep her mind on the chicken leg she nibbled, and not on Josh's long, muscular legs stretched out next to her.

"Another glass of wine?" he asked.

"Yes, please." She held out her glass, hoping the wine would ease her tension.

Josh was having no such trouble. He was feeling relaxed and thoroughly content. "There's one more piece of chicken," he said, offering it to Shadow.

"Oh, I couldn't. I want to save room for one of those blackberry tarts."

"What happened to that hearty appetite?" he

275

asked.

"I don't know," she answered. "Lately I haven't had much of an appetite."

Josh dropped the plate of chicken. "My God, Wildcat, are you pregnant?"

Shadow choked on a sip of wine. "Of course not," she sputtered, her face turning a rosy pink.

Josh took her hand. "It's possible, you know."

She wished it were true, but she knew it wasn't. If she couldn't have Josh, she'd at least like to have his child.

"You don't have to worry, you're not trapped."

Josh was stunned by her words. "I suppose I deserve that," he said sadly.

"I'm sorry. I didn't mean that to sound so callous. I just meant you didn't have to worry about it."

"But I do worry about you," he said, pulling her onto his lap.

"Josh, I'm sitting on your chicken." She laughed.

"Forget the chicken. I'm only hungry for you," he said, nibbling on her neck.

Shadow pulled back from him. "Have you forgotten the tarts?"

Josh thought for a long moment. "They are tempting, but I think I still want you," he teased.

She looked at him from under thick lashes. "I want you, too," she admitted softly.

Suddenly Josh was very serious. "What did you say, Wildcat?"

"I said I wanted you, too, but I can't, Josh."

She buried her face in his shoulder. "It will only make it more difficult when you leave."

Josh smiled and caressed her hair. "Tell me, Wildcat, do you know anything about California?"

"No, very little," she sighed, "but I'd like to know about it if that is where you're going to be."

"There is one particular area I like called San Francisco. The city is built on hills, and the weather is pleasant year round. I've had my eye on a piece of property that overlooks a sapphire-blue bay. I was there one time when the fog rolled off the bay and covered the entire city, except for that hilltop. The sun was still shining brilliantly there. That's where I'd like to build a house and raise a family."

Shadow suddenly jumped up and walked toward the river. Oh, God, how could he be so cruel. She couldn't bear it: the thought of him with another woman and children—someone else's children.

Josh got up and followed her. He put his arms around her waist and pulled her back against him. "Did I say something to upset you, Wildcat?"

"It's nothing." She sighed. "I hope you will be very happy in California."

"I will be if you're there with me, Wildcat."

She leaned her head back against his shoulder. "Don't think I haven't thought about it, Josh. If it wouldn't break my grandfather's heart, I'd be your mistress," she admitted, tears in her eyes. "Because I can't bear to think of you leaving here."

Josh turned her around to face him. For a moment she thought she saw tears in his eyes, but it couldn't be. . . .

"I don't want you as my mistress, Wildcat," he said lovingly. "I want you as my wife."

"Shadow stared at him, dumbfounded. "Your wife . . . you want me to be your wife?"

"That's right." He smiled tenderly. "I think from the first moment I met you, I knew my life would never be the same. It just took me a while to decide what I had to do about it. God help us both, Wildcat, but I love you," he declared.

Shadow threw her arms around his neck. "I love you, Josh Rawlings," she exclaimed. "Oh, God, how I love you."

"Does that mean you'll marry me?" he laughed.

"Yes, yes, yes."

"Will you come to California with me?"

The smile suddenly left Shadow's face. "It will be hard to leave Grandfather, but I think I've always known that one day I would leave Lansing Creek."

Knowing that she would go with him if he asked, Josh felt relieved. "What if I agreed that we stay here, at least for the time being."

"You would do that?" she asked with love in her eyes.

"Yes, but I want you to know beforehand that if the war threatens to come this far, we will pack up and head west. I can't take sides, Wildcat. I'm not for the North, but I don't agree with the South's stand on slavery or secession, either."

"I understand." She smiled. "I have mixed emotions about it myself. Grandfather has always said when he died he would give his slaves their freedom. I always wondered why he didn't do it before then."

"Do you want time to think about this?" he asked softly. It's a very important decision to make quickly."

"You're a fool, Josh Rawlings," she admonished. "My heart has been breaking at the very thought of you leaving me. Why would I need time to think about spending the rest of my life with you?"

"I can't promise I'll be the best husband. I have a lot to learn about loving and sharing my life. But if you'll be patient with me . . ."

"As long as you promise there will never be another woman in your life," she said, remembering the parade of women that panted after him.

"There hasn't been a woman in my life since I met you, Shadow Lansing. You've ruined me for all others."

"Good," she said, pulling his mouth down to hers. "That's the way it should be," she whispered before kissing him.

Alas, regardless of their doom,
The little victims play!
No sense have they of ills to come
Nor care beyond today.

— Thomas Gray

Chapter Sixteen

Josh met with Noble in the library the same evening he proposed to Shadow. As he had expected, Noble was delighted.

"So you finally see the wisdom of my words," Noble said, pouring them both a brandy.

"I'm in love with your granddaughter, Noble," Josh said, accepting the glass. "Our marriage has nothing to do with your offer."

"I can't tell you how happy I am to hear that, but still, Lansing Creek will be yours and your children's. I can die a happy man just knowing that."

"Hell, you'll outlive us all." Josh laughed, unaware that Noble was very serious.

Noble didn't comment. "Have you and Shadow discussed when and where you'd like to get married?"

"As soon as possible," Josh answered, "but I'll leave the rest of the details to Shadow."

Noble laughed. "For a man who has cherished his freedom for as long as you have, you certainly are impatient to end it."

"I suppose I am," Josh mused.

For the next few days Lansing Creek was a hive of activity. Shadow had wanted a small wedding so they wouldn't have to wait more than a few days, but at the insistence of her grandfather, she agreed to a candlelight wedding on the lawn overlooking the river. Noble had insisted that there were some people they had to invite, and he convinced the impatient couple to at least give him two weeks to arrange everything. Shadow finally acquiesced when he reminded her that it would take Camille and her family that long to get there from New Orleans.

The next day, handwritten invitations went out to the close friends who were to be invited. That same day, Martha fitted Shadow in the ivory satin wedding gown her mother had worn.

"I wish your mother could see you in her dress, child," Martha said as she stood back and gazed at Shadow. "You is taller, but you look jus' like her."

"I wish she could, too." Shadow smiled sadly. "I think they would like Josh."

"Sure dey would, jus' like your grandfather. Dat

man is proud as a peacock. He treats Mr. Rawlings like he was a son," she chuckled.

"I know," Shadow laughed. "You'd think he was the one marrying Josh."

"All done," Martha said, placing the last pin in place. "You can git down now."

"I'm glad I didn't decide to get married in the summer," Shadow sighed. "This dress is so heavy."

"Your mama was a Christmas bride," Martha said as she helped Shadow out of the dress. "De whole place was decorated with red and white flowers, and lots of evergreen."

"It sounds like it was beautiful."

"It was, but yours will be beautiful, too," Martha said, hugging Shadow.

"I hope Camille is able to make it by the wedding."

"Sure she will. She's your best friend, isn't she?" Martha assured.

"I know, but it's such short notice. Well, I won't worry about that now. I have enough on my mind," Shadow said.

Martha placed a finger under Shadow's chin, forcing her to look at her. "Child, if you needs to ask questions 'bout your wedding night, you ask old Martha, you hear."

"Thank you, Martha, but I think I'll let my husband tutor me," she smiled shyly. "Speaking of Josh, he and Matt should be here before too long. I'm glad Matt will be staying with us until the wedding. It will give me a chance to get to know him."

There was a tap on the door, and Abraham announced that Mrs. Jardine was in the library, waiting to see her.

"Mrs. Jardine? What in the world does she want?" Shadow asked, annoyed. "Are you sure she didn't ask for Grandfather?"

"No ma'am. She asks for you."

"All right, Abraham. Please tell her I'll be down in just a few minutes, and would you ask Tilly if she'd serve tea?"

Rose Jardine paced the library, still in a fury after learning that Josh planned to marry Shadow Lansing. Her first stop had been at Middleton Place, but to her frustration, she learned that Allen was away on a horse buying trip and wouldn't return for several weeks. So alone she had come to Lansing Creek to put a stop to this farce of a wedding. What she was going to say she wasn't sure, but somehow she had to convince Shadow Lansing that Josh wasn't for her.

"Good afternoon, Mrs. Jardine. How nice of you to pay us a visit," Shadow said, entering the room in a pale green morning dress.

"I had to come, Miss Lansing. I heard the news this morning that you plan to marry Josh Rawlings."

"Yes, that's right. We have set the date for the twenty-ninth of October."

"I must convince you not to go through with it, Miss Lansing," Rose said, twisting her gloves nervously.

Shadow regarded the woman for a moment. "Won't you sit down, Mrs. Jardine."

"Thank you, my dear. I'm afraid I'm in rather a frazzled state. When I heard the news, I just knew I had to warn you."

"Warn me about what?" Shadow asked, annoyed.

"Noble and I have been friends for years, and I don't want to see you or him hurt."

"Get to the point, Mrs. Jardine."

"My dear, I'm afraid Josh is only marrying you for your money," she blurted out.

Shadow laughed. "Mrs. Jardine, we don't have that much money. We've been hanging on to Lansing Creek by the skin of our teeth for the past two years."

"I know that, my dear, but Lansing Creek is a very desirable plantation, and well Josh knows that. I know several people who have been waiting around like vultures hoping Noble would lose it."

"I'm well aware of that, Mrs. Jardine, but I don't see what any of this has to do with Josh."

"Josh is an opportunist, my dear. By marrying you, he sees a fast and efficient way of becoming one of the landed gentry. Surely you realize respectability, next to money, is very important to a man like Josh."

Before Shadow had a chance to retort, Tilly entered with a silver service of tea.

"Never mind the tea, Tilly. Mrs. Jardine won't be staying," Shadow said bluntly.

Tilly looked surprised, but she turned and left without a word.

"You needn't worry about the Lansings, Mrs. Jardine. I can assure you we can take care of ourselves," Shadow said as she stood up, dismissing the woman.

"Just a moment, Miss Lansing. There is more. I had hoped I wouldn't have to tell you this . . . but—"

Shadow sat back down. "Why don't you just admit you're jealous, Mrs. Jardine. I know all about you and Josh, but that's the past."

"Of course I'm jealous, my dear." She laughed. "Josh is an excellent lover, but certainly not husband material. Why, I could have married him months ago," she lied. "He begged me to every time we were together, but I knew he was more interested in my money than in me. And a man like Josh needs a lot of money to keep him living in the style he's accustomed to. Why, I've spent a small fortune on clothes for him, not to mention other personal items."

"Are you through, Mrs. Jardine," Shadow asked angrily.

"My dear, it really doesn't matter to me if he

marries you. Josh is not the type of man to settle for just one woman."

"If he wasn't satisfied with one woman, maybe it was because you weren't keeping him satisfied, Mrs. Jardine," Shadow said, a smile on her face.

Rose's eyes blazed with anger. "Josh Rawlings is a spy, Miss Lansing. A spy for the North. I have been told by very reliable sources that his marriage to you is to give him credibility so he can continue to spy," she blurted out.

Shadow stared at her in disbelief. "That's a lie! Josh has no interest in the North or South."

"Maybe you should talk to your future husband, Miss Lansing. I think you have a lot to learn about the man," Rose said, as she pulled on her gloves.

Shadow didn't know a lot about Josh Rawlings, but she was sure he wasn't a spy.

"I will do that, Mrs. Jardine, and I'll also tell him who accused him of being a spy and a money-hungry opportunist."

Rose chuckled, feeling she finally had the upper hand. "I'll just deny it, my dear."

"And you think he'd believe you and not me?" Shadow asked in disbelief.

"Of course, my dear," she said, heading for the door. "And there is one more thing. Josh will be back to me as soon as the novelty of bedding a virgin wears off."

Shadow smiled confidently. "Don't count on it, Mrs. Jardine."

* * *
287

Shadow wasn't sure what she was going to do about Rose's visit, or if she should even mention it to Josh. Accusations like Rose Jardine had made weren't an easy subject to bring up. She knew Josh had had a hard life growing up, but he seemed to do all right now. My God, he owned Yancey's, so he couldn't be the pauper Rose made him out to be. And as for spying . . . that was totally ludicrous. She decided she was going to forget the whole thing. By God, she wouldn't give the woman the satisfaction of knowing she'd caused her to have any doubt, she decided with determination.

Shadow paced the confines of her room until she heard horses approaching. She regarded her own reflection in the mirror critically, anxious to look her best for Josh and his brother. She had changed into one of her favorite gowns, an aqua silk trimmed with lavender ribbon. Satisfied with the way she looked, Shadow quickly left her room. For a moment she stood at the top of the stairs, listening to her grandfather greet the two men. She smiled as she heard Josh ask where she was.

Slowly she descended the stairs. Josh stopped in midsentence when he saw her. He moved toward her, a smile on his face.

"I missed you," he whispered.

"You have only been gone since this morning," she answered, pleased at his response.

"I know, but I've gotten used to having you near, and when I see you, I realize how much your beauty brightens my day."

"Will you two stop cooing over each other and give me a chance to say hello to my future sister-in-law," Matt interrupted good-naturedly.

"If I have to," Josh smiled.

Matt bowed low over Shadow's hand. "It is a pleasure to view your beauty again, fair Shadow."

"My God, will you listen to him," Josh exclaimed, "the man has become a poet."

"Shadow's beauty does that to me," Matt claimed, winking at Shadow.

"Perhaps I'm marrying the wrong brother," Shadow teased. "I haven't had compliments like this from Josh."

"I think we better retire to the library before we have a war in the foyer," Noble laughed.

Matt offered Shadow his arm, leaving Josh and Noble to follow behind. "There is still time to change your mind," Matt said loud enough for Josh to hear. "Since I'm the *best man,* you would be better off marrying me."

"Enough!" Josh said, removing Shadow's arm from his brother's. "I'm probably going to have to fight men for being too attentive to my beautiful wife for the rest of my life, but I certainly don't intend to have to fight my brother off."

"I am crushed," Matt said, one hand over his heart. "I never realized how selfish you could be, big brother."

The inane chatter lightened Shadow's spirit as she tried to put her conversation with Rose Jardine out of her mind. "You are both most gallant to little ole me," she drawled, "but I think you have both been out in the sun too long."

"Matt, why don't I show you to your room?" Noble suggested, winking at Josh.

"I suppose I should give my brother a few moments alone with his fiancée. But mark my word, big brother, I don't plan to give you many. I'm going to take full advantage of Shadow's company while I'm here."

"I don't doubt that for a moment," Josh laughed, "but be warned, little brother, don't push me too far." He smiled at Shadow. "I'm afraid I am going to be a very jealous husband."

"I like your brother," Shadow said when they were alone.

Josh pulled her into his arms. "He's passable, but remember you are getting the better of the two."

Shadow laughed. "I'll try to remember that."

Abraham poked his head in the door. " 'Cuse me, Miss Shadow, but Tilly says dinner will be served in twenty minutes."

"Thank you, Abraham." Shadow smiled.

"My God, Wildcat, when are we ever going to be alone again?" he asked, nuzzling her neck. "I swear if I last until our wedding night I should be considered for sainthood."

"Saint Josh," she giggled. "No, I don't think that will ever happen."

The evening meal continued with their gay and constant chatter. By the time cordials were served, Shadow was exhausted from laughing at the two of them.

"My dear granddaughter, are you sure you know what you're getting into?" Noble chortled.

"I hope it means there will always be laughter in my home," Shadow smiled at Josh.

"Laughter and love," he assured, taking her hand.

Noble cleared his throat. "Matt, what do you say to joining me in the library for a brandy. I think maybe Josh and Shadow would like to get a breath of fresh air."

Shadow's eyes never left Josh's face. "A walk in the rose garden sounds wonderful," she said softly.

He toyed with a piece of lavender ribbon on her dress, his eyes on her lovely face. "I believe we will have a full moon for our wedding," he said softly.

"Umm," Shadow agreed, trembling at his touch. "Grandfather probably planned it that way."

"How many more days is it?" he asked in a lazy voice as he ran his thumb up and down her neck.

291

"Twelve," she whispered breathly.

"Twelve days of torture," he sighed. "Your grandfather is a foxy old codger; do you know that love? He always manages to give us just enough time together to drive me crazy. Then either he shows up or he sends one of his servants to interrupt us."

Shadow laughed softly. "I've noticed. So you better kiss me now before he shows up."

"You're a saucy wench," he whispered before kissing her hungrily.

Shadow's arms went around his neck to pull him closer. She could feel his heartbeat and wondered if he could feel hers racing wildly. He raised his head and stared down at her. "Twelve days of torture," he repeated.

"They will be torture for me, too," she admitted softly.

"Good. I was afraid you were so enamored of my brother that you wouldn't care."

"Well, you could take a few lessons from him in giving flattery," she teased.

"Oh, so you want to hear how beautiful and desirable you are, um."

"Something like that."

"Mmm, you taste good," he said, running his tongue down her neck. "But I think I've told you that before."

"Yes, but that's all right." She moved sensuously. "Tell me more."

"Your hair smells like flowers . . ."

"Umm," she moaned as he buried his face in the waves of her hair.

"Shadow, Josh, are you out there?" Noble asked.

They both began to laugh. "I told you," Josh whispered before answering Noble.

When Shadow was alone, Rose's words kept coming back to her. She tossed and turned on the bed, trying to go to sleep, but finally she gave up. Getting up, she pulled a thin wrapper on and stepped out on the gallery.

It was jealousy on Rose Jardine's part, she thought as she stared out into the darkness. Josh would be the first to tell her the whole idea was foolish—but she hadn't been able to bring up the subject all evening. She should just ask him and then put the whole thing out of her mind.

"Thinking about me?"

Shadow whirled around, facing a grinning Josh Rawlings in the moonlight.

"I'm sorry, love. I didn't mean to startle you."

"I wasn't expecting anyone else to still be up."

"I've been lying in bed thinking about our kiss in the garden. What's your excuse?"

Shadow began to tremble. She needed to know, yet she was afraid . . .

"Wildcat, what is it?" he asked, taking hold of her shoulders. "Are you cold?"

"No, not really."

"Please tell me you're not having second thoughts about marrying me?"

"Oh, no, Josh, it's nothing like that," she exclaimed. "It's just that Rose Jardine came here today . . . and some of the things she said made me realize I don't know very much about you."

Josh kissed the tip of her nose, then pulled her against him to keep her warm. "Is that really all it is? I can't imagine Rose coming here on a social call."

Shadow shook her head, suddenly feeling very foolish. "Josh she said . . . she said you were a spy for the North."

Josh's arms dropped from around her, and he turned and looked out over the balcony into the blackness.

"Josh . . ." Shadow said, suddenly very frightened.

"I suppose some people would consider it spying."

"Oh, God . . ."

"I've been trying to prevent war, Shadow. The people I have been dealing with are very influential in Washington. They thought if they could convince the war mongers that it would be unwise to secede from the Union that war could be prevented. Unfortunately I've uncovered a very large group in Natchez who want war, and many of them will prosper because of it."

294

"But you said you weren't for the North. . . ."

"I'm not, love, I swear to you. Let me start at the beginning," he said, turning to face her. "Matt and I were on a steamboat traveling from St. Louis to New Orleans. I won Yancey's in a card game while on board from a man who turned out to be an emissary from Washington. He's the one who convinced me I could help prevent a war. After being here a few weeks, I knew it was hopeless. The South is itching for a battle as you well know. Anyway, that's why Yancey's has been robbed so many times, and why I've nearly been killed. They've been trying to run me out of town."

"Who, Josh?" Shadow asked in disbelief.

"I can't put names to them, Wildcat. All I can tell you is it's a group of men who go around with masks on and terrorize anyone who doesn't agree with them."

"I have heard there was such a group," Shadow said, "but I couldn't imagine anyone from around here being involved."

"I think I know who the leader is, but I can't prove anything yet. I have a meeting with my contact Tuesday, so I'll give him this bit of info. Now that I know Rose is involved, perhaps I can get some answers from her."

"She said if I told you she'd deny it."

"I'm sorry you had to find out this way, love. I should have told you myself, but I hadn't intended it to go this far. I planned to find out who the men

295

were who attacked me, and then I was going to inform my contact that there was nothing else I could provide."

"I'm relieved to hear that," she said, leaning her head on his shoulder. "Josh, there is something else. She said you were marrying me to give you credibility so you could gain the trust of the people around here."

"Jesus," he swore. "I can't believe she'd expect you to believe anything like that. You know I didn't even want to stay around here, much less stay around to spy."

Shadow smiled, remembering that Josh had wanted to go back to California. "I knew there had to be a reasonable explanation." She sighed in relief.

"Is there anything else?" he asked against her hair.

She thought about Rose's accusation that he was marrying her for her money, but she knew that had to be foolishness. "No, nothing else."

"Then, how about kissing me to prove you still want to marry me?"

Shadow wrapped her arms around Josh's neck and pulled his head down to meet her mouth. She gave him a long, ardent kiss, her tongue intermingling with his.

Josh could feel her breasts beneath the flimsy material of her nightgown, and for a moment he considered picking her up and taking her back to her room. Suddenly he removed her arms from around his neck and quickly kissed her on the forehead. "Get back to bed." He sighed. "I don't want Noble greeting me with a shotgun. It's only twelve more days," he moaned.

Shadow smiled up at him. "I love you, Josh Rawlings. More tonight than I ever have."

"I'll try to fall asleep with that thought." He grimaced as she ran her hand down his face. "Good night, love. Sleep well, and know that I love you with all my heart."

Our present joys are more to flesh
and blood
Than a dull prospect of a distant good.

—John Dryden

Chapter Seventeen

Shadow couldn't help sneaking a look at the scene on the lawn below her balcony. An aisle lined with candles in hurricane globes lighted the way to a small altar covered with flowers. Chairs for the small group of guests had been set up on each side of the aisle, but at the moment the guests were mingling in the rose garden.

"It's going to be so beautiful," she whispered to herself. "I'm so lucky." She sighed with contentment.

She glanced down the gallery toward Josh's room, wondering what he was doing at the moment. Smiling to herself, she thought of him pacing his room in a bout of nerves.

"Child, git back in here," Martha ordered as she rushed into the room with Shadow's veil over her arm. "You got about two minutes to git downstairs."

"Has Josh already gone down?" Shadow asked as she fixed the veil on her head.

"He's been downstairs a good half hour," Martha answered. "Dat man jus' as cool as a cucumber."

"Are you ready?" Camille bustled into the room, then froze in her tracks. "Oh, Shadow, you are absolutely beautiful," she exclaimed.

"Thank you. The gown was my mother's," she said, running a hand over the smooth satin. "You look beautiful yourself," she exclaimed, admiring the rust-colored velvet gown her friend wore.

"I thought this would be appropriate for an autumn wedding," Camille said, spinning around. "I'm so glad you like it."

"I'm just so glad you're here, I wouldn't care if you dressed in rags." Shadow giggled, hugging her friend.

"Thank you, Shadow," Camille said, clutching Shadow's hands. "I would have been devastated if we hadn't made it in time."

"Come, come," Martha interrupted. "Everyone is taking dere place. Miss Camille, you better hurry. You s'pose to be downstairs right now."

"All right," Camille laughed, giving Shadow a quick kiss. "I'll see you in a few minutes."

* * *
300

On her Grandfather's arm, Shadow walked toward Josh, her blue eyes locked with his. He looked so handsome it took her breath away. He wore a fitted coat of brown velvet, a cream-colored ruffled shirt with a gold-colored neck scarf, and his boots had been polished until they gleamed.

Josh stared at the ravishing beauty who only had eyes for him. There was an achingly familiar feeling he got everytime he looked at her. God, but he was a lucky man, he thought. She looked like an angel with a halo of veil netting around her head.

As the music stopped, Noble gave Shadow's hand into Josh's. For a moment there was silence, then the preacher's deep voice began the ceremony as the sun began to set over the river, casting its golden glow over everything.

Shadow wondered what Josh was thinking as he smiled lovingly at her.

"Joshua, will you take Cassandra to be thy wedded wife . . ." the preacher continued.

"I will," he said firmly.

Shadow started as she realized the preacher was now addressing her. "Cassandra, will thou love Joshua, comfort, honor and obey him?"

"Yes," she whispered, feeling tears of joy slip from her eyes.

The ceremony continued with Josh placing a

beautiful diamond and gold band on her finger.

"I now pronounce you man and wife," the preacher announced. "You may kiss the bride."

Josh took Shadow in his arms and soundly kissed her. A cheer went up from the gathering of guests, and a moment later everyone was congratulating them.

"I'm going to demand my rights as the best man and kiss the bride now"—Matt laughed—"because knowing you, big brother, I may never get to do it again."

Matt took Shadow in his arms and kissed her, in not-too-brotherly a manner.

"Enough!" Josh said, prying Matt's arms from around Shadow. "By God, I'd hate to have to duel my brother on my wedding night." He laughed.

Matt smiled at Shadow. "You have my heart, sweet Shadow. If there is ever anything you need, I'll be your knight in shining armor." He bowed gallantly.

"Thank you, kind sir, but I'm sure your brother will never give me cause to need a shining knight."

"Thank you for your confidence, my love," Josh said, putting his arm around her possessively. "And as for you, little brother, I'll try to be patient with your adoration of my wife, only until you find someone of your own."

"Ah, that I could find someone like your Shadow." He sighed.

Shadow giggled at the attention. "Have you met my friend Camille?"

"Yes, a lovely young lady, but she seems only to have eyes for the red-haired young man who works for you."

"Toby McAllister our overseer," Shadow said. "I'm afraid I instigated the relationship and now they'd like to marry. Unfortunately her father won't allow it."

"Is he against the marriage because Toby is an overseer, or because he doesn't have much money?" Josh asked.

"It's probably the money," Shadow said sadly. "Toby was in school before he came back here to take over after his father became ill, so it isn't like he's uneducated. As a matter of fact, I think Camille's father always admired Toby for his ability to run Lansing Creek."

"Maybe things will work out for them," Josh said, already thinking of a way to help them.

"Matt, Josh tells me that you are planning to go back to California," Shadow said.

"Yes, as soon as we sell Yancey's."

Shadow's gaze went to her husband's face. "I didn't know you were planning to sell Yancey's."

"Matt doesn't want to run it, and I certainly don't want to spend my evenings there when I have a beautiful wife at home."

"I understand you are going to take a wedding

trip to Paris," Matt commented.

"Yes, isn't that exciting," Shadow exclaimed. "Josh told me this morning," she said, looking at her husband with love. "We won't be leaving for a week though, and then we'll be back before Christmas. I wish you'd stay at least until then," she smiled at Matt. "It would be wonderful for all of us to celebrate the holidays together."

"I may just do that." He kissed Shadow on the cheek. "Thank you for the invitation."

While Shadow and Matt talked, Josh came up with an idea to help Toby and Camille. He looked around to see if he saw the young man. "Have you seen Toby?" he asked.

"Not since the ceremony," Shadow said, glancing around the group of guests. "I'd be willing to bet he's sitting alone on the front porch."

"Matt, do you think I can trust you with my wife, long enough for me to talk to the young man?"

Matt wrapped Shadow's arm through his. "Take your time, big brother. I'll guard your lady with my life."

"The only one here I'm worried about is you," he laughed before taking his leave.

Shadow had been right. The young man was sitting alone on the porch, slumped in a chair with a tall glass of whiskey.

"Mind if I join you?" Josh asked.

"Shouldn't you be with your wife?" Toby asked.

Josh sat down and lit up a cheroot. "I think what I'm about to do would make her happy."

"What is that?" Toby asked, his curiosity peaked.

"I'm going to give you the opportunity to marry Camille."

Toby straightened up in his chair and stared at Josh. "What are you talking about?"

"Wouldn't Mr. Deveraux agree to a marriage between you and his daughter if you had the money and means to keep her in the style she's accustomed to?"

"Well, yes, I suppose so, but I still don't understand. I have no way of making that kind of money."

"Perhaps you do," Josh smiled in the darkness. "I own a shipping business that includes two good-size warehouses in New Orleans. It's yours with enough money to give you a good start."

"But why . . . why would you want to do that. You hardly know me. I could run your business in the ground in less than a month."

"It's your business, so I'm sure you'll do everything you can to make a go of it. And I'm doing this because Shadow would like to see you and her friend have a chance."

Toby just shook his head.

"There is something else. I own a house on Chartres Street. It's yours to use for as long as you

305

want. All I ask is that you keep a room for Shadow and me to use whenever we come to New Orleans."

Toby laughed in disbelief. "I don't understand any of this. My God, I must have died and gone to heaven. . . ."

"No man should lose the woman he loves because he's a little short on money." Josh laughed. "I have more holdings and money than I could spend in a lifetime."

"Jesus!" Toby exclaimed standing up. He started pacing, running his hand through his hair. "You really mean this. . . ."

"There is one stipulation. I don't want anyone to know that I helped you. You can tell people that a relative died and left you his heir."

"What about Shadow?"

"It's best she doesn't know, either. She could accidentally let it slip to Camille or her family."

"I don't know what to say, Josh."

"Just say you'll accept my offer. It will ease my conscience for taking Shadow away from you."

"By God, she picked her a winner." Toby laughed, putting his hand out to shake Josh's. "I'll never forget you for this, and I'll pay you back, I swear."

"You might just casually mention your good fortune to Noble before announcing it to Camille's family," Josh suggested. "We don't want your new-found fortune to look too suspicious."

"I will," Toby said, anxious to rejoin the party. "I'll say that I didn't mention it earlier because I wanted it to be Shadow's day, but I just couldn't hold it back any longer."

Josh rejoined Shadow and Matt as they mingled among the guests. "Excuse me, dear brother, but I'm here to claim my wife."

"I was afraid you would come back," Matt teased. "I was just going to get us some more champagne. Would you like some?"

"I'd love some." Josh smiled, taking Shadow's hand. "We'll be in the rose garden."

"Your wife . . ." She smiled. "I like that. Did you find Toby?"

"No, he must have been down at the stables," he answered as they strolled. "I was talking with some of the guests on the front porch. Did my brother behave himself?"

"Like a true gentleman," she replied, "but I missed my husband."

They stopped in the shadows of the house. "How long before we can disappear?" he asked, nibbling on her ear.

"Josh," she blushed, "we haven't even eaten."

"Now your appetite returns." He laughed in pretended exasperation.

"I can't help it if I'm suddenly hungry. I haven't eaten all day," she complained.

"Would you settle for a tray in our room?" he whispered.

"Now that sounds interesting." She wrapped her arms around his neck.

"There you two are," Noble said. "I thought I'd find you here."

"I don't believe this." Josh laughed. "Noble, we're married. You don't have to protect Shadow's virtue any longer."

"Ah, so you realized what I was up to."

"We both did, Grandfather," Shadow said, hugging him. "I love you for it."

"Did you hear Toby's good news?" he asked. "It seems the young man had a relative that remembered him in his will. Toby has inherited a business and some property in New Orleans."

"Oh, Grandfather, that's wonderful. Now maybe he and Camille can get married."

"I'm sure that's what he is hoping. He told me he plans to talk to Andre before they leave."

"Oh, Josh, isn't that wonderful?"

"It certainly is. I'm happy for the young man."

"Now, I came out here to find you to see if you two would like to disappear after you cut the cake? Don't bother eating, though. Tilly has prepared something for you in your room. And Josh," he said, pulling him aside, "I'll be spending a couple of days fishing at the shack down by the river. You and Shadow will have the house to yourselves."

308

He winked.

They cut the cake with the usual ceremony and toasts, then while everyone ate and drank, they disappeared into the house.

Shadow hesitated at the foot of the stairs. "Perhaps I should ask Martha to help me—"

"Let me do it, love. I don't want any more delays," Josh said, leading her up the stairs.

"Is this to be a permanent situation, or just tonight?"

"We'll see." He grinned as he opened the door of the bedroom.

A blazing fire lit the room in a golden glow, and candles had been placed all around the room. A table with china and crystal was set before the fire.

"Who did this?" she asked in awe. "It's so beautiful."

"I wish I could take the credit, but I can't. I think Martha and Tilly are responsible."

"They are romantics," Shadow laughed, running her hand over the satin sheets on the bed. "Look, Josh, champagne. They've thought of everything."

"I hope they left something for me to do," he said, pulling her into his arms. "I've been dreaming about this night for a long time."

"We've only known each other a little over a month," she said, caressing the hair that curled at the back of his neck.

"Oh, I know, Wildcat, but I think I've been dreaming about you all my life," he said as he began to unbutton the small satin-covered buttons at the back of her dress.

"I . . . I think I need a glass of champagne." She quickly pulled away. "I'm so thirsty."

Josh laughed deep in his throat. "Are you a little nervous, my beautiful bride," he asked as he removed his own jacket.

"I know it's foolish, but yes I am," she admitted.

"Don't worry about a thing. We'll just take our time until you feel relaxed," he said as he poured them each a glass of champagne. "Are you still hungry? There is crab meat, ham and too many other things to mention," he said, lifting covers off the dishes.

"No, I think just the champagne for now."

After the second glass, Shadow was feeling a little more relaxed. "It's very warm in here." She sighed, lifting her long hair off her neck.

"I'll open the French doors if you like, but I think you'd be more comfortable if you took that heavy gown off."

Shadow lifted the material. "Yes, I think you're right."

"Your beauty takes my breath away," he said as he deftly undid the buttons.

Before she knew it, the satin dress fell in a rustle

around her ankles. "Oh," she exclaimed, suddenly very shy.

"Just relax, darling. Martha laid your wrapper on the bed. You can put that on if you like, after you get out of those undergarments."

"Maybe I better have another glass of champagne." She giggled.

"I've seen your body, love. Why are you so nervous?"

Shadow placed her hand on his cheek. "Perhaps I'm afraid I'll disappoint you."

"Oh, Shadow," Josh moaned. "There is no way I could ever be disappointed with you. You are the most beautiful, desirable woman I've ever laid eyes on."

"You're just saying that because I'm your wife."

Josh laughed deeply. "You're my wife because I feel that way." He kissed her gently on the eyes and nose. "Now, let me help you out of those things."

When the last garment was discarded, Josh stared at Shadow as she stood naked before him. "So beautiful," he whispered. "So damned beautiful." His mouth found hers, gently forcing her lips apart to explore the inner softness with his silken tongue.

Shadow was weakened by her own passion. She clung to his hard, muscular body for support, whispering his name in an anguished moan.

"Yes, love, I know," he said, picking her up to

311

lay her on the bed. Quickly he began to shed his own clothes.

Shadow admired his muscular physique, the wide shoulders and chest, the narrow waist, and— She quickly looked back at his face, her heart pounding wildly. She hadn't been brave enough to look at him before. . . .

Josh's breathing was ragged as he lay beside her, taking her in his arms. Her reddish-blond hair shone like gold as it fanned out on the pillow. "You look like an angel," he groaned, burying his face in her hair.

"But I'm not." She smiled seductively. "I want you, Josh. I want you very badly."

A sound that was part laughter, part groan escaped him. "Oh, my sweet temptress, I want you, too. I need you more than I need air to breathe. . . ."

His warm mouth closed over her breast, teasing and nipping at her nipple. She drew a ragged breath as he came back to her mouth. He kissed her again and again, determined to keep their pace slow, but Shadow wasn't helping. Her tongue invaded his mouth; her hands were all over him, teasing and torturing.

He knelt above her, whispering soft words of love and endearments as he stroked the soft, sensitive skin of her inner thighs. Then slowly, gently he guided himself into her soft, yielding flesh.

"Oh, yes . . . yes," Shadow cried, arching her hips to accept his thrusts. Her hands gripped his shoulders as he kissed her deeply, his tongue matching his thrusts.

With a cry, Shadow climaxed quickly; an incredible spasm of pleasure washed over her, then his warm seed flooded her.

"I love you, Wildcat," he said, lightly kissing her temple as he held her in his arms. "I'll love you 'til my dying day, and maybe even beyond."

"Shadow snuggled into his shoulder, letting her fingers explore the warm flesh of his chest and stomach. "I love you, too, my husband." She sighed contentedly.

"Are you happy, my wife?"

Shadow leaned across his chest, staring into his warm amber eyes. "More than I ever imagined possible," she said as she traced his full sensual lips with her finger. She brought his lips to hers, caressing his face in both hands as she teased his mouth in sweet provocation. "Do I make you happy?"

"You know you do, my bewitching sorceress," he whispered, caught in the sensual web she was weaving. "Do you have any idea what you're doing to me?" he moaned.

"I have some idea," she smiled, catching his bottom lip with her teeth.

Josh groaned and swiftly rolled over, trapping her beneath him. "Torment me, will you?"

His mouth began a slow, torturing trail down her neck, across her breasts then lower still.

Shadow's entire body quivered with desire. "Oh, Josh, love me," she moaned, raising her hips from the bed. "Please, love me now."

"Not yet, my love," he growled as his fingers and mouth caressed the most private part of her until her body writhed in sweet release.

Floating, dizzy with pleasure, Shadow lay exhausted, unable to move as Josh covered her with the sheet.

"Is my wife still happy?" he asked as he held the champagne glass to her lips.

"Exhausted, but happy." She sighed before falling asleep like a contented kitten.

When lovely woman stoops to folly
And finds too late that men betray
What charm can soothe her melancholy
What art can wash her guilt away?

— Oliver Goldsmith

Chapter Eighteen

Josh brushed at something tickling his nose. Finally opening his yes, he discovered Shadow asleep, curled half across his body, her beautiful hair draped across his face. He carefully shifted her head to the pillow, then studied her sleeping form.

They had made love several times during the night. Three to be exact, he smiled, pleased with the passionate woman at his side.

He touched her soft shoulder, thinking again how her skin felt like velvet. A tender smile curved his lips as he lifted a strand of her golden hair to his lips. He hoped he had planted the seed of a child in her body—a child who would look like her.

Shadow opened her eyes slowly, smiling as she met the loving look in her husband's eyes. Reaching up, she stroked his face.

"Did you sleep well, my husband?"

"When you let me—he grinned lazily—"which wasn't often."

"Umm, I thought it was the other way around." She stretched, letting the sheet slip below her breasts.

Josh kissed her shoulder and each breast, then moved lower over the soft skin of her stomach. "You are all warm and sweet tasting," he moaned.

"What will people think if we don't get out of this bed today?" she asked breathlessly.

"There is no one in the house to know or care," he answered, nipping at her ear.

"No one?" she asked in a hoarse voice. "What about Grandfather?"

Josh smiled down into her face. "Your grandfather said the house was ours for a few days. He's gone to some shack on the river to do some long overdue fishing. He said our meals would be left outside the door, but no one would disturb us until we decided to rejoin the world."

Shadow smiled. "It seems he thought of everything."

"It seems so," he said, taking her face in his hands and kissing her tenderly. "All that's left is for me to keep you happy."

Shadow smiled seductively. "I have no doubt that you will do that, my husband."

His gold eyes were filled with love. "I'll die trying," he professed, before making love to her again.

Shadow woke later, sitting straight up in the bed, a stunned look on her face.

"Umm, what is it, love," Josh mumbled without opening his eyes.

"It must be late afternoon," she exclaimed.

"Do you have someplace to go?" he asked lazily.

"Of course not, but suddenly I'm starving."

"For food?" Josh asked, leaning up on one elbow.

"I hate to wound your male ego," she smiled, running a finger down his chest, "but yes, for food," she said climbing from the bed.

Shadow pulled her wrapper around her, then started for the door. "Please, Tilly, don't fail me now," she said, peeking out into the hallway. "Oh, wonderful," she exclaimed, bending over to pick up a tray. "They didn't forget us."

Josh plumped the pillows up against the headboard and leaned back to watch his wife.

"There's coffee in the silver pot," she said. "I hope it's still warm. There is fruit," she said, lifting a white napkin. "Oh, marvelous, Tilly made us cinnamon buns," she exclaimed, licking her fingers. "Oh, Josh, wait until you taste these."

"Well, are you going to give me one, or do I have

to get out of bed stark naked to get it?"

"Umm, I don't know. Maybe I should let you stay there. There are only a dozen or so of them. I could eat all of them in one sitting."

"Listen to me, Wildcat, or should I say kitten, since you've sheathed your claws and now purr . . ."

"Josh." She laughed delightedly.

"Anyway, if I recall correctly," he continued, "you promised to love, honor and obey."

"Yes, I recall something like that," she said, taking another bite of the sticky bun.

"Then I order you to bring me some of those buns," he said smugly.

"Well, of course, my darling," she smiled, taking him a bun. "Here, let me feed you."

"That's more like it," Josh said. When he opened his mouth to take a bite, Shadow rubbed the bun all over his face, then leaped from the bed laughing.

"You little vixen," he said, slowly climbing from the bed. He bent over and washed his face in the basin, then turned to her.

"You're going to pay for that . . ." He stalked her, a gleam in his gold eyes.

"No!" she screamed, putting the chair between them. He looked splendid in his nakedness; his hair touseled from their lovemaking made him look the rake. "Stay away from me, please . . . I'm sorry,"

318

she laughed. "Give me another chance . . ."

"A wife should be taught from the beginning to show her husband respect."

"I know . . . I know . . . I will . . . I do respect you," she squealed as he lunged for her, grasping the wrapper and pulling it from her body.

"That's better," he smiled. "Now we're even." He captured her, tossing her on the bed and quickly following. "Now I intend to satisfy my appetite."

Shadow laughed and kicked as he took nibbling bites all over her shoulders and neck. "Stop, please. I'll get you food, I promise." She struggled to get away.

Before releasing her, he kissed her, a consuming kiss, branding her his alone. "All right, woman. I'm ready for you to serve my breakfast."

Shadow climbed from the bed. "Are you sure, darling?" she asked, mischief in her eyes.

"On second thought, I think I'll get it myself," he grinned as he climbed from the bed. "But I'm not through with you yet," he warned.

When Allen Middleton returned to Middleton Place, he found Rose Jardine waiting for him. "What brings you out here in the middle of the day," he asked, annoyed that she should be sitting in his home being served tea.

"I just wanted to see your face when I told you

319

what you missed while galavanting all over the countryside."

"I went to Jackson to buy some horses," he answered curtly as he poured himself a drink. "I'd appreciate it if you'd get to the point. I'd like to get out of these dirty clothes and get a bath."

"You told me not to worry about a thing. That you would handle everything," she sneered. "I should have known better. You didn't stand a chance against Josh Rawlings."

"What the hell are you talking about?" he growled.

"Your little sweetheart married Josh Rawlings while you were gone."

"You're lying!" he yelled knocking the teacup from her hand.

"Am I?" She laughed bitterly. "Why don't you go to Lansing Creek and see for yourself, but you better hurry. I understand they will be leaving for Europe in a few days on a wedding trip."

"Damn stupid fool," Allen swore. "I had no idea Noble would let the girl marry that bastard."

"Well he did. Now what are we going to do about it?"

He couldn't tell her he planned to make Shadow a widow. She was too hot to have Josh Rawlings in her bed to agree with killing the bastard. Instead he turned and smiled at her. "Just go home and let me handle everything."

Rose picked up her gloves and purse. "I hope you handle it better this time than you did the last."

Everyone greeted them with knowing smiles when they appeared downstairs for the first time in nearly two days. After sampling some of Tilly's blackberry muffins, they decided to check on Gambler's Lady to be sure she was faring all right after the mating.

"Why don't we take a ride," Josh suggested after examining his horse.

"I was hoping we could go back to our room and isolate ourselves another few days," Shadow said with a twinkle in her eyes.

"All right," he said, grabbing her hand. "That sounds good to me."

"Wait, Josh, I was only teasing. I'd love to take a ride," she said, digging her heels in.

"Are you tired of me already?" he asked, pulling her into his arms.

"No, but it's a beautiful day, and there is always tonight," she said, one eyebrow raised meaningfully.

"All right, until tonight," he smacked her on the bottom.

"Where is the fishing shack your grandfather is using? Josh asked as they rode toward the river.

"About a mile upriver. Can we go by and tell him

how happy we are?" she asked hopefully. "I feel guilty about him staying away from the house."

"I do, too, Shadow. I was going to suggest that we go ask him to come home. We'll have a celebration dinner tonight for just the three of us."

"Oh, Josh, that's so sweet of you," she exclaimed. "If I could reach you right now I'd kiss you."

"If you do that," he grinned, "we may not get to your grandfather for hours."

"Then follow me." She galloped off in the direction of the fishing shack.

With a determined scowl on his face, Noble pretended to be upset about giving up his fishing time. In reality, he had had an attack the night before and was looking forward to getting a good night's sleep on his feather bed.

"All right, if you insist," he agreed, "but in my day, I would have taken all the private time I could get with my bride."

"Josh and I will have plenty of time together in Europe," Shadow assured, helping her grandfather gather the few belongings he had brought with him.

"That's right, Noble. Besides, I'm looking forward to a few hands of poker tonight—"

"Josh!" Shadow exclaimed.

"Only teasing, love." His gold eyes twinkled.

"Why don't you two go on with your ride, and I'll meet you back at the house," Noble suggested.

When Noble reached the house, Allen Middleton was just tying his horse to the hitching post. "Where are the newlyweds?" he asked sarcastically.

"What are you doing here, Middleton?"

"I just heard about the marriage, and I had to see with my own eyes if it was true."

"It's true," he answered, walking past Allen. "Is there anything else you wanted?"

Allen grabbed Noble by the shirtfront. "How could you be such a fool? The man is a spy for the North."

"You're out of your mind." Noble struggled to break the hold the man had on him.

"I have proof, you old fool," he said, shoving Noble away from him.

Noble stumbled and fell off the porch. "You bastard," he growled. As he tried to get up, pain clutched his chest, taking his breath away. "Get off my property," he hissed.

Allen walked past him to his horse. "When the war comes, anyone who isn't faithful to our cause will be burned out," he snarled. He mounted his horse and came dangerously close to where Noble lay in pain. "Of course, if I own Lansing Creek, nothing will happen to it."

323

"You'll never own Lansing Creek, you bastard," Noble gasped in pain.

"Master Lansing," Abraham cried as he came running out of the house. "Oh, my God. Martha, come help me," he shouted as he kneeled beside Noble.

"Help me get to my room, Abraham," Noble said, trying to get to his feet. "I just need a brandy and some rest."

Soon after Shadow and Josh returned, Noble had another attack, this one leaving him weak and disoriented. Abraham had already sent for Dr. Morgan, and he arrived a short time later.

Shadow stayed in the room with him as he examined her grandfather. "He should have told you a long time ago," Dr. Morgan said, shaking his head. "It's his heart."

Shadow stared at the doctor in shock. "His heart?" she repeated in disbelief. "And he knew he was sick?"

"He didn't want anyone to know, Shadow. His hope was that he could live to see you married."

Shadow fought back the tears. "I could have made his life easier . . . oh, God, if only he had told me . . ."

"He's been suffering a long time, Shadow. If he doesn't make it, it will be a blessing."

"Oh, God, how could I have been so blind? I should have seen it," she sobbed.

"He kept it well hidden from everyone," he said, patting her on the shoulder. "I'm glad you have Josh now. He'll take care of you. That's what Noble had hoped for all along."

"I don't need taking care of," she shouted. "My grandfather is the one who needs help. My God, there must be something you can do— No, I'll get Martha . . . she can help," Shadow said jumping up. "I know Martha can help him like she helped Josh," she exclaimed, running from the room.

"Shadow, where are you going?" Josh asked as he stood outside Noble's door.

"I've got to find Martha—"

"I'm sorry, Josh," Dr. Morgan said, seeing the concerned look on his face. "I didn't see any other way but to tell her straight out."

"Is it that bad?" Josh asked.

"It's his heart. He's known about it for a long time, but he wouldn't change his way of living. I told him months ago to stop drinking and smoking. I'm afraid it's finally caught up with him."

"You don't mean he's going to die. . . ."

"I'm afraid that's exactly what I mean, Josh. This last attack took all the strength he had. His pulse is so weak I can barely find it."

"Jesus," Josh hissed, running his hand through his hair. "I had no idea it was this bad. There was

325

no warning."

"No warning that you've seen," Doc said. "I've seen it coming for a long time. Shadow thinks Martha can help him since she helped you, but there's a big difference between having a high fever and your heart giving out."

Josh looked down at Noble's pale figure. Even in sleep his face was contorted in pain. He had always seemed like such a strong man, Josh thought, but now he looked so weak and helpless. His heart ached for the old man he had come to love and respect.

"Isn't there something we can do to ease his pain?"

"I've given him laudanum. There's really nothing else to do but wait."

Martha knew there wasn't anything she could do to help, but to pacify Shadow, she tried giving him some of her herbs while Shadow paced the room. "Child, come with me and have a cup of tea," Martha said after administering what she could of her herbal medicine.

"Go on, Shadow. I'll sit with your grandfather," Josh said.

Shadow's shoulders slumped in weariness. "No, I can't leave him," she said in a shaky voice.

A few minutes later Noble opened his eyes and

smiled at Shadow and Josh. "I didn't mean it to happen like this," he whispered, barely able to find the strength to speak.

Shadow sat on the side of the bed, holding her grandfather's hand, while Josh stood at the foot of the bed.

"Please, just rest, Grandfather. Martha has given you some medicine to make you better."

Noble smiled at his granddaughter. "I'm going to join my family now, Shadow, but I'm ready."

"Please don't say that, Grandfather. I couldn't bear it if you left me."

"You have Josh now. He'll take care of you—" Noble clutched her hand as a spasm of pain clutched him. He looked at Josh with pain-filled, glassy eyes. "It wasn't such a bad deal, was it, my friend."

Josh swallowed with difficulty, knowing that Noble must have forgotten that he told him he was marrying Shadow because he loved her. He saw the puzzled look on Shadow's face, but then she turned and concentrated on her grandfather. "Martha has gone to fix you some honey and brandy. That always makes you feel better."

"I love you, my little Shadow. You brightened my life when I needed it most. Now promise me no mourning clothes. Only bright colors for my Shadow. . . ." Noble closed his eyes and took his last ragged breath.

"Grandfather," Shadow cried, shaking him. "Please, Grandfather, wake up," she pleaded as tears rolled down her face. "No," she wailed, rocking back and forth on the bed. "He can't be gone. . . ."

Josh sat next to her and held her. "I'm so sorry, darling." He stroked her hair. "Just remember he won't have any more pain, he said, trying to comfort her, "and he's gone to join those loved ones who've gone before him."

By the next morning word had spread throughout Natchez that Noble Lansing had died, and friends flocked to offer their sympathy and help.

Allen Middleton was one of those people, catching Shadow alone for a few minutes while Josh was involved in making arrangements for Noble's burial.

"I'm worried about you," he said, leading her to the front porch. "Josh Rawlings will take everything you have now, and there's nothing you can do about it."

Shadow wasn't sure she heard him right. The doctor had given her something to calm her nerves, and she felt dizzy and disoriented. "I'm sorry, Allen. What did you say?"

"Rawlings married you for your money and to get his hands on Lansing Creek, Shadow. I think

Noble had become senile. He made some kind of deal with him to marry you. Rawlings must have known your grandfather was ill, and he convinced him he'd take care of you."

"That couldn't be true," she defended her husband, but her grandfather's last words kept ringing in her brain. *It wasn't such a bad deal . . .*

"I'm afraid it is true, Shadow, but maybe it isn't too late to help you."

Shadow wasn't listening to him. "Thank you for coming, Allen. You will be there tomorrow morning for the funeral service, won't you?"

"Of course, my dear. I'll be there whenever you need me. You know that, but we need to talk soon—"

"Yes . . . we'll talk soon." She fumbled with the doorknob, trying to get back inside, trying to get to the quiet and peace of her room where she could think.

"Darling, are you all right?" Josh asked as he met her in the hallway.

"I need to lie down for a little while," she said, hurrying past him.

Josh attributed her state to grief, and went on handling the affairs of the funeral. When he went to their room later, he found Shadow staring at herself in the mirror and talking to herself. He decided the laudanum must be having a strange effect on her because she acted like she was drunk.

329

"I'm not so bad looking." She weaved away from the mirror. "He shouldn't have had to make any deals. . . ."

"What are you talking about, love?" He asked, crossing the room to comfort her.

"Stay away from me." She moved out of his reach, placing the bed between them. "You must be very pleased with yourself," she said, tears running down her face. "I'd be willing to wager you got Lansing Creek much sooner than you expected."

Remembering Noble's words, Josh could just imagine what Shadow was thinking. "I know you are grief stricken now, Shadow, but don't say anything you will regret."

Shadow laughed bitterly. "You made a deal with my grandfather, and you tell me not to say anything I'll regret."

Again Josh tried to get near her. "I made no deals with your grandfather, love. At one time he mentioned that if I married you Lansing Creek would be mine. I told him I was marrying you because I loved you."

"Liar," she screamed. "You don't love me. Everybody tried to warn me, but I wouldn't listen," she continued hysterically. "All you wanted was Lansing Creek. I remember you saying you didn't ever want to be poor again . . . and you probably lied about being a spy—"

"Shadow, your grandfather wasn't in any condition to know what he was talking about at the end, and you know it. I explained to you about the spying."

"I hate you, Josh Rawlings. I want you out of my room," she cried. "I want you out of my house."

"Shadow, you have to listen to me. . . ." He grabbed her by the wrist and pulled her against him. "I love you, Shadow. Don't do this to us."

"Leave me alone," she sobbed. "You're a money-hungry bastard, a double-crossing trickster. You and Rose Jardine were probably in this together." Her voice rose hysterically. "Do you plan to throw me out and sell Lansing Creek for a quick profit?"

Josh's teeth made a gritting sound as he tried to control his temper. He was genuinely shocked that she could think him capable of making a deal to marry her, yet he was determined that she trust and believe in him without knowing his worth.

"We will talk after the funeral tomorrow," he said, leaving her sobbing in her room.

Josh opened the door and came face to face with Martha, her hand raised ready to knock. "Mr. Josh, your brother is here," Martha said, glancing into the room. "Is she all right?" she whispered, having heard them arguing.

"She's overcome with grief," Josh said, his voice trembling. "Maybe you better go to her. I'll stay in one of the guest rooms tonight."

331

The next day Noble Lansing was buried in the small plot where his wife, son and daughter-in-law were buried. It was a cool blustery day, and Shadow clutched her black cape around her as if it would help keep the cruel world away. Josh stood beside her, but she hadn't spoken to him since their argument the day before. There had been too many people around that morning to bring the subject up, particularly with Shadow walking such a fine line of emotion over her grandfather's death.

He studied his wife, wishing there were something he could do to comfort her. She was so pale, and her eyes were red and swollen from crying. Patience would be best, he told himself—until she gave her arm to Allen Middleton, who stood on her left as the ceremony ended. He started after her, but Matt stopped him.

"Not here, Josh. She's in shock, and any argument now will only make her hysterical."

Josh watched his wife lean on Middleton's shoulder as they walked back toward the house. "I can't believe this," he hissed between gritted teeth. "Three days ago we pledged undying love to each other."

"You could clear this whole misunderstanding up just by telling her the truth, Josh. Tell her you don't need her money," Matt encouraged.

"I'll be damned if I will," Josh swore. "She

should have a little faith. I'm her husband, for better or worse, and when she realizes that, she can come looking for me. In the meantime, I'm going back to Yancey's," he said angrily before striding off toward the stables.

Oh God! Oh God! That it were possible
To undo things done; to call back
yesterday!

— Thomas Heywood

Chapter Nineteen

When Josh returned to Yancey's, he was told by
the bartender that Mandy was packing to leave. He
knocked on her door, then entered.

"What's going on, Mandy?"

"Matt said you would be selling the place," she
said nervously. "I thought I better move on and
find another job."

"Why don't you tell me the real reason you're
leaving in such a hurry?"

Mandy stared at Josh. "I don't understand . . ."

"I think you do."

"Please don't do this, Josh," she said, throwing
clothes in her satchel.

Josh grabbed her by the wrist and pulled her around to face him. "I was nearly killed by three men who knew exactly where I would be."

Mandy forced the tears. "I didn't know they'd do that . . . he sent me to keep an eye on your activities . . . I needed the money, Josh. I had no idea he'd hurt you. . . ."

"I assume *he* is Allen Middleton."

"Yes." She dabbed at her tears. "Please, Josh, let me go. If Allen finds out that I told you, he'll kill me."

"Where are you going?" he asked.

"I'm leaving on the steamer this evening. I may not get off until I reach St. Louis."

Josh headed for the door, then turned around. "You have a good voice, Mandy. If you'd stay away from men like Allen Middleton, you could go places with it."

She nodded her head, realizing how lucky she was that Josh Rawlings hadn't killed her. If Allen knew she had betrayed him, she wouldn't be so lucky.

Josh headed back to the bar and poured himself a drink. He needed to set up a meeting with Will Gregory, then he'd deal with Allen Middleton. He downed his drink, thinking of Shadow. Would she come to her senses, he wondered.

"Did you talk to Mandy?" Matt asked as he joined his brother at the bar.

"She's leaving on the steamer this evening."

Matt studied the grim expression on his brother's face. "There must be something else. I'm sure you're not disappointed that she's leaving. I always had the feeling you didn't care for her."

"I never trusted her, and for good reason. She's been working for Allen Middleton. She just confirmed my suspicions that he is the leader of the group preaching disunion. The bastards are not beyond putting hoods on their heads and killing innocent people to get their point across."

Mandy had opened her door to leave when she heard Matt and Josh talking. She stepped back inside to listen.

"What are you going to do about it?" Matt asked.

"I'm going to see Gregory tomorrow night, then I'll deal with Middleton," Josh growled. "Get the wheels moving on selling this place. I'm suddenly sick to death of Natchez."

"Don't do anything in haste, Josh. When Shadow calms down, she'll realize she was wrong."

Josh downed his glass of whiskey. "Damn all women!" He slammed the glass down on the bar. He closed his eyes, remembering the way Shadow had clung to Allen Middleton for comfort. "How could she, Matt? How could she have turned to him?"

"Josh, tell her you don't need her money," Matt

pleaded, laying a hand on his brother's shoulder. "It would be so simple to clear this whole misunderstanding up."

"No! If she loved me, she wouldn't believe I could be capable of such a thing," he said, grabbing a bottle of whiskey from behind the bar. "I don't want to be disturbed," he said, heading for his room.

Mandy smiled. With this information she might never have to work again.

The morning light streamed across Shadow's bed. She awoke in a fog of laudanum-induced sleep, a dull pounding in her head. Her eyes felt as if there were grains of sand in them from crying so much. She turned over and buried her face in her pillow, wishing she could forget the past two days. *Oh God, how could he have betrayed me,* she wondered in anguish. *I thought he loved me.*

She started at the sound of Martha's voice. "The world ain't gonna go away, child. You need to git up and straighten your life out."

"You know nothing about it," Shadow snapped as she sat up.

"I know youse making a big mistake. Dat nice Mr. Josh loves you."

"He doesn't love me. He made a deal with my grandfather. Don't you understand, the two people

338

I loved the most betrayed me," she cried.

"I understand you think they betrayed you, but they did no such thing. You let your grief cloud your good judgment, child, and youse better do something 'bout it before it's too late."

"I don't need your sermons," Shadow said, throwing the pillow off the bed in a temper. "Just leave me alone!"

Martha picked up the pillow and placed it back on the bed. "You gonna be *all* alone if you're not careful," she said before turning to leave, "and you better not let dat Mr. Middleton give you any more of dat medicine."

Shadow leaned back against the bed, holding her head. She vaguely remembered Allen insisting she take something before he left her yesterday. God, she couldn't remember anything else, though.

Shadow swung her feet off the bed, but found it difficult to stand up. Martha was right about one thing, she thought. She wouldn't take any more medicine. She had some very important decisions to make, and she needed a clear mind to do it.

She would talk to Toby. That always helped — Oh, no, Toby was gone, she remembered. He'd left for New Orleans with the Deverauxs the day after her wedding. God, how she'd miss him.

She took a tentative step away from the bed, but was too weak. "Damn," she swore. "Martha! I know you're out there. Come in here. I need you."

Martha opened the door and smiled. "You come to your senses yet, child?"

"I need some food and coffee," Shadow snapped, "and no more of your sermons."

Allen Middleton stood across the street from Yancey's waiting for Josh to leave for his meeting. This time he planned to handle getting rid of Rawlings himself. If the fools he'd sent to kill the bastard the last time had done their job, he would already own Lansing Creek and Shadow.

He straightened away from the post he leaned on as he spotted Josh coming through the swinging doors. He was surprised when he crossed the street and walked along the river. This was going to be easier than he thought.

He fell into step behind Josh, staying in the shadows. He could have picked him off easily at that moment, but he wanted to get the man Rawlings had been passing information to at the same time.

Josh followed a path up a bluff overlooking the river and stopped at the top of the hill.

Allen could hear their low voices as he crept up behind a rock.

"I'm glad to see you are well," Gregory said. "You had me concerned. I'm really sorry it had to happen."

"I wish the hell I hadn't gotten involved with you and your cause," Josh said bitterly. "It's all been futile. There is going to be war, and there is nothing you or I can do about it."

"I know," Gregory agreed. "I really thought we could do something to stop it."

"There are too many people like Allen Middleton promoting war as the only way the South can survive."

"I'm afraid they are going to be in for a rude awakening," Gregory said.

Allen stood up, aiming his Colt revolver at Josh. He smiled as he pulled the trigger.

Shadow paced the gallery outside her bedroom, only the moonlight guiding her steps. The loneliness was too much to bear. Her grandfather gone, Toby in New Orleans, and Josh . . .

She clutched the railing, staring out into the darkness. There weren't even enough memories to last a lifetime. Two days of married life . . . two days of happiness.

She sighed into the silence. Did it really make a difference that her grandfather had picked Josh, and even sweetened the deal. She was sure he had feelings for her—and she loved him. If he wanted Lansing Creek, then he would just have to take her with it. She was his wife, and tomorrow she would go to Yancey's and tell him how she felt.

Suddenly a cold wind blew off the river. Icy fingers gripped her heart, and she began to tremble. Something was wrong. She backed into her room, fear gripping her. She was letting her grief make her crazy, she told herself, pulling the quilt off the bed to wrap around her while she waited for morning.

Allen downed his cognac in a single gulp. He had done it; he'd gotten rid of Josh Rawlings and the man he was spying for. He gave a restless glance around his library, finding it difficult to remain there until news came of Josh's death.

He laughed aloud as he thought of his deed. The bastard wouldn't cross him again, he thought smugly as he poured himself another drink. He took out his watch and checked the time. Three o'clock. It would be a long time before he could ride to Lansing Creek without looking suspicious. Hell, what was his hurry, he thought as he settled in a comfortable chair before the fire. Everything would be his now.

Will Gregory crawled to his knees and stared over the cliff where Josh had fallen after being shot. Blood dripped in his eyes from a wound in the head, but he knew he had to get to Matt. He had to tell someone what happened before he bled to death, he thought struggling to his feet. He didn't know how long he'd been unconscious, but the sky was beginning to get light. The bastard that had shot them was probably long gone, he thought bitterly.

When Shadow entered Yancey's, Matt was coming from Josh's room. He froze in his tracks, his face as white as his shirt. "Shadow, I was just getting ready to ride out to see you."

"I have to talk to Josh," she said, walking toward Josh's room.

"Shadow, sit down," Matt said, grabbing her by the arm.

"What's wrong?" she asked, panic in her eyes.

"Please, sit down," he said softly.

"He's been hurt. I knew it," tears glistened in her eyes. "I felt it during the night."

"Shadow, Josh is dead."

"Josh," she whispered. "No . . . no," she began to sob. "He can't be." She shook her head violently, as if denying it would keep it from being true. "I have to talk to Josh." She tried pulling away from Matt. "I have to straighten things out between us. I wasn't fair to Josh."

"Shadow, stop it!" Matt pulled her around to

343

face him. "I know how hard this is to accept, but there's a man lying in Josh's room right now who was with him. Just before he was shot, he saw Josh take a bullet in the chest, before falling over the bluffs into the river."

"Oh, God." Shadow slumped against him.

"I'm so sorry, Shadow," he said, stroking her hair. "I feel the same pain. Josh and I were so close. I really thought he was invincible."

"I came to tell him it didn't matter why he married me. I wanted to tell him that I loved him. Oh, God, Matt, this couldn't be happening. He died thinking I hated him," she sobbed.

"He never thought that, Shadow." He lifted her face to look into her eyes. "He blamed the misunderstanding on your grief."

"I've lost everyone," she said, a dazed look in her eyes. "Everyone I cared for . . ."

"Let me take you home now, Shadow."

"No, I have my horse." She stumbled away from him toward the door.

Matt took her by the arm. "I'll get a carriage, and your horse can follow behind."

Shadow was too stunned to argue. She let Matt lead her to the stables where he rented a carriage. Then she rode silently beside him back to Lansing Creek.

"May I stay for a while," he asked as he helped Shadow from the carriage.

344

"Yes," she answered, but Matt wondered if she even knew what he had asked.

Josh is dead! Agony tore through her. He couldn't be. Not Josh. Not her husband, too. She suddenly swayed with the grief, and strong arms picked her up, carrying her up the stairs.

"Martha, get something strong for her to drink," Matt ordered. "She's had another terrible shock."

"Oh, Lordie, what's happened to her now?" Martha wrung her hands.

"Josh has been killed," he said, laying Shadow on the settee.

"Josh has been killed," Shadow repeated, staring into space.

"Oh, child." Martha knelt beside Shadow, smoothing back her hair. "My poor baby can't take much more," she cried. She looked up at Matt, who fought back tears himself. "She was gonna make things right with him. Dats why she went into Yancey's."

"I know." He sighed. "Josh was killed sometime after midnight."

"Lordie, Lordie," Martha moaned. "Mr. Noble wanted her to have someone . . . someone good and loving . . . dat's all he wanted for her. . . ."

"Martha, can you handle her all right. I should get back to Yancey's. Someone who is interested in buying the place is supposed to come by this afternoon."

345

"You will come back?" Martha asked, hoping he could help Shadow.

"Yes, I'll be back tomorrow. If you need me before then, just send someone for me."

Shortly after Matt left, Shadow brought herself under control, refusing to take anything to calm her nerves. "Josh would expect me to be in control," she said, straightening her black dress. "Please ask all our people to meet with me on the front lawn in fifteen minutes," she instructed Martha.

Everyone milled around on the lawn, feeling the loss of Noble Lansing and their young mistress's husband.

Shadow stepped out on the porch, forcing a smile. "Thank you for coming so quickly," she said. "In memory of my grandfather and husband—" she took a deep breath, naked, uncontrollable pain on her face—"I will start drawing up papers with my lawyer tomorrow to give each of you your freedom."

There was an audible gasp from the group as a whole.

"I don't want to let my grandfather or Josh down by letting Lansing Creek fall apart," she continued. "So I hope you will all stay and help me. I will give each of you a parcel of land and enough

346

seeds for your own crop. Then, whoever helps me plant and harvest the cotton crop next year will share in the profits of that. This is all I can offer you for now," she said, tears in her eyes. "My grandfather loved you all and considered you family."

They filed past her, shaking her hand and offering sympathy for her double loss.

"Our little Shadow has grown up," Tilly said, wiping a tear from her cheek.

"De hard way," Martha agreed.

Everyone's attention was drawn to the horse and rider coming down the drive. "More trouble," Martha said in disgust as she recognized Allen Middleton.

Allen leaped off his horse and came running to Shadow. "My dear, I just heard," he said, taking her hands. "God, I can't believe it. First your grandfather and now your husband."

"Will you come inside for tea, Allen?"

He stared at her, deciding she must be in shock. "Yes, tea is certainly called for," he said, following her into the house.

"Please have a seat," Shadow instructed, sitting on the settee across from him. "Tilly will be here with tea in just a moment."

"What is going on with all your servants milling around on the front lawn?" he asked.

"I just gave them all their freedom," Shadow

answered calmly.

Allen came out of his chair in one quick movement. "Their freedom? Are you out of your mind, Shadow. My God, you can't do that," he screamed at her.

"Don't tell me what I can and can't do. Lansing Creek belongs to me, and I'll run it the way I see fit."

Allen forced a patient smile. "We can correct this situation when you are feeling better, my dear. Grief does strange things to people." He lifted her hand and patted it.

"Don't be condescending to me, Allen Middleton," she yanked her hand away. "I know exactly what I'm doing."

Allen realized he was making it worse by arguing with her. Once she tried to run Lansing Creek without a man around, she'd come crawling to him for help. "I'm just a few miles away," he smiled. "You can come to me whenever you need anything."

"Thank you, Allen, that's very kind of you, but I think we'll do just fine. I'm confident that most of my people will stay with me."

"You don't know these people very well," he laughed bitterly. "They'll run as soon as they have their papers. What makes it even worse is Lincoln was elected today. The black bastards will probably go to war against us."

348

"Enough!" Shadow turned on him. "If it wasn't for people like you, we wouldn't have to worry about a war."

"You sound just like your husband," he snarled.

"I hope so, because he didn't want to see the South go to war, and neither do I. Now if you don't mind, Allen, I'm very tired and I'd like to rest for a while."

"All right, Shadow. May I call on you later this week?" he asked, kissing her hand.

"If you like."

When Matt rode out to Lansing Creek, he was told by Martha that Shadow was at the stables.

"I'm glad to hear that. I was afraid I'd find her pining away in her room."

"She is hurting terribly, but she's making plans for de future," Martha said.

"That's the best way to deal with grief. Has she heard the news of the election?"

"Yes, Mr. Middleton was here earlier today."

"Was he?" Matt asked bitterly. "Well, I suppose he'd delighted to hear that war is inevitable now."

"He's a fool," Martha spat as they walked out onto the porch. "Dat's Mr. Josh's horse," she exclaimed, seeing the silver mare tied to the post.

"I thought Josh would want Shadow to have her."

349

Shadow stood at the fence, rubbing Rapscallion's nose. "It's just you and me, boy," she whispered. "Somehow we'll make it."

She gazed across the field, thinking about riding to her secret place along the river. No, she wasn't ready for that yet, she decided. She stroked the horse's nose, so lost in thought that she didn't hear Matt approach.

"I'm glad to see you out," he said behind her.

"Oh, Matt, you startled me."

"I'm sorry," he smiled. "I brought Gambler's Lady with me. I thought you'd like to have her."

"Gambler's Lady," she repeated, walking over to the horse. "We bred her to Rapscallion, you know," she said, stroking the horse's side. "I hope it took," she sniffed.

"It would be a very special horse," Matt said.

"Yes, it would," she agreed, taking a deep breath. "Tell me, Matt, is the man who was shot . . . is he going to make it?"

"I think so."

"I'm glad to hear that. I'd like to talk with him when he's better."

"Shadow, I think I have a buyer for Yancey's. If it goes through, I'm going back to California."

Shadow continued to rub the mare's nose. "I thought you would."

"There is something I need to tell you, but I didn't have the heart to tell you yesterday. Hell, maybe I wouldn't tell you at all if I didn't know that when Josh's lawyers finish going through his papers they'd be in touch with you."

"Matt, what are you talking about?"

"Josh was an extremely rich man, Shadow."

There is no greater sorrow
Than to be mindful of the happy time
In misery.

— Dante Alighieri

Chapter Twenty

Shadow leaned against the railing of the porch,
looking out over the muddy brown river. A light
mist was falling, adding to her depressed state. The
holidays would begin in a few weeks, holidays she
would most likely spend alone, unless she decided
to accept Camille's invitation to come to New Orleans.

Turning around, she walked back into the house,
thinking she had some time before planting season,
and she had to admit it would be wonderful to see
Camille and Toby. The only problem was she would
have to make the trip by steamboat alone. Martha
claimed she was too old to leave Lansing Creek,
and Tilly had just announced she was expecting her

first child.

A child, Shadow thought, feeling her own flat stomach. She had hoped she was pregnant, but she knew now she wasn't. It would have been nice to have had some part of Josh with her, she sighed.

She stared down at the papers on her desk — papers that Josh's lawyer had delivered. There had been so much she didn't know about her husband, she thought as she flipped the pages: gold, ships, lumber . . .

Why hadn't he told her, she wondered for the hundredth time. She tossed the papers back on the desk. She knew only too well why he hadn't told her. It was because he wanted her to have faith, and she had failed him.

Unconsciously she rubbed the sapphire and diamond pendant at her throat. It was supposed to have been a wedding present from Josh, but they had been so busy making love. It was only a few days ago that she had found the beautiful crystal music box and the necklace among his things. It was ironic, she thought. There had been a beautiful note telling her that he would love her until his dying day.

She poured herself a cup of tea and sat before the blazing fire. They would be in Europe now, she thought as she sipped the hot liquid. She leaned her head back and closed her eyes. Josh's sparkling smile came to mind, his amber eyes filled with mischief. "Oh Josh, I miss you so much. . . ."

She set her cup down and laced her fingers together as she stared into the fire. Matt had already gone back to California. He had been as devastated and lost as she was, she thought sadly. At least she had Allen. He had turned out to be a good friend when she needed him the most. At first she had objected to his daily visits, but after a while, she realized she looked forward to them, even though she had to put up with Martha's grumbling the entire time he was there.

She knew Allen still had notions about their marrying eventually, but she knew it would never be. She could never think of Allen as anything but a friend.

She closed her eyes and unconsciously compared the two men: Josh's strong, handsome features against the weaker features of Allen Middleton; Josh's blond curly hair opposed to Allen's lank, thinning hair; Josh's steady, amber eyes opposed to Allen's ice-blue eyes.

"Oh, God, what am I doing?" she said aloud, rubbing her temples. Cursing herself, she stood up, thumbing through the papers on her desk again. She needed to sign them and get them back to Mr. Davis, Josh's lawyer. She didn't know why she kept holding on to them.

"Miz Shadow, Mr. Middleton is here," Abraham announced.

"Please show him in," Shadow said.

"Hello, my dear. How are you on this miserable

355

day?" he asked, kissing her on the cheek.

"I'm well, but I was hoping you might come by for a game of chess. Please, sit down near the fire. It will take the chill off. Would you like a brandy?"

"That would be marvelous. Before I forget, Samuel Burton's plantation is being auctioned off next week."

"I had heard he died," Shadow said, handing him his drink. "I was sorry to hear it. It seems all the old-timers are gone."

"Yes, well, his overseer Lloyd Wicker will be looking for a position. I think he would work out very well for you."

"I'm not interested," she said, sitting down with her tea. "I've heard how he treats the blacks."

"He's only doing what is necessary, my dear. You're much too easy with your slaves."

"I don't have slaves, Allen," she corrected. "My people are free. They also have a stake in the crop now, so I don't think I'll need an overseer."

Allen took a sip of his brandy. "I'm afraid you'll sing a different tune when planting season comes."

"We'll have to wait and see, won't we?" she answered, sipping her tea. "I had a letter from Camille yesterday. She has invited me to come to New Orleans for the holidays."

Allen almost choked on his brandy. He couldn't let her leave now . . . not when things were going so well. She was starting to depend on him. . . .

"Surely you're not thinking of going. I mean the

weather—it isn't a good time to be traveling."

"I have to disagree. I have nothing but time on my hands at the moment. I think it would do me good to get away until after Christmas. By the time I come back, it will be time to start thinking about the planting. Yes, I'm very seriously considering it," she said more to herself than Allen. "I need to keep busy."

Allen was at a loss for words for a few moments. "You see, this is a perfect example of why you need an overseer. You have no one to leave in charge," he said, hoping to discourage her.

"Of course I do. Tilly's husband Jake is quite capable of running things for me," Shadow laughed, "and Abraham and Martha will see that the house runs smoothly."

"I don't like you doing this." Allen began to pace. "I thought we would spend the holidays together."

"I'm sorry, Allen," she said, becoming more determined by the minute. "Would you like to play a game of chess now?" she asked, changing the subject.

Allen's mind was in a turmoil. He was so close. What the hell was he going to do? Suddenly he stopped pacing. Perhaps if they were away from there . . . away from her memories.

"Shadow, if you insist on making this trip, then I will accompany you."

Shadow almost dropped her teacup. "That's very

kind of you, Allen, but I can't allow it. It wouldn't be proper."

"Since when did Shadow Lansing start worrying about what was proper," he laughed.

"Shadow Rawlings," she corrected, "and you are right, I don't usually worry about such things; but I would never want the Deverauxs to think . . . well, you know what I'm talking about."

"I will escort you until we reach New Orleans. Then I'll go about my own. We will accidentally meet while we're in the city, and then travel back together. You see, it's very simple, my dear. This way I will still get to spend the holidays with you. And of course we will have separate accommodations on the steamer. You could pretend we met while on board if you like."

Shadow studied her teacup. This would solve her problems. She was concerned about traveling alone. "Are you sure you can get away at this time?"

"Of course. As you said, this is our slow time."

It was settled. Shadow had to admit she felt excited about something for the first time in weeks. She just knew she'd feel better once she saw Camille and Toby again, and preparing for the trip would keep her mind off her grandfather and Josh.

On the morning the steamer was to leave, Martha was still grumbling about Allen Middleton escorting her.

"Please trust me, Martha. You know I would never do anything to bring shame on my grandfather's name."

"I knows you wouldn't, child, but dat doan mean Allen Middleton wouldn't."

"Everything will be just fine, Martha. Now stop worrying and give me a hug."

The old black woman hugged Shadow, tears in her eyes. "Ise gonna miss you."

"Will you change your mind?" Shadow asked hopefully. "Will you come with me?"

"Lordie, no." Martha shook her gray head. "Not me . . . no sir, not me on any boat on any river."

"All right," Shadow laughed. "Just see that things go smoothly here. I've talked to Luke about Gambler's Lady, but be sure he keeps a close eye on her. And he should exercise Rapscallion every day." Shadow noticed the smile on Martha's face. "I'm sorry, I've told you this a half dozen times already."

"A dozen times." Martha laughed.

"I should be back shortly after Christmas. If I decide to stay any longer, I'll send word."

"You can write us. We'll get Mr. Jerome to read it to us," Martha said.

"All right," Shadow said, a lump in her throat. She hugged Martha again. "Oh, God, I'm going to miss you. Have I ever told you how much I love you, Martha? How much I appreciate your being a mother to me after my own mother died?"

359

"I know, child, I know. I love you, too. Now git on your way before dat boat leaves without you."

Shadow climbed into the waiting carriage. "Don't forget to have a wonderful celebration during the holidays," Shadow instructed. "Spare no expense to make it special. I'll bring back presents for everyone," she waved.

A holiday mood prevailed on the *Mississippi Lady* as she left the dock at Natchez Under the Hill. Shadow stood on the deck, listening to the sweet music of the steamboat whistle. She was already settled in her beautiful cabin, but she hadn't seen Allen yet. Just as well, she thought. She didn't want anyone to think they had come aboard together.

Everyone seemed very congenial. In the first thirty minutes aboard, she had made the acquaintance of several lovely couples. When the air became too cool, Shadow descended the gingerbread decorated stairway to the main salon. She stared in awe at the elaborate room. In spite of more than fifty people milling around, the room was so large it seemed empty. Intricate hand-carved moldings encrusted the walls and ceilings, and a row of huge crystal chandeliers hung over the emerald-green carpeted floors.

"What do you think of our *Lady*, Mrs. Rawlings?" the captain asked.

360

"She is beautiful, Captain Sinclair. I never imagined she would be so elegant."

"I think you will enjoy the trip to New Orleans. We have an excellent chef aboard."

"I'm sure I will," Shadow smiled.

"Ah, Captain Sinclair. I wanted to compliment you on the beauty of the *Mississippi Lady*." Allen Middleton offered his hand to the captain.

"Thank you, sir. It is Mr. Middleton, isn't it?"

"Yes, you have a remarkable memory for names, Captain."

"I pride myself on that," the captain smiled. "Have you met Mrs. Rawlings?" he asked, just as Allen had assumed he would.

"No, I haven't had the pleasure." He kissed her hand. "Is your husband aboard, madam. Perhaps he would be interested in a few hands of cards."

Shadow had been momentarily stunned by his question. "No. No, I'm a widow."

"I'm sorry to hear that. I'm also traveling alone, Mrs. Rawlings. Perhaps we could dine together."

Shadow felt the heat rise to her face. She didn't like deceiving people, even people she didn't know.

"Yes, perhaps we can. If you will excuse me," she said, hurrying off toward her cabin.

Shadow entered her cabin, sighing as she leaned against the door. Why had she let him come along? She already felt nervous and apprehensive about the charade, and the trip was just beginning.

Seeing her trunk in the corner, Shadow decided

to hang some of her clothing in the wardrobe. She had deferred to her grandfather's wishes that she not wear mourning clothes, but she had chosen dark dresses: browns, deep greens and dark blues. All were colors that highlighted her ivory skin and strawberry-blond hair, but Shadow was unaware of that.

The evening meal was formal, and the setting was sumptuous elegance. Sterling flatware and china that bore the ship's monogram gleamed on Irish linen tableclothes. The best wines and champagnes were served in beautiful crystal goblets. The stewards were all Negroes, and they moved through the dining room quietly and efficiently.

Shadow thought again of the trip she and Josh had planned to Europe. She glanced at Allen Middleton across the table from her and forced a smile. Why couldn't it be Josh with her, she wondered bitterly.

Shadow had just dipped her spoon in a steaming bowl of chowder when the woman next to her spoke.

"I understand you and Mr. Middleton are both from Natchez?" the gray-haired woman said.

"Yes," Shadow acknowledged.

"I had met Mrs. Rawlings' late husband several times," Allen interrupted, "but unfortunately I had never met the lovely Mrs. Rawlings until now."

"Aren't you fortunate to have found someone else traveling alone," the woman said with a knowing smile on her face, "and someone from Natchez at that."

"Yes, I am." Shadow's flush deepened until her cheeks were tinted a deep rose. Lowering her head, she made a determined effort to concentrate on her food.

The food was excellent, but Shadow barely ate. She wasn't good at lying, and this lie was making it look like something was going on between her and Allen instead of protecting her reputation. The worst part was, she had a feeling Allen knew that and was taking pleasure in adding fuel to the gossip.

"Will you be joining us for a few hands of cards, Mr. Middleton?" one of the gentleman asked.

"A card game," he rubbed his hands together. "That sounds very interesting. Perhaps I will after I enjoy my stroll around the deck with Mrs. Rawlings."

Damn him, Shadow gritted her teeth. "I don't believe I'll take that stroll, Mr. Middleton. I'm afraid I'm quite tired, and I plan to retire early."

"Are you sure, my dear?" he asked.

"I am positive." She glared at him.

Shadow collapsed into one of the plush chairs in her cabin. Maybe she'd just stay right there the rest of the trip, she decided as she noticed a bowl of fruit and a pot of tea had been left for her to enjoy. She certainly couldn't take much more of the embarrassing questions she had had to put up with this evening. At least it wasn't a long trip, she sighed. As for Allen Middleton, she would straighten him out good and proper in the morning.

Shadow stepped out of her dress and underwear, then washed in the warm water left in a porcelain basin. After drying, she slipped a soft, white cotton nightgown over her head.

It's been a long day, she thought as she slipped between the sheets.

Shadow dozed off without any trouble, waking only when she realized the steamer was stopping. She turned over and pulled the blanket higher, remembering that the captain had said they would be stopping in St. Francisville during the night, but would make up the time.

Allen was pleased with the arrangements he had been able to make before boarding the steamer. Shadow's cabin was directly across from his, and they were in the aft section where they had considerable more privacy than up forward.

He removed his jacket and freshened up, whistling a little tune as he thought about the night ahead. She would put up a fight, but once he had a chance to tame her . . .

Shadow pulled the pillow over her head. What

was going on now, she wondered, hearing the annoying sound in her sleep. She could tell the steamer was moving swiftly through the night; perhaps it was the paddle wheel knocking. Suddenly she sat up, realizing someone was knocking on her door.

She hadn't laid her robe out, so she stumbled to the door in only her nightgown. "Yes, who is it?" she asked, lighting a lamp.

"It's me, Shadow. I must talk with you."

Shadow cracked the door open. "Allen? What's wrong?" she asked rubbing her eyes.

"I need your help," he said, pushing past her.

Shadow closed the door, thinking only of her friend's problem. "What is it, Allen. What has happened?"

Allen turned toward her and smiled. "I need you, Shadow."

She stared at him in disbelief. "What in the world are you talking about?"

"You know I love you. I can't bear to be this close without holding you in my arms. No one on board has to know."

"Get out, Allen!"

"Now, my dear, there is no harm in us enjoying each other tonight. I plan to marry you, so it isn't like—"

"You plan to marry me?" she screamed in disbelief. "How dare you assume I will just fall in your arms. I thought you were my friend. I trusted you."

"Dammit, Shadow, don't act so high and mighty with me. You're a widow. You know the facts of life."

Shadow opened the door of her cabin. "Get out before I scream rape," she said between gritted teeth.

Suddenly there was a tremendous explosion that rocked the entire ship. Shadow had been thrown back into the room. As she tried to get to her feet another explosion followed, this time sending timbers and debris falling down around them.

"We've got to get out of here," Allen shouted. "The boilers have blown." He looked down at Shadow and found her pinned beneath debris. "Jesus! Shadow, get up. We've got to get out of here," he screamed.

"I can't, Allen. Help me. Try to lift this timber off me, please."

Hearing the screams of people all over the ship, Allen panicked and ran from the cabin.

"Allen, help me!" Shadow screamed.

She struggled against the weight on her legs, trying with every ounce of strength to lift the timber that trapped her. "Oh, God, help me," she cried. Smoke began to stream into the cabin, choking her as she continued to struggle against the weight holding her. Finally, her strength sapped, she leaned back, gasping for breath. She was going to die, she thought as she shivered. She would be joining her grandfather, her mother and father, and Josh. "Josh," she cried out in pain.

Suddenly a figure, larger than life, appeared in the doorway. He was silhouetted by smoke and flames, and Shadow wasn't sure if she was imagining him.

"Shadow, where are you?"

"I'm here, near the bed. Please help me," she cried. I'm trapped beneath the timbers."

She stared in disbelief as Josh lifted the timbers and picked her up. "Josh . . . have I died? she asked.

"You haven't died," he said, picking his way through the timbers and planks that were strewn everywhere. When they reached the main cabin, Shadow gasped, seeing the passengers sprawled dead from scalding steam.

"Do you have any feeling in your legs?" he asked as they reached the deck.

"Some pain," she answered, still unable to believe he was there. "Josh, how did you get here?"

"We'll probably have to swim," he said, ignoring her question.

The lifeboats were already filled, but people still jumped overboard, hanging on to the boats and anything else they could find in the cold water.

Shadow looked around, unable to believe the carnage on the deck. Less than thirty minutes had passed since the first boiler exploded, and already most of those aboard the *Mississippi Lady* were

367

dead: drowned, scalded to death, or crushed by falling masts and timbers.

"No matter what happens, don't let go of me," he ordered. One minute they were standing on the bow, the next they hit the cold water. They were going down, down. Shadow felt as if her lungs were going to burst, but she didn't release her hold on Josh, even though she knew the weight of the two of them was probably pulling them down. Suddenly their descent stopped . . . they were going back up. She felt Josh kicking his feet and tried to do the same. She gasped for air when they finally came to the surface.

"Lie back and try to float for a minute," he ordered. "You're going to need your strength."

"I'm all right." she panted. "I can't believe you're here," she said with a sob. "How did you find me?"

"Don't talk," he said.

Shadow floated on her back, her hand clasping Josh's hand. She could still hear the wails and cries of people around them, people who were helpless and lost as to what to do.

"We are not far from land," Josh shouted to anyone who could hear him. "Grab hold of anything in the water and start kicking toward shore."

There was a murmur of voices, then Shadow could hear water splashing. "Is that true, Josh? Are we close to shore?"

Josh grabbed a piece of planking that floated by.

"Not as close as I'd like to be. Hang on to this. I'll do the kicking."

Shadow did as he ordered, wondering why he sounded so cold. Was he still angry that she hadn't had faith in him. She closed her eyes and sniffed back a tear. At least now she would have a chance to explain. Oh God, he was alive . . .

Love conquers all things;
let us too surrender to Love.

— Virgil

Chapter Twenty-one

Shadow didn't know how it happened, but after they had safely reached the shore they had become separated. As they struggled out of the water they found Allen's body washed up on shore. She had looked up at Josh, expecting some words of sympathy, even though she knew Allen had left her to die. But Josh's words had shocked her. *If he hadn't died, I would have killed the bastard,* he had growled.

They immediately became involved in helping the survivors, and then flat boats had come to take them the rest of the way to New Orleans. She had searched everywhere for Josh, but to no avail. As she was helped aboard the boat, she even wondered

371

if she had imagined him being there.

Camille's family was waiting in New Orleans for her. They had heard of the disaster and that the survivors were being brought down the river in flatboats and had waited all night and part of the next day for news. Shadow had become hysterical when she saw them.

When she kept asking if they had seen Josh, they assumed she was in shock. It had taken hours before she convinced them what she said was true. Josh was alive. He had saved her from a sure death on the burning ship.

Now she waited while Toby tried to find him — waited and prayed that she would find him before he went back to California.

Shadow lifted the lace curtain and stared out the window of the Deverauxs' brick house on Royal Street. She watched people strolling along the brick sidewalks. It was a beautiful day in November, yet she felt a depression like she had never known before. She could hardly breathe, it weighed so heavily on her. He was alive, only to disappear from her life again.

She had asked Toby to leave word with the steamship line where she would be if Josh should be looking for her, but Shadow knew he was aware that the Deverauxs lived in the city. It would be natural for him to look for her there — if he wanted to find her.

Why hadn't he stayed with her? she wondered with a heavy heart. She sighed, moving away from the window. Curling up in a chair, she stared into the fire with hot, dry eyes. She would not cry. She had to be strong and work this thing out.

Hearing voices in the foyer, she rushed from the room, hoping to find Josh. Instead Toby was talking with Camille.

"Did you find him, Toby?"

Toby took her by the hand and led her back into the sitting room. "I know where he is, Shadow, but he won't see you."

"Won't see me!" she exclaimed. "Surely he isn't still angry because I thought he married me for my money. . . ."

"I'm afraid it's a little more than that, Shadow. Why don't you sit down and I'll try to explain."

"I don't want to sit down," she said, pacing. "I want to know why my husband won't see me," she insisted, fighting back the tears.

Toby sighed, finding it very difficult to explain Josh's motives, when he didn't understand them himself.

"Josh thinks you betrayed him to Allen Middleton, Shadow. He thinks you told Middleton that he was meeting with Will Gregory on that Tuesday night he was shot."

Shadow looked bewildered. "Told Middleton . . . I don't understand. What do you mean betrayed him to Allen."

"It was Allen who shot him, Shadow."

"Oh, my God." Her hand went to her mouth.

"Rose Jardine admitted that she begged Middleton to help her end your marriage, but she was horrified when she learned Josh had been killed. Her conscience finally got the better of her, and she went to the authorities."

"Rose Jardine," Shadow snorted. "Is that who he's been with all this time?"

"You know better than that, Shadow," he said patiently.

"Yes, I suppose I do," she sighed. "But what I don't understand is why Allen would want to kill Josh."

"There were several reasons. He knew Josh was spying for Washington, and he wanted you and Lansing Creek. I suppose he thought with Josh out of the way he would have everything."

Shadow shook her head in disbelief. "How could Josh think I had anything to do with it? I love him," she cried.

"Josh was just lucky Middleton was a poor shot. He took the bullet in the shoulder and fell into the river. Luckily an old fisherman downstream pulled him out of the water and saved his life. It was a touch and go for quite a while, but when he was well enough, he made his way back to Natchez to find his assailants. Instead he found that Matt was gone, and you had left on a steamer for New Orleans with Allen Middleton. I suppose it was only natural that he came to the conclusion he did."

"But he was on the ship," Shadow interrupted. "He must have come for me."

Toby poured both of them a drink and handed one to her.

"I don't want this."

"I think you better drink it. There's more."

"What could be worse than what you've already told me?" she asked impatiently.

"Josh boarded in St. Francisville with the intention of killing Allen Middleton . . . and you."

Shadow whirled away from Toby, holding her arms tightly around her body. "Oh, God," she moaned. "How could he . . . how could he think I'd want to see him dead . . . how could he want to kill me?"

Toby put his arms around Shadow. "I told him he was wrong, Shadow. I told him that you and Allen weren't really traveling together, but he insisted he confronted Allen coming out of your cabin."

"He did," Shadow sighed, leaning against Toby's shoulder. "But it wasn't what he thought. Josh is the only man I've ever loved."

"I'm so sorry, Shadow. He's a good man, but he's the most stubborn, hardheaded individual I've ever met. I felt like I was pleading with a stone wall."

"I know. Thank you for your help, Toby."

"I had promised Josh I'd never tell anyone, but I feel I have to tell you, Shadow. Josh is the one who set me up in business and gave me a house on Chartres Street."

Shadow stared at her friend. "Josh did that. But

375

why?"

"He did it because we were your friends, even though he didn't want you to know. He said it wasn't fair that Camille and I couldn't marry just because I didn't have any money."

Shadow leaned her head against his shoulder and cried. After a few minutes, she calmed down. "I'm sorry, Toby. I suppose that's been coming for days." She sniffed into Toby's handkerchief.

"I've always heard a good cry would help," he smiled sympathetically. "What will you do now, Shadow?"

"I don't know. I think it would probably be best if I go back to Lansing Creek. The mood I'm in, I'd just ruin the holidays for everyone."

"I wish you'd stay, Shadow. Camille and I can help you."

"I don't think anyone can help me, Toby."

All Shadow's clothes had been lost in the explosion, so she had to arrange for several dresses to be made before she could make the trip back to Natchez. While she had a few days before leaving, she and Camille shopped for Christmas presents for her to take back home, but her heart just wasn't in the spirit of things. She should have enjoyed her first visit to this exciting city of sights, sounds and smells, but she couldn't. She couldn't get rid of the heavy melancholy that hung over her.

On the morning of the afternoon she was to

leave, Shadow paced her room, feeling as if she could scream. She had to do something. She had to make some attempt at talking with Josh before giving up completely.

She rushed down the stairs and interrupted Mr. Deveraux's breakfast. "Where can I find Toby?" she asked breathlessly.

"His house is at 410 Chartres Street."

"How far is that from here?"

"Only a few blocks. Can I take you there, dear?"

"No, thank you. I have some business to take care of, but I'll be back shortly."

Shadow had no idea that Josh would be at the house on Chartres Street. Her hope had been that Toby would tell her where Josh was staying. She knocked on the door, expecting Toby to answer. Instead she stared into the amber eyes of her husband. He looked so handsome it took her breath away.

Josh stared at his wife, dressed in a sapphire-blue velvet cape and a matching hat. She looked thin and tired, but she was still the most beautiful woman he'd ever seen.

"We have to talk," she said, pushing her way past him.

"I don't think we have anything to say to each other," he said, following her into the library.

"Have you been here all along?" she asked, confused.

"Is that what you came to ask me?"

"No," she replied, removing her gloves, trying to keep her hands from trembling. "I came to ask you how you could possibly think I had anything to do with shooting you."

"Don't make me laugh," he said, walking over to the desk and pouring himself a drink. "You were the only one besides Matt who knew I met Gregory on Tuesday nights."

"And that makes me a murderer?" she asked in disbelief.

"A murderer no, since I'm still alive, but certainly my prime suspect," he said coldly. "Particularly since you and Middleton became so chummy before I was even out of the house."

Her eyes widened in shock. "Allen was nothing more than a friend to me, though I have to admit, I was a poor judge of character, since he left me to die."

Josh laughed bitterly. "That's putting it mildly, my love."

He had said my love, but there was nothing but cold contempt in his voice.

"I'm a very busy man, Shadow. I'm leaving for California today, so I'd appreciate it if you'd get to the point of why you came here."

Shadow couldn't bear the hatred in his voice. He really believed she tried to kill him, and he was leaving her for good. They would be miles apart, never to see each other again . . .

"Why did you save me when the boat exploded?"

she asked.

Her question caught him off guard. He'd been asking himself the same thing for days. "I don't know," he answered.

"You had come aboard to kill me, but you couldn't do it, Josh. You couldn't do it because you still love me."

"Don't flatter yourself, Shadow. I stopped loving you the day you walked away from your grandfather's grave on Allen Middleton's arm. At that moment I realized you were like all the others," he said bitterly. "You didn't give a damn about anyone or anything except yourself."

"That's not true," she pleaded, reaching out to touch him.

He shoved her hand away, knowing if he let her near him he'd be lost. "Of course it's true. You and Middleton didn't waste any time going off to celebrate, did you? A trip down the Mississippi to New Orleans. How cozy," he growled.

"It wasn't like that. I was coming here to visit Camille. Allen insisted on escorting me to protect me," Shadow tried to explain. "We were not sharing a cabin. Josh, please believe me. I had nothing to do with anyone shooting you. I didn't even know about it until I went to Yancey's to tell you I didn't care why you married me, that I still loved you."

"How magnanimous of you." He laughed bitterly.

"Josh, you must believe me." Her blue eyes

pleaded.

He had to turn away from her to stay firm. "Believe a cold-hearted bitch like you?" he asked, his voice thick with mockery.

Shadow stared at him in defeat. He hated her. Nothing she could say or do would change that. She pulled her gloves on. "I'm sorry to have taken up so much of your time, but I had to try to make you understand before I left New Orleans," she said.

Josh turned and faced her. She was leaving . . . he could stop her with a word, but he didn't.

"I made one mistake, Josh, and one mistake only. I believed you married me for my money. For my money" — she laughed bitterly — "isn't that ironic, when you were rich beyond belief. I wonder why you didn't bother to mention that," she commented, fighting back the tears. "Well, no matter," she shrugged. "Just let me say that you are making the worst mistake of your life, Josh. I love you," she said, hoping his eyes would tell her something, but there was nothing there. "Well, I guess words don't matter if the feelings are gone," she said, heading for the door. "Good-bye, Josh."

Josh stared after her. One part of him wanted to stop her, yet another warned him that she'd only betray him again. He was better off alone, he told himself as he closed the door. If he didn't love, he wouldn't be hurt. But God, why was he hurting so bad now?

* * *

Shadow bid a tearful farewell to Camille and Toby, promising to return for their wedding in the spring. Then she slowly climbed the gangplank to the steamer.

Please God, let this be a safe trip, she prayed silently as she stood on the deck and waved goodbye to her friends.

"Mrs. Rawlings, I've placed your luggage in your cabin. May I show you there," a steward asked.

"Yes, please," she smiled, following him.

"I understand you were one of the passengers on the *Mississippi Lady,*" he commented.

Shadow trembled at the mention of the ship. "Yes, I was."

"Don't worry about a thing on this trip, ma'am. The *Marietta* is the safest ship afloat."

"I hope you're right," she forced a smile as he unlocked the door of her cabin.

Shadow was about to step inside when she noticed someone else's luggage next to hers. "Just a minute," she called after the young man. "There is someone else's luggage here."

The young man had a strange look on his face. "Yes, ma'am. It's your husband's luggage."

"My husband . . ." Shadow stepped back into the room and saw Josh sitting in a chair. The pulse in her throat quickened as she stared at him.

"I hope you don't mind," he said, coming to his feet. "If you want me to go, I will."

He was there, looking very unsure of himself,

381

but he was there. Shadow wanted to throw herself in his arms, yet she was afraid to. She wasn't sure just why he had come. "Why are you here?" She managed to get the words out.

"Since you don't fare very well on these things, I thought you might like some company," he said lamely.

He still hadn't made a move to come near her. "Is that the only reason you're here, Josh."

Josh stared at the slender trembling figure before him. "No. You said something to me earlier today that finally penetrated by stubborn brain. You said I was making the biggest mistake of my life, Shadow, and I realized you were right. I couldn't let you go. I couldn't face life without you. I knew if we were to ever straighten our problems out, we had to be together."

"You said you were going to California. . . ."

"Life is where you are, Wildcat. I want to be with you."

Shadow ran into his waiting arms.

"I'm so sorry, Wildcat," he said, kissing her all over her face. "I love you so much. Is there any hope for us? I can't take back any of the hateful words or thoughts I had . . . my only excuse is that I love you too much, Shadow. When you walked off with Middleton, I nearly went crazy—I did go crazy!"

His impassioned declaration was choked off when Shadow pulled his head down to her mouth and kissed him soundly, nearly taking his breath away.

"You talk too much," she whispered against his mouth.

Josh held her away at arm's length. "We will never doubt one another again," he said firmly. "If we ever have any questions or concerns, we will talk about it. Is that agreed?"

"Agreed, my husband." She looked at him with loving eyes. "But right now do we have to talk?"

"Oh, Wildcat," he said, swinging her up into his arms. "I will never let you out of my sight again," he swore.